ACCIDENTALLY LIVING WITH THE CAPTAIN

CHICAGO AWAKENINGS
BOOK THREE

LEXI AMBER

DEDICATION

For everyone who helped make my first year as an author so amazing. Thank you!

CONTENT WARNING

- Sudden divorce
- Discussion of parent having had a major, disabling stroke
- Mention of being a spouse to someone who needs full-time care
- Adoption (open, domestic, arranged during pregnancy)
- Discussion of off-page past neglect/emotional abuse from parents for being queer
- Mention of being a homeless 18yo teen before college
- Pregnancy & birth, including high blood pressure, induction, heart decelerations, emergency C-section

NOTE TO THE READER

Reminder- suspend disbelief

Although the cities/states in this book are real, they are fake
versions of them that only exist in my head. The laws and
procedures mentioned may not be 100% accurate, particularly
when it comes to divorce, adoption, and an entire fake town
recovering from being victims of a cult. Although these are all
things that I researched and tried to keep as true to real life as the
story allowed, I'm sure that I missed something.

Same thing for the hockey league. The NHL that the Werewolves
play for is the fake version in my head. Any statements about the
teams/cities/organizations/schedule/etc. are all fake. The hockey
is fake.

I wrote this for fun because it made me happy. I think that reading
is fun, and I hope that reading this story makes some people
happy. If you're looking for a super low-angst cozy read, this
might be for you. If you need angst and drama (the real kind, not
Adrian's normal state) and can't stand when the idiots should just
talk to each other... maybe skip this one.

A NOTE SPECIFICALLY ON ADOPTION

I am not adopted, nor have I adopted anyone. I do have many family members who were adopted, though, and I am so grateful to have each and every one of them in my life and family.

Again, suspend disbelief, but I did do a lot of research on adoption, the process, and the different options available for everyone involved. Hudson's situation is unique and specific to him as a fictional person, but there are very real children who are in need of loving homes. If you think adoption might be right for you, I encourage you to look into your local options as they vary by state/country.

That being said, I am very pro-choice and nothing in this book is intended to read as otherwise.

A NOTE ON STROKES

I was a nurse working on neurology units for years before I ever wrote anything. I feel like the nursing part of my brain needs to say something in case someone out there doesn't already know.

Time is brain. Do not hesitate to seek treatment if you think someone is having a stroke. Strokes are the second leading cause of death worldwide. There are treatments available to help treat and even reverse the effects of a stroke, BUT ONLY IF YOU ACT QUICKLY.

The BE FAST acronym can help you remember the symptoms of a stroke, and in my opinion, is something that everyone should know.

B- Balance impairment/dizzy

E- Eyes/vision problems

F- Face drooping

A- Arms/legs weakness

S- Speech difficulties (understanding or producing)

T- Time: call 911 or whatever emergency medical treatment is available in your area.

I have this memorized from my years of doing patient and

family education, but there are excellent resources I can direct you to if requested.

Medical Advice Disclaimer: I cannot give personal medical advice or answer personal medical questions.

SPOILER WARNING:

Although this book can be read as a stand-alone, it will contain many spoilers for Accidentally Joining His Cult and is recommended to be read AFTER it.

HUDSON

End of September

"Hudson, this is your third year now as captain, how are you feeling about the team culture going into this season?" one of the many reporters surrounding me asks.

I'm sitting on the bench in front of my stall in the locker room after winning our final preseason home game, stripped down to my base layers with a towel draped around my shoulders, answering the media's questions. Each reporter has a microphone or phone held out toward me, hoping to get something interesting to report on, and I'm happy to play along.

I've been in the NHL for thirteen years now, and the AHL before that, so I'm no stranger to these post-game interviews. Some of the guys despise any and all media interaction, but I've never minded flashing a smile to the cameras or talking about how great my life is.

Even on the days that we lose, we're still out there getting paid to play hockey, and until recently, I wouldn't trade that for anything.

"I'm feeling great about the team," I answer honestly. "We've got a lot of young talent moving up this year, and it's been awesome to see how hard they're working to earn their spot. They really want it, ya know? That's only going to help us out on the ice."

"Are you hoping for another year with Bell and Martin on your line? Or do you think Coach will switch things up with all the new names?"

"I mean, yeah, I'd love to finish things out with them. Our line had the highest points last year for a reason, that chemistry is solid, but I wouldn't be surprised if he tries out some other options, too. Especially with it being my last season."

The crowd murmurs at the reminder of my retirement. For some reason after I made the announcement that I'd be done after my current contract, almost no one believed me. There were countless articles about how I was using my retirement "threat" to negotiate a better deal, that the Werewolves weren't offering me enough money, that I was too young to really be done, so it had to be a ploy.

But thirty-four doesn't feel young when I've spent most of my life being slammed into the boards and taking punches from the best of them.

"Hudson, are you still planning to be done at the end of the season?" another reporter asks, because apparently, if I don't officially confirm my retirement plans after every game, they aren't happening.

If possible, my smile grows even more as I look right at the camera that's aimed at me. I don't want them to misinterpret my answer. "Hockey has always been my focus, and I'll always love it, but I'm also excited for the next chapter in my life. I've been lucky to have a long career, but I don't think I'll be able to keep up with these young guys much longer." I nod my head to the side in Oliver Bell's direction where he's surrounded by his own media crowd.

"It's been an honor to play for the Werewolves for as long as I have, and to be their captain, helping guide so many young players at the start of their time in the NHL. I'm really looking forward to this final season skating with them, I hope it's a long one. When it ends, though, whether that's in April or in June, I'll be happy to hang up my skates. I'm ready to focus on my family. My beautiful wife, Shelby, has put up with my crazy travel schedule for long enough. I can't wait for us to finally expand our family and become parents."

"Hudson Roy?" a man in a plain black suit, just like other reporters, asks as he presses his outstretched phone even closer to me. I don't recognize the media outlet on his press pass, and maybe he's new, because I only heard him ask my name, but I don't want to embarrass the guy on his first day by calling him out on not knowing the players or what the typical interview style is.

"That's me," I reply easily with another smile, earning a few laughs from the rest of the people surrounding me.

He reaches into his laptop bag and pulls out a thick manilla envelope, holding it out to me. "You've been served."

"Served?" I repeat, my smile faltering a bit, because I have no idea what he's talking about. The crowd around me has gone silent, and without really thinking it through, I open the envelope.

I'm used to being given direction and following it without complaint. One of the coaches wants us to run through a drill? Or have me skate with a different line? I do it, no questions asked. That's part of why they like having me as their captain. I set a good example, both on the ice and off it. I have the experience, good instincts; I know the other players and what works in a game. I've always been one of the top scoring players on the team. I'm also easygoing and approachable. I handle the media well. I'm not in any news headlines. I'm married, not out hooking up and partying after games.

But outside of hockey? I might not be the smartest guy out there. Following my gut to act quickly on the ice also means I tend to act before considering the consequences. Like right now, as I skim the document this stranger just handed me, reading some of it aloud in my confusion.

"State of Illinois… Summons? Petition for the dissolution of marriage? You have thirty days to file a response? What the fuck does any of that mean?" I mutter to myself, the lack of understanding overwhelming my media training so I completely forget where I am and who can hear me.

"Are you getting a divorce?" someone asks.

"Hudson, you just said you were planning to focus on your family; is there trouble at home? Is that the real reason you're retiring?"

"Now that your wife is leaving you, will you want to stay in the league?"

Each question sounds further away as the reality of what's happening finally sinks in.

Shelby is leaving me.

With no warning, no discussion, no attempts at therapy. She's already filed legal paperwork for a divorce.

I thought we were happy. In love.

We've been talking about having kids. I wasn't just saying that for the cameras.

Maybe it's a joke? Everyone knows that Shelby and I are married. There was no hiding her name from the media when she used to be a supermodel. Maybe someone thought this would be a funny way to convince me not to retire.

I need to talk to her.

"Excuse me," I finally mutter, standing and weaving my way

past the crowd of reporters that seems to have doubled since I was handed this envelope.

I duck into a dark hallway that leads to some of the assistant coaches' offices and PT rooms, not really sure where I'm going, but I know I can't be around all those people. I don't bother to see if anyone follows, but I hear someone say "No media access back there, leave him alone" pretty harshly.

God, I hate that my team has to step up and defend me. That's supposed to be my job.

Luckily I'd already grabbed my phone from my bag, so I pull up Shelby's number. After what feels like an agonizing pause where the phone rings far too many times, she finally answers.

"Hey."

"Sweetie, what's going on? A man just handed me what looks like divorce papers. Is it real?" The silence on the other end of the call has my stomach twisting. The hope that this was all a misunderstanding is fading fast, stealing my future and all my hopes and plans with it. "Can't we talk about this?" I practically beg, my voice cracking.

"Hudson, you had to have seen this coming," she finally answers, sounding like this conversation is already exhausting her. "I've told you that I didn't want kids."

Um, no. She didn't. That would have definitely stood out to me. "But we talk about having kids all the time."

"No, you've been talking about having kids constantly. I've been trying to talk about literally anything else. I told you a few months ago that I wasn't getting pregnant."

"I thought you meant while I was traveling so much, not forever. I'll be retired, I'll be home all the time now."

"Yeah, that's not the selling point you think it is," she says dismissively. "I have no desire to volunteer to get fat and be tired all the time. There's just no way I would willingly get pregnant."

What the actual fuck is happening right now? How could I

have been so wrong about what my wife had planned for us? Maybe it's just cold feet about the *being* pregnant part. Maybe there's a chance I could still fix this.

Feeling desperate, I try to come up with a compromise. "Well, don't celebrities hire people to grow their babies? We could do that."

Shelby sighs loudly into the phone. "You don't get it, Hudson. Babies are always there. If I have a baby to take care of, how will I go on trips or go shopping or do all of the things I need to do for myself?"

"You'd really rather go shopping than be a mother?"

"Don't make it sound so awful, not everyone wants to be a parent. Plus, if you're retiring soon, how will I afford that stuff anyway? It's been fun but it's over. Don't come home. This place is mine. I picked it out and designed everything. You're never here anyway so it won't even matter. I'll have my lawyer call your lawyer."

She hangs up.

And just like that my marriage is… over?

All the plans I'd been making in my head, the two of us decorating a nursery, singing to the baby, teaching them how to walk and talk, none of that will happen now. I had all these ideas of what our family would look like: what sports the kids might play, that I could help coach, the vacations I wanted to take them on, even the books I was excited to read to them.

What the fuck do I do now?

My future hasn't felt this uncertain since I entered the draft.

I think I might be breathing too quickly, or maybe not enough? Whatever my problem is, I'm dizzy. I feel like I've lost all sense of what's real. My vision isn't focusing on anything in particular and it's taking all my mental energy to stay standing instead of sinking down onto the floor.

Fuck, am I actually having vision and balance problems? Should I be calling 911? No, no. I'm not Dad. I'm okay.

I take a deep breath, stand up straight, and focus on the sheet that's posted on the wall in front of me with our PT's schedule.

I can read it fine, my vision isn't really blurring, I'm not actually losing my balance. *I'm okay.*

I numbly turn back toward the locker room. I can't go back in there. I can't be around the media or my teammates when I can't even remember how to breathe properly. I'm the team's fucking captain for god's sake. I'm supposed to have my shit together and be the example they look up to. Not be hiding alone in a dark hallway while my life falls apart.

But as I finally focus, I realize I'm not even alone for this freak out.

Awesome.

God, I hope it's not another reporter.

It's too dark for me to see much more than their silhouette as they approach, but when they hesitantly say "Hey, I'm so sorry," I instantly relax. My whole body calms as I focus on Adrian.

My eyes adjust as he stands right in front of me so I can finally make out his styled blond hair and delicate features. Adrian is smaller than I am, both in height and build, but his confidence means he commands the attention of whatever room he's in easily. I've admired that about him since he started working for the team years ago, and I latch onto his steady presence now.

Adrian has probably never run away to hide in a dark hallway before. He would have said some sarcastic remark that had the media distracted and moving on before they even realized what'd happened. He might only be the assistant to our president, but I swear this man is more involved than anyone else in the organization. If someone has a problem, usually by the time they think to ask for Adrian's help, he's already solving it.

Actually, he might be the perfect person for me to talk to right now.

He clearly overheard everything—which is so embarrassing, but also great because he always knows what to do. My shoulders relax even more; I hadn't realized how much tension I was holding in my body, but I feel like I can finally breathe again.

Adrian will be able to tell me what to do next.

He's looking at me warily, like he's approaching a frightened animal, and I hate it. We usually get along great, and I don't want him to ever feel uncomfortable around me. "Hey, Charming, so I know you just heard all that," I start, using the nickname I usually do for him. It started a few years back when he got a haircut that looked like Prince Charming from *Shrek 2*, and I couldn't help but point it out. Plus it fits him and his whole perfectly-put-together-all-the-time vibe. Sometimes I'll call him "Prince" too, just depends on my mood.

Adrian is flirty in a very over-the-top way with all the players, and he can't say no to me when I'm flirty back, so I do it a lot. Plus, it's just fun. A good ego boost. It doesn't mean anything when Adrian knows I'm straight and married. That's just the friendship we've fallen into over the years.

Or at least, I was married. Shit, I can't believe this is happening.

"Fuck. Yeah, I did," he confirms. "Ugh. And it sounds like you had no warning either? I'm going to figure out how that asshole lowlife got his grubby hands on a press pass, and I promise whoever in the communications department let him in will be reprimanded. Hudson, I can't believe you not only had this happen but that it was so public. It's just awful, I'm so sorry, please let me know if there's anything I can do to help."

Wow, somehow Adrian sounds even more pissed off than I feel. I think I must still need time to process everything. "Yeah, so what now?" I ask.

"You'll be okay. I know it seems awful right now, but you're such a strong person. You'll look back on this one day and be glad that it happened. You're so much better off without someone who is cold enough to orchestrate all that," he promises.

It's a kind sentiment, and I really do appreciate how supportive he's being. But that's not exactly what I meant. "Oh yeah, cool. I hope so," I agree awkwardly before I try again. "But I meant literally. What now? Shelby told me not to go home, so what do I do right now? Where should I go tonight?"

Adrian just stares up at me, blinking a few times before he finally speaks again. "Why are you asking me?"

"Well, you always know what to do. You can fix anything," I say seriously.

Adrian doesn't look as confident in that statement as I am though. "Um, that's nice of you to say." Then he lowers his volume even more so no one else can hear. "But, aren't you closer with the other players? Do you want me to go grab one of them to talk to? Maybe you can crash with them until you figure things out."

"Fuck no," I scoff. "I'm the captain, I'm supposed to have my shit together. I can't 'crash with' one of the players I'm supposed to set the example for."

Adrian crosses his arms over his chest, looking at me with even more concern than a few moments ago. "Well, you can't go to a hotel after all the media just saw you get served divorce papers and be obviously surprised by it. Even if they didn't hear that phone call, they'll definitely swarm a hotel if they find out you're staying there."

Damn it, he's right. "See, I wouldn't have thought of that." I run my hands through my hair, trying to think of another option when I realize there's one standing right in front of me.

"What about you?"

"What about me?" Adrian asks, not following my train of thought.

"Well, can I come stay with you?" I ask eagerly. "Until I find a new place. I'll be traveling so much now that the season's starting, I don't know if I'll have much time to find somewhere, but I promise I'll be a good roommate. The best you've ever had. Whatever you need from me, just let me know and I'll do it."

"Oh my god, stop talking before you manage to make that sound even more sexual," he warns. Then he gives me a once-over, his bright blue eyes assessing my expression as if he's searching for something that isn't there. "Wait, you're serious?"

The more I think about it, the more perfect the idea seems. Adrian offered to help, he'll have me back on my feet in no time, and I'll get to hang out with him outside of work, which sounds like a definite perk. We've always been friendly, but in that coworker way where I know we get along great, but I don't actually know many details about his life. I'd like to change that. "Yeah, Prince, you make everything better." Then I aim my very best pleading eyes his way. "Pleeease."

He doesn't look nearly as excited about the idea as I'd like him to be, but after another head-to-toe glance, he sags a little where he stands. "Fiiine. I suppose you can come stay with me for a few days," he says with a roll of his eyes. But it also looks like he's fighting to hold back a smile, which feels like a definite win to me.

All I know is, with Adrian at my side, I no longer feel like my life is over.

2

ADRIAN

"Welcome home," I say as I swing open the door to my condo.

And, oh my god, why did I say that? This obviously *isn't* his home. He's crashing here for a few days while his life falls apart. Nothing more. It'll probably be even less than that once he processes everything that happened tonight.

This man is a millionaire. I know with his salary, plus with all the endorsement deals he has, there is absolutely no reason he can't get on the phone tomorrow and end up with a gorgeous new place that's private and away from the media by the end of the day. Two days, tops.

No need for my imagination to run wild with his suggestion that it might take longer or the fact that he called us roommates. And I'm definitely ignoring the breathy way he sounded as he promised "whatever I need from him," or that he'd be "the best I ever had."

Nope. I am not thinking about that.

At all.

Only very innocent, completely PG thoughts happening as my dream man moves in with me.

Because, despite the fact that Hudson frequents my fantasies, and let's be real, he is at the very top of my if-I-could-magically-make-anyone-gay-and-they'd-be-happy-about-it list, I know he does not think about me like that. He's straight. And technically still married on top of that.

The flirting and calling me "Prince Charming" is just Hudson's way of joking around with me. It doesn't matter that when he does it butterflies swarm in my stomach even after all these years.

We're coworkers, and barely even coworkers, that's all. We work for the same team, we cross paths, and we're friendly. I might intentionally make my path cross his more than necessary, but no one needs to know that, especially not him.

And I flirt with everyone. It's harmless fun. It doesn't mean anything when I do it with any of the other players. So what if Hudson has no idea I wish it could mean something when I do it with him? I'm going to ignore the crush I've had on this man since the day we met and chill the fuck out.

Because this is real life, not my fantasies.

I was pinching myself the entire ride home, convinced that Hudson would call me any second and say he'd changed his mind. But nope. He's here, looking around my apartment, and it still hurts like hell when I pinch my wrist, so I think it's actually happening.

Hudson fucking Roy is moving in with me.

And he's single.

And I'm freaking out a completely appropriate amount about it.

"Wow, this place is awesome," he comments, looking around as he heads further into the space.

"Down the hall we passed coming in are the two bedrooms. The bathroom in that hallway can be yours. There's another off the kitchen, and the laundry room is small but right next to your bathroom. That door is my office, and this is obviously the main living space," I ramble, gesturing to the open concept kitchen, dining, and family room.

"I love it. Nothing is white," he points out, sounding really excited about that for some reason.

"Uh, yeah, I guess I don't love white either," I agree, looking at the oak upper cabinets and the black stainless-steel appliances that blend in with the lower ones. The island is a gray quartz, and all my furniture is similar cool wood or dark metal with some leather mixed in. It's modern and moody and each detail was carefully picked out by me. "I know it's popular, but I've always found white to be kind of boring. I like my home to have a bit more character."

"I think I would too, but I've always been pretty bad at that sort of thing. Shelby insisted on everything being white; she said it didn't feel clean otherwise, but I hated how sterile it always seemed. I used to joke that we'd have to redecorate before we had kids since they'll obviously be messy, but I guess that won't be happening now..." He trails off, and his expression falls again.

I hate it.

Before tonight, I don't think I've ever seen Hudson without a smile on his handsome face, and how crushed he looks right now has my heart literally breaking.

Fuck Shelby and her stupid ex-supermodel perfect looks with zero personality. I've always hated her. It had nothing to do with being jealous either—she was always way too cold for Hudson. He lights up every room he's in. He needs someone who can reflect his light back at him and make him just as happy as he makes everyone else, not a black hole that sucks it all in, taking and taking and never giving him anything in return.

I need to find a way to get that smile back.

"Well, I'll be happy to help you decorate your new place however you'd like," I promise, feeling like I've won something when the corners of his mouth lift at the suggestion. "You could color drench everything so that there's no white at all."

"What's color drench mean?"

My god, has this man never seen HGTV? Been inside of a Home Depot? I don't expect him to own any design magazines, but still. "If you're sick of white, you'll love it. Come see." I grab his hand without thinking, do my best to ignore how perfect his large, callused hand feels around mine, and quickly lead him back to the guest bedroom that will now be his room.

I throw the door open with a dramatic "ta-da." Every wall, baseboard, crown molding, and even the ceiling, are painted the same deep blue color. My bedroom is designed similarly in a dark green.

He walks into the room and spins around. "Wait, this is really cool. Is this your room?"

"No, it's yours."

He blinks at me a few times, his gray-blue eyes full of wonder, before another smile slowly takes over his face. "Holy shit, Adrian, this is really nice. I don't know if you'll ever be able to get rid of me."

As if I want him to leave.

Be cool, I remind myself. *Don't tell him he can stay forever, and while he's at it, my room is actually even nicer, just stay in there with me.*

"No rush, but I'm sure you'll get bored of me in no time," I say with a shrug. Yeah, we get along, but we're not close friends. I'm confident if he stayed here long enough to get to know me, he'd get bored and forget all about our casual teasing and flirting exchanges at work.

Hudson sits down on the bed, looking like a fucking model with his perfectly styled brown hair, short beard, and stylish game-day suit still on. He turns to look right at me with his megawatt smile before he responds, and this whole moment is surreal. "I could never get bored of you, Charming. You're one of the most interesting people I've ever met."

Fucking swoon.

Calm down. He said "interesting." That doesn't necessarily mean a good thing. It's probably the mystery because he doesn't know that much about me.

A nervous chuckle escapes my throat before I ask—because I can't help myself—"Is interesting good? Or are we talking more of an 'I can't look away from that car crash' interesting."

Hudson bursts out laughing before reassuring me. "Interesting is very good."

And then he fucking winks.

Hudson winks while sitting on my bed.

Well, it's my guest bed, but it's still a bed I own in my apartment.

What is happening?

Nothing. Nothing is happening. Hudson is just being his normal, friendly self, probably distracting himself from everything that happened tonight. And if he needs to flirt with me to not focus on his divorce and how shitty his soon to be ex-wife is, then I will gladly let him.

Except there *are* a few details I need to update him on…

"Well, good. I would hate to find out you think I'm boring," I finally joke before I quickly move on, not wanting him to notice that I might be less confident than I want to be. "I obviously don't have any clothes that would fit you, but I spoke to Shelby, and she agreed to let me come over first thing tomorrow to pack up your belongings. So, hopefully, you'll be able to get through one night without extra clothes."

"Yeah, I sleep naked anyway," he says dismissively.

And I did not need that visual while he's *on my bed.*

"But wait, how did you already talk to her? Or convince her to let you in the house? On the phone earlier it sounded like she'd planned to throw me out without any of my things."

"I have all the WAGs numbers and most of them love me," I remind him. "I called her while I drove over here. I didn't tell her you'd be staying with me, but I did say I'd heard about your situation and informed her that the team was not happy with the public nature of her having the papers served the way they were. I might have reminded her that you're a beloved star player with a multimillion-dollar contract and a giant organization behind you, and that it was in her best interest to cooperate and make your transition smoother to avoid involving the team lawyers."

Hudson smirks. "See, I knew you'd know what to do. You always do. I hadn't even really thought about my things, and you've already made and confirmed a plan. You're amazing."

"Well, I'm happy to help. Especially if you keep reminding me how great I am," I tease, proud of how confident I sound when his words are making me feel like I could float away with how happy they make me. "If you want to give me a list of everything you need, it's probably better if I go while you're at your morning skate. I have a friend that offered to help if there's any heavy lifting needed."

Hudson pushes off the bed, standing to his full height. "God Adrian, you really are the best." Then he walks right over to me and wraps me up in his big professional athlete arms, and I have to cough to cover a whimper. We might joke around a lot, but Hudson has never hugged me before. Never surrounded me with his warmth and muscles and intoxicating woodsy cologne like this.

I can't help it; I sink into his embrace as I wrap my arms around his trim waist. I have no idea if this will ever happen again, so I might as well enjoy the moment.

"Thanks again for everything. I don't know what I would have done without you tonight," he says into the top of my head, squeezing me even tighter.

"Don't mention it. I'm sure anyone on the team would have done the same."

"Well, I'm glad it was you," he adds earnestly.

Can I die from swooning too many times? God, I wish that there were cameras in here to record this perfect moment. Pretty sure my heart stopped there for a second. And how does breathing work again? Right, okay. Focus. In. Out. I'm a responsible adult man fully capable of not freaking out at that comment.

"Me too," I manage to get out, sounding mostly casual. *Go me.*

We finally break apart from the best hug of my life, and Hudson smiles at me. It's too much. My heart can't take any more compliments from him tonight. I would actually drop dead.

"Well, the guest bathroom has extra toiletries in the drawer. I'll let you get some rest," I say, and then I spin on my heel before he can add anything else and head right into my room next to his.

Only one wall between us.

Where I now know Hudson will be sleeping naked.

This is definitely not how I thought my day would end when I woke up this morning.

Does it make me a completely horrible person if I'm happy that someone I care about is getting divorced?

Do I even care if it does?

I grab the emergency chocolate I always keep stashed in my nightstand and immediately pull out my phone to update my group chat with my friends. I want to shout from the rooftops that Hudson fucking Roy is sleeping in my guestroom tonight, that he hugged me and said I was one of the most interesting people he's ever met!

But I don't think anyone would actually hear me since the city is pretty loud.

So my friends will get to hear about every little detail of my night instead.

3

HUDSON

Early October

"Ready for tomorrow?" Oliver Bell, one of my favorite guys on the team, asks as I sit next to him on the bench in front of my locker to unlace my skates. "Your final home opener."

"Yeah, the crowd is always great for the first game, I love it. What about you? No longer your rookie season, anything you want to do differently?"

"Oh, thank god I caught you," a very out-of-breath Adrian interrupts before Ollie can respond, and I glance up to see him leaning against the doorframe.

"Hey, Charming, did you want to drive home together?" I ask, trying to remember if I forgot something we'd talked about. Living with Adrian has been amazing. We were just gone for another away preseason game, but the few days in Chicago have been so much better spent with him at his condo than if I'd been stuck alone in a hotel. He's always happy to hang out with me, and I've loved the distraction of his company. When he's there, it's easy to forget that my life is kind of a mess right now.

Admittedly, finding a new place hasn't exactly been a priority with everything else going on, but Adrian doesn't seem to mind having me around.

"What? No, we both drove our own cars today," he reminds me.

"Well, we should look at our schedules and see if we can ever do that," I suggest. No need for us to both waste the gas, and it sounds way better than sitting in my car alone.

"Um, yeah, sure. But that's not why I practically sprinted across the building to find you. And let me remind you, I am not an athlete, I feel like I'm dying." He puts his hand over his heart, chest still heaving, and I can't help but smile at his theatrics.

"Well, you look great," I assure him. And he does, his hair is still perfectly styled, and his stylish suit isn't even wrinkled. Adrian always looks so put together; I don't know how he does it.

His eyes widen a little, and then he shakes his head like he's trying to clear it before he stands to his full height. "I ran here because we need to go to HR before they're all gone for the day."

HR? I can't catch a break. "Did I not turn in all my paper-work? Am I in trouble?"

Adrian lets out a short laugh. "No, you're not in trouble. But we should let them know you're living with me. A few days is one thing, but as far as I know, you still haven't had any luck with your realtor, so we need to let them know we're roommates."

Haven't had any luck with the realtor, haven't called him yet... Same difference.

"We actually have to do that?" I ask, not doubting Adrian so much as I'm surprised that it would be a thing. "It's not like we're dating."

"We're obviously not dating," he agrees quickly, cheeks growing red. I love that I seem to be able to break through his seemingly perfect act that he puts on for everyone else, that I get to earn those little reminders that, as put together as I might think Adrian always is, he's also just a regular guy like me.

Even living with him, I still feel like I barely know anything about him. He's always so upbeat and positive, but I'm hoping that with a little more time, he'll be comfortable enough to let me get to know more.

"We probably don't need to, but living together, being room-mates, is still a type of relationship that we should notify them of," he explains. "It would be different if we were both players or both back of house, but we don't want anyone to accuse either of us of taking advantage of our job to pressure the other into anything."

"See, this is another one of those things I never would have thought of. Thanks for always being five steps ahead." He smiles softly and nods at my gratitude as his cheeks darken even more, a hint of his dimples shining through. "I need to take a quick shower, but I'll meet you there in fifteen?" I offer.

"Okay, I'll see if they can have the paperwork ready for when you get there. Thanks, Hudson." And as quickly as he came, he's gone.

"You're still living with him?" Bell asks.

Honestly, I'd kind of forgotten he was there. Adrian has a way of demanding my full attention. "Yeah, he's the best," I reply easily, hurrying to get out of the rest of my gear so I can shower.

"And it doesn't bother you that he's gay? Are you worried about what people might say about you moving in with him two seconds after your wife kicks you out?"

I turn to face Ollie. I might be in a hurry, but I can't rush this. "I can't tell if that comment was homophobic or not, but it's important that you know I have a zero tolerance policy for that shit. Adrian is an amazing person, and we're lucky to have him working for our team. I don't care how good you are out on the ice, this team is accepting of everyone, and if you can't get behind that, I won't hesitate to harass the coaching staff to trade you."

Ollie puts up his hands like he's trying to prove his innocence as he lets out a surprised laugh. "Hey, man, I'm the last person you have to worry about that with. I was just surprised. I thought that ancient people like you were more concerned about that bullshit," he teases, and I drop my warning glare.

"Fuck off, man, I'm not that old," I say with a laugh, glad that this kid is a good one. He's so young, and the team has invested pretty heavily in his success, plus we've always gotten along well, so it would really suck to find out he was an asshole. I'm relieved he isn't. "But nah, people can talk shit all they want. At the end of the day, the only thing that matters is the truth. And hockey. They should always focus more on hockey."

"So true," he agrees with a shake of his head. "Well, have fun with HR."

"Thanks, man."

"I'LL HAVE one small iced coffee with a splash of cream and a large iced chocolate almond milk shaken espresso," I order, relieved that the coffee cart is still open. I know Adrian seemed like he was in a rush, but hopefully he'll appreciate the coffee enough to not care if I'm an extra minute or two late.

"That will be right out," the barista promises with a smile. I leave a generous tip before moving to the pickup area, and in no time, I'm walking into the reception area of Human Resources.

I wonder how people end up with these jobs. I always wanted to play professional hockey, but do people actually grow up wanting to work in HR? I used to love daydreaming about all the random things my kids might want to be one day, but now when I have those sorts of thoughts, it bums me out.

I know my life isn't actually over, and my chance of having kids isn't completely gone. But what used to feel like such a close future plan now feels like more of a fantasy, and the time that it'll take to get me back to that I-could-be-a-dad-soon feeling seems horribly long. My parents had me in their twenties. I'm almost ten years older than they were, and they know better than anyone how quickly life can change; how future plans can be gone in an instant.

I don't like to focus on such negative thoughts, but it's hard to ignore them sometimes. I know I should probably be more upset about losing Shelby, but she showed her true colors with how she ended things, and I honestly haven't missed her like I probably should.

"Oh my god, what is that?" Adrian asks as he steps out of one of the conference rooms off the reception area I'm standing in.

"Your coffee?" I check, glancing behind me before holding it out to him, not completely sure if that's what he's asking about or if I missed something.

"You got me coffee?"

"Yeah, of course." I shrug, taking a sip of mine as he does the same.

His eyes widen, and he stares at me in shock as he slowly lowers the cup. "You got me *my* coffee. Like, the correct order and size and everything."

"Should I not have done that? You don't need to drink it if you don't want it."

He gasps, holding the cup closer to his chest and turning away slightly to guard the cup like I'm going to try to take it back. "Of course I want it. Chocolate and caffeine are my love languages. I just wasn't expecting it is all. Thank you."

I smile and wink. "Anytime, Prince. So what's the plan here, do we sign something, or…?"

Adrian's cheeks darken before he straightens like he's physically going back into professional mode. I immediately miss the more relaxed posture he's had more and more around me, but I appreciate how on top of everything he is, so I try to focus on why we're here like he is.

"Yes, Natasha was kind enough to stay a little late to help us get everything done before the home opener tomorrow. I've already explained the situation and the importance of avoiding media involvement around your separation. She agreed it was better to do it now while less people are around. We started the paperwork so I think you'll just have to sign a few things. It should be easy."

"Thanks, Adrian. Hey, Natasha, sorry to keep you here so late," I apologize as I follow him into the conference room. I take a seat across the table from her and Adrian sits next to me. It looks like he's already signed some things and there's a stack in front of me with highlights next to where I assume my signature is needed.

I don't know why I'm so nervous all of a sudden. This should be no big deal.

But for some reason that stack of papers feels more important than the ones Shelby served me. *That probably says something about how shitty my marriage actually was.*

"Hello, Hudson. It's no problem. I'm sorry to hear about your divorce," she says sweetly.

"Thank you," I respond, and I know that's all I really need to say, but I can't seem to stop talking. "Yeah, I had no idea we even had to do this or I would have come in sooner. I've heard of people needing to declare when they date a coworker, but it's not like we're dating, so I had no idea." I shrug apologetically, but then I realize how that sounded, so I rush to add, "Not that dating Adrian would be a bad thing. It wouldn't be; Adrian is great."

Fuck, did that make it sound like I wanted to date him?

I should probably just shut up, but I also feel the need to clarify so she doesn't think we're trying to cover up a relationship. "If I was gay, he would probably be my first choice, but unfortunately I'm straight," I explain. *But damn, that sounded bad too.* "Not unfortunately, because being straight isn't bad. Not that being gay is bad either," I add.

"Oh my god, how do you manage to be so endearing even when you're bumbling?" Adrian asks with a laugh. "Stop stressing, this is a formality. We don't actually directly work together, so you can calm down. It's not like I'm your boss."

Natasha laughs too. "Yeah, thank God Beckett Caldwell has never tried to date a player. That would have been a problem. But Adrian is right, no need to stress. And honestly, even if you two *were* dating, I don't think it would matter. It's the same form, you're just disclosing a personal relationship outside of your professional one, and like Adrian said, you're not reporting to each other, so there's no real conflict. This is just so that the team can have your back in case anyone tries to point fingers and make anything up later on. But thank you for sharing so much about your opinion on sexuality," she says with an amused smile.

"Can we all just pretend that I handled this whole thing very calmly and professionally?" I ask with a wince.

"Nah, this was way more fun," Adrian teases.

And yeah, if Adrian looks that happy, I don't mind embarrassing myself a little. I wink at him, waiting to see his cheeks turn pink again before turning back to Natasha, and pulling the papers closer. "So I sign these?"

"Yes, everything is highlighted so it should be pretty straightforward."

"Thank you."

And a few minutes later, my nonprofessional roommate relationship with Adrian is official.

"Should we celebrate declaring our relationship?" I tease as we walk back to our cars.

"Oh my god, Hudson, you can't say it like that, what if the media heard you?"

"Who cares." I shrug, earning a very confused look from him. "They always say whatever they want to anyway. I have a game tomorrow, so I can't really eat anything fancy, but I could watch you eat something more fun if you want me to pick up food on the way home," I offer. "I can enjoy the smells and live vicariously through you."

He smiles at that, shaking his head a little. "Want to do that takeout place right next to my building that has the grilled chicken and veggies and stuff you liked last time?"

I groan and my mouth is already watering from picturing the pasta he had. "Hell yeah, you want the same rigatoni with breaded chicken?"

"As long as you don't mind me having a way better meal."

"Not at all. Like I said, I'll pretend I'm enjoying it too," I assure him. "Plus, you should always have whatever you want. Don't let me hold you back."

He smiles up at me as we get to his car, his dimples drawing my focus for a moment as he looks around. "Where are you parked?"

"The other side of the lot."

He turns back to me, wide eyed and staring at me like I'm crazy. "Then why the hell did you keep walking with me?"

"We weren't done talking." I shrug. "Plus it's dark. Can't I make sure you get to your car okay?"

"I am perfectly capable of walking myself to my car," he insists, crossing his arms over his chest defensively.

"Obviously," I agree with a short laugh. "But I still wanted to.

Anyway, I'll call and order the food now so it's ready when I get there. Want to watch that design show you introduced me to last week while we eat?"

He uncrosses his arms, eyeing me skeptically. "Do you actually like it, or are you just suggesting that because I like it?"

"I liked it too!" I insist. "And I need to study before I have my own place for the first time in years." Shelby moved in shortly after we started dating almost six years ago. We got married about a year later, but that all feels like a different lifetime now.

"Fine, I'll get everything ready for when you're back. You sure you don't want me to pick up the food?"

"Fuck no, I'm living with you and you refuse to take any money, so buying food is the least I can do." I turn away before he can argue and shout "See you at home" over my shoulder, ready for another fun night of ignoring the fact that my life looks nothing like I thought it would a month ago.

At least it'll be with Adrian.

4

ADRIAN

I just finished emailing the documents I need Beck to sign to approve the latest marketing campaign, focusing on ticket sales for different theme nights, when he walks up to my desk in the small lobby outside of his office and hands me my large iced chocolate almond milk shaken espresso. I've already confirmed everything the marketing department put together after our last meeting with them, and it looks great, so he literally just needs to sign it.

It would be so much easier if I could tell everyone he trusts my judgment, no need for Beck to see it, but for some reason people don't love that answer. The *actual* team president needs to give the approval, not his executive assistant. Honestly, it's really annoying, but I guess I'm used to it, even if I do enjoy complaining about it to Beck.

My title sounds kind of basic for what I do. I don't know many people with multiple Master's degrees in Business Administration who are still "assistants," but my salary reflects my role here, and that's what really matters. I love working for the Werewolves. This team is my passion; I wouldn't want any other job.

Plus, Beck is my best friend, so I like that so much of my job is to make his life easier. Helping people, especially my friends, always makes me happy, so I try to do it whenever I can.

Beck likes to remind me that he would still want to be my friend if I wasn't always making his life easier at work, and I love that we spend so much time together outside of our jobs, but I can't seem to completely quiet that voice in my head that's always worried people wouldn't want me around if I wasn't doing things for them.

"Got a minute?" he asks, already continuing into his office. I stand to follow, shut the door behind me, and sit in one of the chairs across from him at his desk.

"What's up?"

"I'm hoping you can help me out," he starts with a sigh, taking a large sip of his disgusting plain black coffee.

"Anything," I respond automatically.

"I'd like to try to help save Linna."

I immediately perk up; that isn't at all what I was expecting him to say, but I shouldn't be surprised. Despite Beckett's intimidating appearance, covered in tattoos with a great resting bitch face, he's a really great guy. *Obviously*, or he wouldn't be my best friend.

Linna is the small town in Montana where Beckett's boyfriend, Cody, used to live and work until Beck visited and realized the company Cody worked for was actually a cult, and the two of them—with a little help from me and our other friends, *no big deal*—helped expose the truth. The story got enough attention that their leader, Viktor, and some of the other top executives were arrested on racketeering charges, and there are talks of more charges being added as the investigation continues.

"I'd love to help, what can we do?" I ask eagerly.

"Well, all of Viktor's victims are stuck there now that Kyla has been shut down, and so many people are out of work. I know some of them have already left, but the majority of ex-Kyla members are still there. They were so invested and isolated that most of them have nowhere else to go," he explains, sounding defeated.

"Do you know what's happening to the giant campus with all the businesses around their headquarters? Are they all shut down?"

"The government seized all of Kyla's former assets and demanded any of the businesses in town affiliated with the company halt operation as a part of the investigation, but I've already expressed interest in purchasing the properties after they've concluded. I'd like to eventually use the campus to help rebuild Linna, turn it into something more positive, and find a way to give all those people employment again."

"Beck, that sounds like an amazing idea," I enthusiastically agree. "What do you need from me?"

"Mostly to cover for me here," he admits apologetically. "I know you already do so much—"

"Consider it done," I interrupt with a wave of my hand. "Anything else? Do you need help organizing donations to the victims in the meantime, or researching therapists to hire to help them?"

"The therapist thing would be great. I already talked to Jordan about running another article specifically drawing attention to donation opportunities." Jordan is one of our other best friends, and it was his investigation and reporting that officially broke the truth about Kyla.

"My family is working on starting a nonprofit in Linna," he continues. "We've agreed to start with a fifty-million-dollar donation, but we know that will only go so far with the thousands of people out of work, so we'd really like to focus our efforts on rebuilding the economy and infrastructure of the city so people aren't relying on that for the long run."

Beck looks exhausted, and I can't imagine how stressful the last few months have been for him. I'm so happy he managed to find Cody during all of that. Despite the stress, I know Beck is happier than he ever was before meeting Cody.

He lets out a big sigh, taking another big sip of his drink. "So what's new with you? I know I've been pretty MIA dealing with the investigation. Did Hudson finally move out?"

I let out a little snort laugh. "Nope. My dream man is still very much living with me."

"Still? Does he need a different realtor?" Beck offers.

I glare at him. "Absolutely not. Hudson can stay in my guest room for as long as he needs. I have no idea why he doesn't seem to be in a hurry to find his own place but we are not questioning my good fortune."

"So I take it he's a decent roommate?" he asks with a smirk.

"Ugh, he's literally perfect. Like, I thought I was in love with this man before when he was just some hot hockey player I got to flirt with at work. But now he's somehow even better."

Beck arches a brow. "Better than perfect?"

"He walked me to my car the other night before buying us dinner from my favorite restaurant."

"The one right next to your place that the rest of us never want to go to because you've taken us way too many times?"

"The very same," I confirm. "Then he suggested we watch design shows while we eat, and we spent the whole night making fun of the couple's impossible standards and commenting on how we would have made everything look so much better."

"Wow. Are you sure he's straight? Because that does sound like a perfect night for you."

"I knooooow," I whine. "And yes, unfortunately for me, he has made no declarations of any secret attraction to me, or any other men for that matter. So I will just continue to enjoy the eye candy while he somehow raises my already impossibly high standards for what I want in my partner." And I'll continue to blame my high standards on why I'm still single and ignore the fact that there aren't exactly men lining up to ask me out.

"Sorry, A."

"Thank you, my life really is so hard," I tease with an eyeroll. "You're only exposing cults and rebuilding communities. Meanwhile I have to pretend to ignore how hot the half-naked hockey player walking around my condo in grey sweatpants is every morning."

"A real modern-day hero," Beck deadpans.

"You get me," I say with a dramatic sigh. "Okay, I'll look up therapists and cult specialists and get recommendations to you by lunch. If you can just sign everything I've sent over, that should be all I need from you around here, and honestly you can e-sign almost any document these days, so don't stress if you can't make it in."

"You're the best," he replies, sounding relieved. I'm glad I can help alleviate some of his stress, no matter how small.

"I know," I tease with a shrug and a smirk, earning a slight corner of the mouth lift from him before we both get back to work.

I really do love my job. If only the hot man I'm living with wanted to be with me, then my life would be perfect.

5

HUDSON

I know I've put this off for long enough, but I'm still anxious as I wait for my parents to answer my video call. We've texted, and I had a brief phone call with my mom when the first news stories broke about the divorce, but I haven't had the chance to sit down and actually talk about the situation yet.

I'm in my room at Adrian's place, lounging on the bed and propped up by his seemingly endless supply of pillows with my laptop balanced on even more pillows next to me. One thing I've learned Adrian takes very seriously is comfort, and every pillow, blanket, couch, and bed in his condo are high quality, super soft, and more comfortable than anything else I've ever experienced.

Well, I guess I'm assuming his bed is too. I obviously haven't been on it. But my bed here is way nicer than any I've had in the past. I'll seriously need him to help me pick out furniture when I get my own place, because after living like this, I don't think I can go back to my previous scratchy blankets and boring, normal number of pillows.

"Hey, sweetie," my mom finally greets. It looks like she's got their computer on the kitchen table, the same one that's been there since I was a kid. I've tried to buy them a nicer home. I'd love to move them closer to me, but my mom insists it's better for my dad's routine if he stays in the same house they've lived in for almost forty years.

"Hi, guys." I attempt a big smile. My mom is huddled close to my dad so they can both be seen on the screen, and although my dad doesn't say anything, half of his face lights up when he sees me.

It's still hard to look at the man my father has become sometimes, but I know that we're really lucky to still have him around at all.

"Sorry I haven't called sooner, things have been kind of crazy since Shelby filed the papers."

"Oh, don't you dare apologize. I feel just awful that you were so blindsided by that girl. Is there any way you can come visit us soon? You know I'd love to see you, but I'm not sure if your dad's overnight nurses would be able to coordinate me being gone for more than a day or two."

"Go," my dad grunts. He isn't able to enunciate well, and long phrases are really hard for him, especially because it can take so long, but my mom and I can understand him. Speech therapy has definitely helped over the years.

My mom waves him off though. Even though I know my dad's home healthcare staff is the best of the best—I've made sure of it—she still really struggles with being away from him.

"Sorry, Mom, I don't play in Minnesota until December. Let me know how many tickets you want for the game, though, and we can see each other then."

"Hockey… game?" my dad grits out slowly, checking if he'll get to be a part of it.

"Yeah, Dad, I'll make sure you can come see me play in my last season. I got a wheelchair accessible box again so you guys can come, and hopefully it'll be a bit quieter, or you can turn off the lights if the arena gets to be too much," I remind them.

My dad still gets bad headaches sometimes, and the overstimulation of a pro hockey game isn't great for him. But my mom has assured me that he's always so happy when he gets to come to my games, and he talks about it leading up to and after them, even if we both know they're a lot for him to handle. So I try to make the experience as painless as I can.

"And don't worry about me, I'll be fine," I assure them with a shrug. They've been through so much worse than what I am dealing with right now, and I really admire how they've managed to remain so positive. I'm doing my best to do the same. "Unless you want me to move you guys out here?" I offer hopefully for the millionth time. "I know I was promising grandbabies soon, but I would still love to live closer to you both."

"Oh, Hudson, don't worry about us either," she says, taking my dad's mobile hand in hers. "I know you were looking forward to that next chapter, but don't give up hope, sweetie. I also know you've never liked being alone, but you are going to make someone else so happy one day, I have no doubt. You truly will be such an amazing father when the time comes. Try not to stress too much about when it'll happen."

My dad is nodding, and it's hard to know how much he's following along, but I so appreciate his encouragement.

"Thanks, guys. Yeah, I'm trying not to be too hard on myself. It's just such a big change."

"Are you still living with that friend from work? Or did you find your own place yet?"

"I'm still at Adrian's."

"And is he another player? I don't recognize that name."

"No, he works for the team."

"Is he there?" she asks, looking around behind me like he

might have been waiting to pop out at the first mention of his name. "Can I say hello and thank him for his hospitality?"

I snort a laugh. "No, he's still at work. We had a morning skate and are traveling early tomorrow, so I just did a light work-out, but I have the rest of the day off. He seems to work all the time."

"Well, make sure you thank him for me then."

"I'll get him extra chocolate tonight from you." She nods, happy with that idea. "Actually, I should probably let you guys go so I can order our dinner."

"Alright, sweetie, we love you so much, and we're so proud of you."

"Love you, too."

I make sure to add both a piece of chocolate cake and a triple fudge brownie to our usual order. Adrian said he'll be back in about an hour, so it should get here just before him, and I have plenty of time to shower and put away the load of dishes I started earlier so everything is ready for him when he gets home.

6

ADRIAN

I'm starting to wonder if the whole pinch-me-I-must-be-dreaming thing is complete bullshit.

Because it definitely hurts when I pinch myself, but Hudson Roy is still living in my apartment. And he isn't just living here—everything I told Beck the other day is true. He's the ideal roommate.

He can't possibly be real.

"Sorry, what did you say?" I ask when I realize I've just been standing in the entry to my kitchen, staring.

But really, it isn't my fault. Hudson is moving around my kitchen, looking perfectly at home like he owns the damn place—which I'm obviously not complaining about. He's shirtless, his muscles look like they're carved from marble, his tattoos are on display, his hair is wet like he must have just gotten out of a shower, and to top it all off, he's only wearing loose, gray sweatpants. Nothing is being left up to my imagination.

"Dinner got here just before you did, so it should be hot. Your stuff is on the table. I'm grabbing some real plates and we'll be all set," he says, flashing me his perfect smile.

Aren't hockey players supposed to have bad smiles? Missing

teeth and all that. Why does he have all his teeth? Asking that seems rude though… right? More of a personal question.

"You ordered me dinner?" I ask instead, focusing on my surprise that he did that. Hudson and I have eaten together a few times now, but always when we were already together beforehand.

"Yeah, I finally coordinated with my chef to deliver my prepped meals when I get back from the away games next Tuesday. But for now, I figured our favorite place would be good." He gestures to the bag in the center of the table.

He said "our" favorite. As if it's totally normal to lump the two of us together. I'm not imagining that, right? While he was talking about buying me food… My favorite food… Which he knows. As though he actually knows and cares about me in a way that goes so above and beyond what he needs to.

I'm not used to having anyone other than my best friends care enough to pay that much attention to me, and even with them, it took years before I trusted that they intended to be in my life long-term. I have no idea how to respond to Hudson doing it so casually, so I sit down quietly at the table across from him.

"I wasn't sure what food you'd want me to request, but he said it's no problem to add on meals for you as well."

"From your chef?" I squeak out, making sure I'm still following. He nods. "Hudson, you don't need to have your private chef cook for me!" *Why the hell would he even think to offer that?* "That's so nice, but I wouldn't like that healthy stuff anyway," I remind him with an awkward laugh.

He laughs too. "Yeah, I know you'd hate my food. He said he'd make whatever you *do* like. He used to do the same for Shelby. So if you have any menu ideas, I'll give you his number, otherwise he can make suggestions. I was going to give him your number, but I wasn't sure if you'd be comfortable with me handing it out, so I told him you'd reach out to him instead."

My jaw is open, practically on the floor. I can't remember how to shut it, and I'm probably going to really embarrass myself when I start drooling in a minute, but I can't help it.

There is just no way this walking green flag of a man is real.

And did he just compare me to his wife? Ex-wife? God, I fucking wish our titles were comparable.

"Hudson, I so, so appreciate it, but you don't need to do that. Shelby was your wife. That's totally different."

"Is it though? We're living together," he points out, as though I might have somehow forgotten the most amazing thing that's ever happened to me. Then he tilts his head and gives me his pleading "come on, do it for me" flirty look and… how do I know what his exact expression means so well?

"He's already cooking for me. I want him to also cook for you, Charming. Don't overthink it. I know I don't *have* to have him do that, but I *want* to," he insists.

"Well, how the hell am I supposed to say no to that?" I ask aloud, too confused to keep that as an inside thought.

"You don't." He smiles triumphantly and pulls out his phone, apparently to text me the contact info because my phone buzzes in my pocket. "And make sure to text him, otherwise he'll guess, and he won't know to make you chocolatey desserts."

"Oh my god, I don't need desserts from him too."

He rolls his eyes as he takes our food out of the to-go bag. "Adrian, you don't *need* anything. I know that. But if you want it, if it's going to make you happy, then you should ask him for whatever you'd like." Instead of handing me my container, he opens it and starts plating my meal for me, as if on autopilot, like that's a totally normal thing to do for your friends. Then he pulls out not one but two very chocolatey dessert options and sets them both down in front of me.

That's it.

This seriously can't be real.

I look around my apartment, convinced there must be hidden cameras. "Okay, I'm sorry, but am I getting Punk'd? Is this some sort of test to see how nice the perfect straight man can be before the innocent gay man cracks and offers to blow him or something?"

Hudson chokes on nothing and starts coughing as I continue. "Sorry, that was probably very inappropriate, but it was the first thing that popped into my head. I'm trying really hard to pretend this is all very normal friendly behavior, but you're definitely acting way nicer than any friend—or even boyfriend—ever has, and I am very confused."

When he recovers, he tilts his head again. "Kindness isn't transactional. Your friends aren't nice to you?"

I shake my head. "They're normal nice! Not 'serve me dinner and get me extra dessert' nice."

He glances down at my plate, then back up at me. "I didn't even think about serving you. I wasn't trying to make you uncomfortable. I guess I just like taking care of the people I care about." He shrugs.

The people he cares about?

This man will be the death of me.

Then he scrunches his brows together, and when our gazes meet, I feel like he's looking right into my soul. "Is there a reason you don't think you deserve for people to be nice to you, to take care of you? It seems like you're always helping everyone else. Does anyone look out for you?"

I blink at him a few times because... what the fuck? How does he seem to see me in a way that no one else ever has? "Is this a therapy session now? Hudson, I promise I'm okay, my friends are great, and they look out for me plenty. Yes, I like to help people; it makes me happy. All I meant to point out was that you could dial it back if you want to." And yes, it probably is because of my fucked-up childhood, feeling like I need to earn affection and approval that I never will, but that's a story for another day.

"What if I don't want to?" he challenges with that big smile of his.

I cross my arms. I honestly have no idea how to respond to him. I've never met anyone like Hudson. "Fine. I'm not going to stop you from being weirdly nice. As long as you know you don't have to be. I'm not Shelby. I won't be kicking you out or blind-siding you. You can stay as long as you'd like, even if you don't do all the dishes or watch my favorite shows. Kindness isn't transactional," I repeat to him with a smirk.

He chuckles. "I'm not great at being idle. I like to keep busy and moving so I end up cleaning when I'm just sitting at home. And I really do enjoy those shows, too."

"Fine." I roll my eyes, but the more serious tone we both had moments ago has been replaced with a teasing one. "Keep being perfect. Somehow I'll find a way to manage."

His smile somehow grows. "Good."

"One more thing though," I add before we completely move on. "It's okay if you're not okay. I know we aren't all that close, but I am here if you want to talk about any of the stuff you're dealing with. You've seemed to be handling the split really well, but this is your home, however temporary. You don't have to be strong all of the time. Not around me."

His smile softens to one that's a little sadder. "Thanks, Prince." He shrugs again. "I keep waiting for it to all sink in or something. It's, like, I think I should be more upset, or angry, or more... I don't know, *something* about her leaving me, but I'm just not. I'm really bummed about losing the future I had planned for us and the life I was picturing for my retirement. I was so excited to expand our family, to finally get to be a dad." He shakes his head again, and I fight the urge to go to him, to wrap him in a hug. Sure, he hugged me when he moved in, but that was him initiating comforting contact. I don't know if he'd want the same from me.

"But when I think about Shelby specifically, I'm kind of… numb. I'm annoyed that things ended the way they did, sure. But I don't think I miss *her* so much as the idea of her and the role I assumed she'd play in my future family. So…" He takes a big breath and finally confidently continues. "I guess that means she probably wasn't the person I was supposed to be with anyway."

Wow. I guess I had assumed he was putting on a brave face. I'm relieved to hear he's taking it so well though. "That is a very mature outlook to have," I commend.

And I try to stop there, I really do. But I can't help myself. I want to know more. I want to know everything about Hudson, and he seems comfortable with sharing right now. I just hope I don't overstep. "Would it be horribly nosey and rude for me to ask why you got married if you seem kind of indifferent about her? Did things change between you two over the years?"

He smiles and glances around like he's searching for the answer himself. "Looking back at everything now, I think I met her at the right time. I was ready to settle down, get married. She was successful enough on her own that I didn't think she was just after my money or title of 'NHL wife.' Maybe she didn't think I'd care if she didn't actually want kids. Or maybe she thought one of us would change our mind before the time came, but now that I really think about it, I guess I was the one doing all the future planning. Plus she's really hot," he adds with a short laugh.

I snort. "Well, other than how attractive she might be, and I'll have to take your word on that part," I joke, trying to avoid things getting too dark, "that really sucks, Hudson. For what it's worth, you deserve to be treated nicely too. I'm sorry if I made it weird calling out how nice you are or made it seem like I don't appreciate you. I hope that you can find someone who's excited about planning that future with you."

His smile is so genuine as his gray-blue eyes meet mine. "Thanks, Adrian."

See, I can be kind and supportive too. So mature. No blowjobs offered.

I didn't even suggest that I could be that person and would love to plan a future with him, even if the little voice in my head is screaming it on repeat. I know he'd never think about me in that way.

I really do deserve double chocolate treats though.

Speaking of. "So what did I do to earn multiple desserts today?"

"Oh! Thanks for reminding me. One is from my mom."

Now I'm the one choking on air because… What? Did I hear that correctly? "Why would it be from your mom?"

"She told me to thank you for letting me stay with you. She knows how much I hate living alone and made me promise to get you something from her, and I told her that you love chocolate. So don't be surprised if more gets delivered here from her too."

Aww. He hates living alone? Does that mean he's choosing to stay here? It isn't a real estate thing? I'll obsess over *that* little nugget of info later. And of course the sweetest man would have the sweetest mom. Not that I'm a reflection of mine, because that woman was not nearly as great as I am.

"Well, please thank your mom for me and assure her that you are the ideal roommate."

His smile is back to its full size, filling my heart right along with it. "Will do."

7

HUDSON

"If they don't go with the second house, they're actually crazy," I comment to Adrian.

"Oh, absolutely. I don't know why they even showed them anything after that."

We're done with dinner, and I still have about an hour before I'll realistically be able to fall asleep. We've moved to Adrian's insanely comfortable couch. It's one of those big L-shaped ones, so I'm sitting in the middle with my feet extended toward the TV, and he's on the other end with his feet stretched out toward me.

I don't think I'd normally even notice how close he is, but I can't stop thinking about his comments at dinner that he isn't Shelby while implying I was treating him like I would her.

Have I subconsciously replaced my relationship with Shelby with my friendship with Adrian because we're living together?

I don't think so… Shelby and I didn't spend a ton of time together with how much I traveled, and her social calendar was always so full that we didn't spend much time at home. When we did, we tended to focus on our physical relationship, making up for that time apart. We certainly didn't spend a lot of time doing anything as innocent as what Adrian and I are doing now.

But that thought only reminds me of his blowjob comment.

Not sure what to do with that.

He obviously didn't mean anything by it.

Right?

He wasn't saying he *wanted* to offer to blow me. He was just trying to demonstrate that I was apparently acting more like someone would with their partner than a friend they live with.

At least, I'm pretty sure that's what he meant. Not that it even matters. Obviously.

I mean, it would be a nice offer. If he was making it. Really nice. I bet that someone as detail oriented and enthusiastic about life as Adrian is would give excellent head. But I'm not into guys, so I would probably have to politely turn him down. Even if a blowjob sounds like exactly what I need right now.

Fuck, I should not be thinking about that while I'm not alone. My sweats aren't hiding a thing as my dick thickens, so I shift to try to make it less obvious, but I'm not sure how successful that attempt even was.

And I definitely shouldn't be picturing Adrian's mouth wrapped around my cock. Shouldn't be wondering what I would do if he crawled over to my side of the couch and offered. Would I really say no? And if I did, would I be saying no because he's a guy, or because he's my friend and I wouldn't want to complicate that?

I've never wanted a man to give me a blowjob before. But with how fucking hard I am right now, I definitely don't hate the idea if Adrian is the one I'm picturing doing it.

What does that say about me?

Am I less straight than I thought I was? Or am I just horny now that Shelby and I aren't together? I have enough big changes happening in my life right now, why not throw in a sexual identity crisis too?

"Time for one more?" Adrian asks, interrupting my internal

monologuing as he glances my way, the remote in his hand aimed at the TV.

I need to stop thinking about blowjobs. It doesn't matter what I would do or say in this hypothetical situation because Adrian wasn't offering. And if no men are offering to blow me, then I don't need to be having this debate with myself right now.

Probably a good one to come back to later though…

"Yeah, I have time," I manage to answer. He starts the next episode and immediately locks in on the new couple, but my attention is still on him.

I wonder if he's dating anyone… Adrian *would* be an awesome partner. He keeps things pretty tidy just like I do, but he isn't super picky about it in a way that makes me nervous to be in his space. He's fun to hang out with and always checks in to make sure I'm enjoying what we're doing. He's so funny; I've always thought that. And he was so kind and supportive when I was explaining my feelings about the split. I didn't feel judged at all. He listened and really wanted to help.

Adrian would kind of make the ideal partner.

I wonder if *he* wants kids.

Okay, now I'm definitely overstepping normal friendship boundaries.

And I'm still not convinced that being able to picture getting a blowjob from a guy means I'm suddenly not straight. So jumping to relationship thoughts is definitely out of the question. Adrian wouldn't want that from me anyway. He's just being a good friend, helping me hide away from media attention, and letting me stay with him. He would probably be uncomfortable to find out I've been thinking any of this. Just because he's attracted to guys and he flirts with me, it doesn't mean he'd actually be interested in me anyway. What a horribly conceited assumption for me to make. Not all gay men are into their straight friends.

I wonder where I could find someone who shares those qualities though. Like a female version of Adrian, maybe. Okay, now I'm literally just picturing him with longer hair, what is wrong with me? Adrian *is* objectively attractive though. Like, he's just pretty, there's no other word for it. His blond hair and bright blue eyes, the way his confidence shines though and draws people in. He's certainly prettier than most of the women I know. And I've always had a thing for blonds.

Wow, I must be hornier than I realized if I'm this focused on dating and wondering what it would be like to be in a relationship with someone exactly like Adrian.

Maybe what I should be focusing on is that this all means I'm ready to move on from Shelby. Should I try dating again? How do people even find someone they want to date these days?

"Are dating apps still a thing?" I ask.

Adrian tilts his head to the side and raises a brow as he stares at me before hesitantly answering. "Yes. Why?"

"I was just thinking that maybe I should try dating again."

Adrian pauses the show to give me his full attention. "Like, you want to hook up with someone, or, like, *dating* dating?"

His question doesn't sound judgmental, and I take a second to really think about it before I answer, glad I have something other than oral to focus on as my dick calms down. "Well, I definitely miss that part of being in a relationship, but it's not the most important thing to me. I still want that future I was telling you about. And I'm not going to end up happily married with kids if I don't put myself out there again."

He nods. "Okay, got it. So you want a real dating app with common interests and life goals and stuff. Not just pictures of abs and late night 'wyd?' messages."

I cringe a bit at the thought of sending a text like that. "Yeah, that's not my thing," I confirm. "I've always preferred to be in a committed relationship over casual hookups. I don't judge the people who do though. It just didn't take long for me to realize I wanted the real deal, the overnights and cuddles and knowing their coffee preferences, not just an easy orgasm."

"That's fine, those types of dating apps exist too," he assures me.

"What about you?" I ask, too curious at this point not to. I've been dying for Adrian to open up more on his own terms, but maybe I need to be more direct about wanting to know more.

"What about me?"

"Well, are you seeing anyone? Or are you on any of the apps? Are you more of a late-night booty call kind of guy, or do you prefer a long-term thing?"

"Now who's nosey," he teases, looking a little surprised by my questions. I smile apologetically, but I'm also glad when he actually answers. "I'm not seeing anyone, and I have dating profiles on a lot of different apps. I would love to be in a relationship, but I've found my standards for the men who seem to be interested in me are much higher than I've had luck with, so here I am." He shrugs.

"Good, I'm glad you're not settling. You deserve someone as amazing as you are."

His cheeks darken before he responds. "So do you."

"Well, do you think you could help me figure out what apps to try? Maybe help me set up my profile?" I flash him my biggest smile, pleading with my eyes for his help. The thought of attempting that on my own is overwhelming. But having Adrian help me actually sounds kind of fun.

He hesitates, side-eyeing me before he finally lets out a big sigh. "Fiiine. But not tonight. You need to sleep before your flight tomorrow, and I'm invested in this episode now."

I laugh as he resumes the show. "Thanks, Charming. I seriously don't know what I'd do without you."

"Probably be really bored," he deadpans, making me laugh again.

"So bored," I agree.

And I feel a bit better than I did even an hour ago. I might not have a whole big, detailed plan for my future like I did before my split with Shelby, but at least now I have a plan that feels like a step in the right direction.

One more thing to thank Adrian for.

8

ADRIAN

"And how would you describe your ideal partner?" I ask Hudson.

I quickly took over as the one typing as we fill this out so I could have something to focus on other than how hot he looks right now in his faded black Werewolves sweats. He is, yet again, not wearing a shirt.

Have I kept the place a little warmer than necessary since he moved in? So what? He hasn't complained.

"Umm, kind, funny, smart. I've always been attracted to confidence too," he answers, pulling my focus back to this stupid app I'm setting up for him.

Ugh. Why did I agree to do this again? Creating a dating profile for your perfect man to help him start seeing someone else —probably another hot confident blond supermodel with big tits —should be considered a cruel and unusual form of torture.

Hudson was gone for a few days with a stretch of away games, and I was kind of hoping that he'd have gotten impatient and started this whole thing without me.

Or better yet, decided he didn't actually need to create any dating profiles because he was already living with the perfect candidate.

Except that obviously didn't happen. He flew in late last night, and when I got home from work today, he was already waiting for me with our fancy pre-made-by-his-personal-chef meals heating up. And as soon as we started eating, he asked if we could work on this after dinner.

I had no excuse not to help him. The truth of "sorry but I'm far too jealous to help when all I want to do is sabotage any date you ever try to go on with anyone other than me" probably wouldn't have gone over well.

And I do want him to be happy.

So now here we are, sitting side by side at the table, building a dating profile so he can finally move on from his ex-wife… with someone who isn't me. It's not a surprise—*he's straight,* I remind myself for the millionth time—but somehow knowing that doesn't stop it from stinging.

After he let that little comment slip about preferring to not be alone, I've realized he's *never* actually talked about trying to find his own place. I've been afraid to ask and remind him that it was even an option, but as far as I know, he's content to stay with me for now.

And I'm more than happy with that arrangement. But I also know exactly how this is going to go when he starts dating again. Anyone he shows the slightest interest in is going to fall head-over-heels in about two seconds. *I know I have.*

And then he'll realize bringing home his date to my guest bedroom isn't as appealing as it would be if he had a house of his own. I'll be lucky if he's still here in a week.

My nights of coming home to dinner, chatting about our days, and ending with relaxing on the couch together watching TV are numbered.

I guess I already knew they were, he could find his own house tomorrow, but for some reason, creating a dating profile for him makes his leaving seem far more real than I care to focus on.

I just hope they deserve him, that it isn't another Shelby situation where he settles for the first woman that checks his boxes.

I wonder if he'd let me screen his dates to make sure they're worth his time. Or maybe I can meet them after he actually likes someone enough for a second date, see if they seem like a good fit.

Ugh. That would be weird, right? Hudson and I are friends, and honestly new friends at that. Just because we're living together doesn't mean he owes me any extra access to his life. The fact he's asked me to help with this at all is more than I would have expected.

"What's your ideal first date?" I prompt.

He takes a second to think about it, because he actually cares about this. He's so invested in finding his person, and it's so fucking sweet I could puke.

"I'd love somewhere public enough that they're comfortable, but private enough that we can talk and get to know each other. Maybe dinner in a quiet restaurant overlooking the lake. Oh, at sunset, that's my favorite."

Of course it is. Every answer he's giving is so endearing that if I didn't know him, I would think this was a fake profile with how perfect he seems. But no, the man sitting next to me is very real, and he genuinely enjoys all the cliché things his profile will advertise.

I love them too, damn it.

And his pictures are so hot, like, what the actual fuck? Does this man not have one bad angle, maybe an off-putting picture of him holding up a big fish or something?

No.

Of course not. His pictures are him in gameday suits, posing with people at charity events, and hanging out with other professional hockey players. And somehow none of them come across as him showing off or like he's pretending for the cameras.

At this point I'm convinced Hudson has no flaws, and honestly, it's rude.

"Okay, what age range would you like me to include?" I ask, trying my best to stay focused and get this thing done as quickly as I can. He talked about wanting to try multiple websites, but I'm really hoping the one will be enough for tonight.

"Ummm. I don't really know. I guess like twenty-five to forty? Is that bad if I cap it at forty? Maybe forty-five? I don't want to judge anyone based on their age, but I'd like someone who's in the same phase of life as I am of wanting to start a family."

I glance at him as I try to picture him with someone over ten years older than him. "Can women have kids at forty-five?"

"Well, a woman could have fertility issues at any age. I'm not necessarily looking for the biological mother of my children. I just want a partner that wants to raise kids with me," he explains with a shrug.

Interesting. He's been talking about wanting to be a dad so much, I guess I had assumed he meant his own biological children, but if he's open to other options…

What else is he open to?

Focus. He wants to date a woman. Not me. Although the next question is certainly interesting. "Okay, do you have any other preferences? I put that you're straight, but would you prefer to only match with cisgender women?"

"Oh, they ask you that right away? Wow, things have really updated since I was last dating. That's pretty cool, though, that people can be so open about everything upfront." He sits back in his chair and crosses his arms over his bare chest, dark brows furrowed, deep in thought, and somehow as gorgeous as ever. "I honestly haven't considered it before now. I've been with Shelby for so long, but no, I don't think I would have any reservations about dating a woman who happens to be transgender."

My fucking heart, this man.

I know Hudson is an ally, so I'm not completely shocked by his answer. He has always made his support of the LGBTQIA+ community obvious, not in a showy way, but he's always the first to volunteer when Beckett or I have asked for team support for Pride events, and he's never hesitated to use Pride Tape or wear the Pride jerseys like some players. But dating preferences are so personal, and yet he didn't hesitate to share his with me. Not only did I like his answer but the fact that he is so comfortable with me already makes me way happier than it should.

I want to ask if I was right in labeling him as straight, but he didn't correct me, so I don't need to make him repeat it unnecessarily. Even if I could probably use the reminder when he's looking as attractive as he does right now, continuing with his green-flag behavior.

"Okay, let's move on, I think we're almost done. Do you want me to include any hobbies or interests?"

"Hockey, obviously," he says with a laugh. "But other than that, I'm pretty boring. Everything in my life has revolved around hockey for so long, I'm not sure what else I like."

"A workaholic? I wouldn't know anything about that," I tease. "But I'm sure there's something. Do you enjoy working out? Like, is that something you only do because you need to for work, or do you think you'll still do that when you retire?"

"Yeah, I enjoy it. I can't imagine stopping."

"Then we'll put fitness as an interest. And hockey. Maybe design TV shows? Or has that just been while I'm around?"

"Oh, you can definitely add interior design shows. I'm officially hooked. Half of my algorithm is interior design now."

I can't help but smile at the thought of Hudson scrolling through endless videos of wallpaper and mirror shapes. I'll be so curious to see how he decorates his place when he does move out.

I hope that he shows me, and that we'll remain friends. I know it hasn't been all that long since he moved in here, only a couple of weeks really, and he's been gone for a lot of it with his travel schedule, but we fell into our routine so quickly that it's hard to think about how quiet it will be when he's gone. How empty my condo will feel.

I'll be fine. I've always been fine living on my own. I'm just being dramatic. *Dramatic? Me? Never.*

I put the finishing touches on his profile and realize I have one more question. "Have you thought about how you'll handle it if you match with a fan? Would you prefer to date someone who doesn't really care about hockey or…?"

"I've never had a strong opinion either way. Shelby didn't really care about hockey, but she got really into the idea of it after we started dating. Looking back, I think it was more the WAG lifestyle she was into than anything else. I could see the benefits of dating someone who doesn't care at all, who's interested in me for me and not because of my job." He tilts his head back and forth as he considers. "But, like I said, hockey is such a big part of my life, I also think it would be nice to be with someone who genuinely enjoyed the sport, so they don't get bored of me talking about it all the time."

I nod. "Yeah, I get that. My last boyfriend was so confused when I'd want to watch every Werewolves game live, like if I wasn't at work, why should I care about watching it as it happened? I could just look up the score later, right? *Wrong, Kevin.* And that is one of the many reasons he's an ex."

Hudson laughs, and it lights up his whole face. As great as all the pictures on his profile are, nothing compares to seeing him like this in person, relaxed and enjoying his life, laughing at something I said because he thinks I'm funny. It's intoxicating. I already feel addicted to being in his presence, soaking up his positive energy.

Seriously. What the hell am I going to do when he leaves?

"It sounds like you made the right decision with Kevin," he says with another laugh. "So when do I start looking at other people's profiles? How do I match?"

Yeah… I don't think I can sit here and watch him pick out the next Mrs. Roy. I need to start mentally preparing for when he moves on and I'm still here, all alone.

"Everything is set up, so whenever you'd like, you can start," I say, pushing the computer over toward him. "But I'm going to call it a night. I've got to go in early to prepare for a big meeting, so I'll probably see you around before the game tomorrow night."

"Oh, okay." I hate how disappointed he sounds, but I know I'm not in the right headspace to be any help. I'm going to focus on every single flaw I can find and that isn't going to actually be helpful.

But instead of going through the profile on the screen like I'm expecting, he shuts the laptop. "Ya know what, I should go to bed too. I'll look at that when I'm more rested."

Or never. Never is good too. God, what would Hudson say if he knew how pathetic my internal monologue about him is? "That's a good plan," I agree instead, forcing a smile.

Then, as if to make sure I have no hope of thinking of anything else tonight, he winks at me. "Goodnight, Prince."

"Night, Hudson."

Trying to fall asleep, I imagine a world where Hudson changes his preferences in the app to all genders, that we match, and he realizes we're perfect for each other.

If only.

He wouldn't even need to do it on the app. He could just knock on my door. It's so easy to picture him there, asking to come in. Obviously I'd let him, and he'd confess that he misses sleeping with someone, and I'd easily agree to having him in my bed, but we would both know it was just an excuse. In this fantasy, Hudson has always wanted to be with a man, but before me there was never anyone worth risking his career over.

Now, though, this fantasy Hudson can't keep his hands off me. My dick is rock hard as I imagine him exploring my body with his hands, maybe even his mouth. I take off my sleep shorts, grab some lube out of my nightstand, and coat my hand with it before moving it back to my aching erection.

I slowly work my hand up and down my cock as I picture a hesitant Hudson, unsure what to do with another man's dick but eager to learn like he is about everything else in life. I'd assure him that he has nothing to worry about, that I can show him exactly what to do. I rub my thumb over the leaking tip as I imagine him licking it clean instead, and my hips jerk involuntarily.

I'd offer to blow him first though, talking him through it so that when it was his turn, he'd be more confident. I imagine fitting all of him inside of my mouth as I grip my cock a little harder. The sweats he's always wearing do absolutely nothing to hide how big of a feat that would be, and I love the idea of proving to him that I could.

If I already had my mouth on his cock though, I'd want to go even further, move to give his balls some attention and see if he likes that. I use my other hand to play with my own as I picture slipping a finger even further, imagine teasing his hole to see how he reacts.

Obviously, in this made-up version, Hudson loves it and begs for more, begs me to fuck him, and even though he's never been with a man before, he's ready. He trusts me. More than anything else, the idea of Hudson asking me to be the first man inside him is too much for me to handle. I can't hold off any longer, and my release crashes over me. The high of my orgasm distracts me from any coherent thought, and I have no idea how loud I've been during this little fantasy.

Usually when all the half-naked perfect eye candy that is Hudson gets to be too much, I wait until I'm locked away in my ensuite where I know he won't hear me jerking off.

I need to be more careful. I'd hate to scare him away because I make him uncomfortable with my solo sex noises.

I have no idea how long it'll be before he finds someone on his new dating app, so I probably don't have much time left anyway. I can't risk losing him a moment before I need to.

Having him here has probably been one of the best things that ever happened to me. I don't think I'll ever be ready to say goodbye.

9

HUDSON

Martin takes advantage of the shift change chaos and gets possession as I jump back onto the ice. I wait until he crosses the blue line into the offensive zone, and then I'm flying toward the net. I'm not nearly as fast as Ollie, though, and he's ahead of me to accept Martin's pass before LA's defense can get anywhere near him. He takes a shot, but at the last second, their goalie is able to block it from going in.

Luckily, my "old" ass has caught up by now, and I'm in the perfect spot to snag the puck on the deflection. Their goalie anticipates my shot, so I line up like I'm going to go for it but pass it back to Ollie who just circled the net instead. He snaps it in behind the goalie who was focused on me.

The lamp lights up and everyone crowds around Ollie, who just earned his second goal of the night, and we're only five minutes into the second. We all know there's about to be a mad rush for the fans to buy hats, but none of us will say anything and risk jinxing his chance of getting a hat trick.

Our line returns to the bench, and I try to focus on the face-off while I rehydrate. We're only five games into the season, but it's been our strongest start in years. We've won our two home games and two away so far. We lost to Pittsburgh in overtime, but we still got the point for the tie there. Ollie's goal brought us up to three points; meanwhile, Anderson, our goalie, hasn't let LA get anything in.

It's way too early in the season to even be thinking about our standings. But team morale is high, and I know I'm not the only one strictly sticking to their routine, afraid to fuck something up when things seem to be going so well. I've certainly wondered if my new roommate might be a good luck charm with how many points I've already gotten in our other games. Our line has a few more shifts before the end of the period, but it isn't until the third that Ollie is able to take advantage of the empty net and earn his first hat trick of the season.

A shutout and a hat trick at home, on a Saturday? This city, or at least the part surrounding the Caldwell Center, is about to be crazy.

"Congrats, man." I bump Ollie's helmet with mine, getting out of the way for everyone else to do the same. Coach tells us both to hang back for the stars of the game to be announced, and I quickly wave when my three stars are announced for my assists, getting out of the way for Anderson and Bell to be awarded their two and one stars, respectively.

The next hour is a blur of the quick post-game team meeting, media, and showering. Unlike most of the guys, I'm not in any hurry to get out of here to go party. I'll go out with them if anyone really wants me to, especially on the road or after a big win, but I'm doing that to support my teammates, not because I really want to go drink in a crowded bar after giving it my all during the game.

Ollie is the last one in the locker room with me since he was stuck in even more interviews than normal. "You going out?" he asks, looking over at me where I'm sitting on the bench next to him.

"Do you want me to?"

He shrugs. "I don't particularly want to go, but I was told it wasn't optional. So, yeah, I think you should be forced to come with me."

I laugh before letting out a dramatic sigh. "Fine, I'll go."

He laughs too. "You don't really need to if you have plans or something."

"Hot date with myself, actually. I was hoping to be asleep in the next hour." I should be scheduling real dates, but this morning when I was telling myself to go through other profiles on the dating app to try to get matches, it sounded way too overwhelming to do on my own.

Adrian was so helpful with setting it all up, maybe he'll help me with this part too?

"Come on, you're not that old," Ollie teases, lightly shoving my shoulder. "You should be going on a real date."

"Oh yeah, and what about you?"

His expression falls, and his face pales. "Me?"

Shit. I don't think I've ever seen him look like that before. Almost like he's scared? I hold my hands up in surrender. "Whoa, whatever I just said to make you that upset after a hat trick, I'm sorry."

"Fuck," he mutters, burying his face in his hands. "Why am I so awkward?"

"Hey, man, you're not awkward." I shift closer to him on the bench so I can put a comforting hand on his back. "What is it?"

He looks back up at me, and then glances around the empty locker room. "It's nothing. Sorry, I misunderstood."

"You seemed pretty upset for a second, are you sure you don't want to talk about it?" He glances at the door again, so I try a different approach. "Maybe I could drive you to the bar? If you change your mind, we can chat on the way."

He takes a deep breath before finally nodding. "Yeah, okay. I probably should have told you by now anyway."

Well, that sounds ominous.

"Perfect. You ready to go?" He nods so I grab my stuff and head toward the exit. After walking in silence for a bit, I decide to change the topic, hoping small talk will get him to relax before whatever it is he wants to tell me. "Any idea if staff are coming?" I ask.

"Not sure. Is there someone specific you're hoping is there?"

"Just wondering if I should text Adrian that I'll be home late or if he'll also be out."

He stops walking. "You're still living with Adrian?" Ollie sounds shocked, but I have no idea why.

"Uh, yeah, I would have mentioned it if I moved," I say with a short laugh as we start walking again. "What's that look for?" He doesn't say anything, staring at me like he has no idea what I'm talking about, but when we get to my car, he shakes his head and gets in.

"Seriously, what did I say wrong?" I push when we're settled and I'm pulling out of the lot.

"Nothing… I just—" His shoulders sink before he turns to look at me. "Can we be honest with each other? Like totally off the record? I feel like we've known each other for long enough, and we're friends, not just teammates, right? You're not going to say anything?"

"Of course I wouldn't say anything." I assure him, although I have no idea what he's talking about, so hopefully I'm not agreeing to anything illegal.

"Are you dating him?"

"Dating who?" I ask. I thought he was about to tell me some big secret, so I'm surprised by the question, although as I say that, I immediately realize I know who he's talking about. "Adrian?"

"Yes, Adrian! The gay man you've been living with for almost a month now."

Why would he think we're dating? Because he's gay? I thought we went over this… "No, we're just friends," I remind him. I'd like to lecture him again about making those kinds of assumptions, but he already seems upset, so I'll save that for a better time when he'll be more likely to listen to my feedback.

Ollie hangs his head back against his seat with a groan. "And we're being honest here. This isn't a 'just friends' situation that's hiding more?"

"Yeah, I'm being honest. Why are you even asking?" I'm focusing on the road, but in my periphery, I see him turn to look at me again.

He stares for a long moment, finally turning away to look out the window, crossing his arms over his chest before he answers. "Because I've had those types of friends, and it's never ended well."

"Oh," I say before I can stop myself. That is not where I saw this conversation going. "Wait, are you coming out to me right now? Have you been hiding that this whole time? I'm so sorry if you felt like you had to, Ollie. I had no idea."

He groans, turning back to look at me. "It wasn't anything you did. It was my stupid agent. He's convinced that I can't be the next big name in hockey if everyone finds out I'm gay."

"Well, that's bullshit." I huff. "You're still *you* no matter who you want to date. And you *are* the next big name in hockey. The Werewolves have invested enough in you that you should know that. Plus, the team's owner is very publicly gay, they wouldn't care if you came out. Is that why you looked scared when I mentioned dating back there?"

He laughs, shaking his head. "No, Hudson, that was because I'm painfully awkward." He laughs again. "I should probably quit while I'm ahead and never admit this, but when I said you should go on a date, and you asked 'what about you?' the secretly gay kid that used to have a huge crush on his idol had a freakout moment where I thought you were asking me on a date. And then I was mortified when I realized that you obviously were not."

Holy shit, he had a crush on me? That's flattering.

"Fuck, Ollie, I'm so sorry. I wasn't trying to make you uncomfortable—or disappoint you? I don't really know what you were feeling, but I was just trying to joke around and give you shit for also being single. I had no idea… You said 'used to'?"

"Oh god yes, definitely in the past, way before I met you."

"Should I be offended that my personality was apparently so off-putting?" I joke, trying to keep the mood lighter so he doesn't think I care about his confession.

"You're way too nice. I don't know if you'll be offended by that, but when I found out you weren't as tough as I'd pictured, the illusion was shattered," he teases.

"Probably for the best. I'm sorry that your agent isn't being more supportive though."

"Yeah, I get their concern, I really do. But I've also accidentally almost let something slip that would give myself away so many times. I'm sick of always having to filter myself."

"That sounds exhausting."

"It is."

"Well, maybe we can keep winning, and then you can announce that you're into guys after your next hat trick or something, and no one can claim you aren't the next hockey star."

"God, I wish it was that easy."

"We'll figure something out," I assure him. "You've got my support now. If it's what will make you happy, we'll find a way for you to do it, don't worry."

"Thanks, Cap."

"Now that we talked, do we actually have to go out?" I joke.

"Probably."

We get to the same crowded bar the players always go to after games, hurrying to the back private section they reserve for us and say hello to the rest of the team. After a few minutes, I give up looking around for Adrian and realize I should have just texted him before we even got here.

HUDSON

Any chance you decided to come out with the team tonight, and I just haven't seen you here yet?

ADRIAN

LOL no. I'm already in bed.

HUDSON

Jealous! But also boo, wish you were here. I feel like we haven't gotten to hang out much lately.

ADRIAN

We hung out last night...

HUDSON

How dare I want to do it again.

ADRIAN

Hey, I'm not the one who went out, you could have come home.

HUDSON

Should I leave? It wouldn't take me long to get there. I can bring snacks

ADRIAN

I mean... I'm not going to turn down snacks... but shouldn't you hang out with your teammates? Great game by the way! Amazing assist in the second!

HUDSON

Thanks! Nah, I've already said hello to everyone, I should be good to go.

ADRIAN

If you're sure...

HUDSON

See you soon!

I confirm with Ollie that he's got a sober ride home before I leave, stopping to pick up the promised snacks. Hopefully Adrian isn't too tired. I'll feel bad if he really was already in bed, and I'm demanding that he hang out with me.

But I'm also looking forward to spending time with him too much to consider changing our plans now.

ADRIAN

I was surprised that Hudson even texted to see if I was out.

I was completely shocked when he offered to leave the bar to hang out with me instead. Why would he want to hang out with me when he has another option? Still, I jumped out of bed, even though I wasn't convinced that he was actually going to ditch his team. I debated if I should change out of my pajamas, but that felt like I was jinxing it, so I'm still in my matching silk sleep shorts and button-up shirt.

Not that Hudson cares what I'm wearing, so it doesn't even matter.

Barely twenty minutes after he made the plan, Hudson walked in with a bag full of treats, looking thrilled to spend the rest of his night at home with me. He changed into his pajamas too, aka his loose sleep pants and no shirt, and is preparing our snacks.

I don't need to be focusing on that, though, so I go over to the couch, get comfortable wrapped up in one of my favorite blankets, and pull up our usual home design channel.

"Hey, would you want to watch a movie tonight instead?" he asks from the kitchen.

"Sure. What kind of movie?"

"Maybe a comedy? I don't really care; I just thought we could mix it up."

"Okay, I'll put on one of my favorites." Then, as if I wasn't surprised enough, instead of going to the opposite corner of the couch like he normally does, Hudson sits down *right* next to me.

His thigh is touching mine, and I can't seem to remember how to breathe.

What is happening?

"Chocolate?" Hudson asks, handing me a bowl of mini Reeses. If I thought I was dreaming before when a half-naked Hudson was just walking around my apartment being all domestic… I have no idea what's happening now. Did I die? Were all those religious people I grew up with right and heaven is real?

Well, they weren't completely right if it is, because they claimed I wouldn't be going.

"Thanks," I manage to get out without sounding too breathless as I take another piece.

"Want any of mine, too?" he offers, holding out his bag of pistachios toward me.

"Gross."

"You're not allergic, are you?" he asks, dramatically pulling the bag away from me.

"No, you're fine, I'm not allergic to anything. I just have no desire to eat something even vaguely healthy when there's a much better *chocolate* option," I explain, holding up my bowl.

"Right. How silly of me to even suggest it," he teases. "So what are we watching?"

"*Miss Congeniality*," I hesitantly answer, waiting to gauge his reaction.

"Cool, I've never seen it." He settles in further, focusing on the screen.

Well, it's a damn good thing I've already seen it, because how the hell am I supposed to focus on anything when Hudson is *this* close to me?

Every time he shifts I want to cry, because our thighs brush against each other, and all I can think about is how I wish we were even closer, how I wish I could eliminate any and all space between us and maybe crawl right into his lap.

He's so nice he probably wouldn't even care.

But that would be weird. Right?

As the movie goes on, Hudson seems to sink further into the couch, and as great as the movie is, I'm honestly surprised he's still awake after how hard he worked tonight.

"Would you rather lay down?" I whisper. We can finish this another time. He certainly doesn't need to stay awake for my benefit when I could probably recite this whole movie from memory.

"You wouldn't mind?"

"Not at all," I assure him, reaching for the remote, but instead of standing up to move to his bed, he shifts even lower to lay down on the couch. And he doesn't just stretch out—Hudson puts his head *on my thigh* like a pillow.

That is so not at all what I was suggesting, and yet I've never been happier for a misunderstanding. Even if I have no idea why this straight man would assume I was offering to basically cuddle or why he would agree so quickly. I'm not going to question a good thing.

I was just wishing we could cuddle… Did I manifest this? I need to start a Hudson vision board or something.

The blanket means his face isn't touching my bare leg, but it's all too easy for my imagination to run wild right now, picturing a far less heterosexual Hudson moving the blanket out of the way, turning his head so his face was aimed at my crotch instead of the screen. The things he could be doing with his mouth in that position.

Deep breaths. Calm down. I do not need to make my erection any more obvious right now. Thank God he's low enough on my leg that he doesn't seem to have noticed.

On a slightly more innocent note, I want to reach out and run my hand through his hair, play with it while he watches the movie, but that would most certainly be crossing the line of friends and roommates.

Where that line is right now, I'm not entirely sure, but I know it still exists, and I'm doing my very best to not overstep, damn it.

I have no idea how long I sit here, staring at all the varying shades in his chocolate brown hair, wondering what it feels like before I realize that Hudson has fallen asleep.

What the fuck do I do now?

Obviously, I could wake him up… *But I don't want to*. I don't want to cut off this perfect moment.

Before Hudson moved in, I had a mostly innocent, but definitely harmless, crush on him. It was fine. I wasn't obsessive and it didn't prevent me from dating anyone else. But now? Hudson has spent every moment since he moved in proving to me that he isn't just a good guy, he isn't just exactly my type—he's truly the perfect man. The gold standard, and no one else will ever compare. That little crush has evolved into something I no longer have any control over.

And now this perfect man is asleep in my lap, and my imagination decides to be even more cruel. Sexual fantasies are one thing, but now I'm picturing lazy nights at home, *exactly like this one,* because tonight was everything I've ever wanted to have with a partner. Hudson put me first, not because I asked him to, not because I did something to earn it, but because he genuinely wanted to spend time with me. We didn't need to leave the house, he went out of his way to get me chocolate, and he even let me pick the movie.

I don't think I've ever felt more wanted in my life and it's platonic.

If I were to wake him up right now so we could move into the same bed, even if all we did was sleep, then it would probably be one of the best nights of my life. It's still up there as is.

But I can't wake him up. Can't shatter this illusion of what a night with Hudson as my partner would be like. Not yet.

He'll probably wake up when the movie ends anyway.

Except, he doesn't, and I tell myself just another minute. Just one more moment to enjoy this.

Just one more.

HUDSON

*D*id I get a new pillow?

And leave the curtains open? Adrian's black-out curtains are no joke—there's never this much sunlight in the morning.

I finally open my eyes enough to look around and realize I'm still on the couch. I must have fallen asleep watching the movie last night. Damn. I was enjoying it too, but once Adrian offered to have me lay down, I didn't stand a chance after a game.

I shift and realize that my pillow is not actually a pillow. I'm still laying on Adrian's leg. *Holy shit,* he didn't move all night? He looks far less comfortable than I was, half sitting up and slumped against the arm of the chair. I sit up fully and check the time. Still way earlier than he needs to be awake for the day on a Sunday.

I nudge him. "Hey, did you want to move into your bed? That doesn't look very comfy."

"Hmm?" he hums sleepily. "You want to go to my bed?"

I chuckle. "Nah, I have to go in for conditioning soon, but you should sleep."

"M'fine," he mumbles, but his brow is furrowed and there is just no way his neck isn't going to hurt with the angle it's at.

"I've got you." I stand and position one arm under his knees and the other behind his back. "Put your arms around my neck, and I'll carry you."

He does what I say without actually opening his eyes, and he's small enough that I lift him easily. He rests his head on my chest, and the way he trusts me so easily, even in sleep, makes me smile. Luckily his bedroom door is open, so even though it's dark and I can't really make out the details of the room, I'm able to carry him all the way to his bed without any obstacles. But when I lay him down, he doesn't remove his arms from around me.

"Alright, Charming, you're in bed, you can let go now."

"Don't wanna," he grumbles, eyes still closed, hugging me closer.

"I wish I could stay too, but I have to go to work," I remind him with a laugh. I can't help it, Adrian is usually so put together, so energetic, and seeing this sleepy side of him that just wants to cuddle is adorable. He still hasn't let go, and I really did enjoy how comfortable we were laying together on the couch last night. "We can cuddle later if you'd like," I promise, peeling his hand away from my neck.

"Fiiiine," he says through a yawn.

"Sweet dreams, Adrian."

"Night, babe."

Babe? Who does Adrian think I am right now in his half-asleep state? There's a twisting sensation in my stomach as it sinks in that he probably wishes I was someone else. He said he wasn't seeing anyone, but maybe it isn't serious, or maybe there's someone he wishes he was seeing.

I hope he isn't holding back from having anyone over because of me.

But I also don't love the idea of giving up the time we have to hang out together.

That's selfish though; if he wants to have a guy over, to his own house, he obviously should. I'll have to ask him about it later.

I should really look at that dating app too.

ADRIAN IS TALKING LOUDLY in his office when I get back a few hours later, so I head to my room to call my parents. My dad is napping, but my mom gushes about our game last night, going on and on about how excited they are to see us play in person soon. I'm excited too, but it's weird to think it'll be the last time with me retiring.

Hopefully we'll have other things to celebrate though. Maybe I'll meet someone soon, and they'll also be eager to have kids. I'm trying to remain optimistic even if those new life milestones I'm hoping to reach seem further away than ever.

With that thought in mind, I think it's time to really sit down and look through who's on the dating app, no matter how much I don't love the idea of trying to weed through profiles by myself. I go back into the living room, determined to make some progress while I wait for Adrian to be done with whatever he's working on in his office, and am excited to see he's already moved into the kitchen, grabbing some water.

"Hey! Did you end up having to work too?" I ask.

He snorts a laugh. "Yeah, I don't really take any days off. It works out pretty well that my boss is one of my best friends, so it doesn't always feel like work."

"That must be nice. So how did you guys meet? Did you ever

date?" I ask, wondering if Beckett Caldwell could be the "babe" he was picturing this morning. I know he has a boyfriend now, but maybe Adrian is jealous?

He scoffs. "Definitely not. We met in college, but we never dated. He and our other friend, Jordan, gave me a place to stay when I had issues with a roommate, and we've all been friends since."

I don't know why, but I'm relieved by his answer, and I love how freely he shared it. I want to ask about the issues with the roommate. I actually want to know everything about him that he's willing to share, but I don't want to sound too eager. And I shouldn't care who he's dated; I should be supportive of my friend. "That's awesome you're all still close. Most of my friends are also current or former hockey players, so we don't have a ton of time to spend together. Hopefully I can catch up with some of them after this season."

"Yeah, that'll be such a change of pace for you to have free time."

Shit. I shouldn't have made it about me again when he was talking about himself. Well, maybe if I open up more, he'll be more comfortable doing the same. "I'm just hoping I won't be alone for too long. I had all these visions of becoming a dad and having all that time to dedicate to my family."

"It'll happen," he assures me with a supportive smile. "I might be overstepping by saying this, but Shelby was an idiot who didn't know how good she had it. Anyone would be lucky to end up with you."

I let out a relieved breath, feeling like a weight has been lifted from my chest at Adrian's assurance. He makes it so easy to open up to him. "No overstepping. I actually really appreciate you saying that. I've been trying to tell myself that we just wanted different things, but it's still hard not to second-guess myself, or wonder what I did wrong and if I'll make the same mistakes when I do try dating again."

"Be yourself, and whoever you give attention to will fall for you in no time. And make sure you're clear that you eventually want to have kids. Maybe ease them into your ideal timeline for that though," he teases.

"Is 'I want to be a dad' not a good first date topic?" I joke.

"Just make sure you don't say 'daddy' because then you'll be setting them up with very different expectations," he teases. "Unless of course you're into that, I'm not kink shaming."

I burst out laughing at the thought of asking my date to call me that. "Not my thing," I confirm when I calm down. "But thank you for the advice. So, do you have more work to do? Or do you want to hang out?"

"Nah, I should be free for a bit. Did you want to finish the movie?"

"Eventually, yes, because I was really enjoying it, even if I fell asleep, but I was actually wondering if you might be able to help me look through the dating profiles?" I flash a hopeful smile. "Doing it on my own seems overwhelming, and I know you already helped so much setting it up, but I'd love to be able to talk through it with you."

He hesitates, and for a moment, I worry he's going to turn me down. Is it bad that I asked? Before I can panic too much though, he answers. "Sure." Then he's smirking. "What would you do without me?"

"I'm seriously starting to wonder," I chuckle.

I move to the couch, getting comfortable in the corner and stretch my legs out. "I got the app on my phone too," I comment as I log in. Adrian comes around the couch and hesitates, so I pat the cushion next to me. "We'll need to both see the screen."

"Right," he says quietly before joining me on the couch. But when he does, he's kind of stiff, sitting up straight, not a blanket or extra pillow in sight.

I pull up the first woman's profile, but right away I don't think she'd be a good match. She reminds me too much of Shelby, so I move on. The next person has similar vibes, based on the very posed and curated images, I'm just getting a sense that they care more about their appearance than I'm hoping for in my partner.

"Sooo are you going to show me anything, or am I here in more of a moral support capacity?" Adrian jokes when the next profile is also not my vibe.

I playfully roll my eyes. "Well, you're all the way over there, how are we both supposed to see the screen?"

He looks around then back at me with a disbelieving smile. "Over where? I am literally right next to you on this giant couch."

"I know, but your posture is so proper it's like you're on high-alert or something. Scooch in closer and get comfy. I won't bite," I tease.

He lets out a surprised laugh. "Okay, what the fuck are you expecting? Any closer and we'll basically be cuddling."

"Yes! That would be perfect actually, great idea," I agree. "You can lay your head on my chest, and then we'll both be able to see the screen."

He stares at me, blinking a few times without responding or making any moves to lay on me. "You want to cuddle with me?" he finally asks.

"Well, don't sound so surprised. I did promise you this morning that we could cuddle later," I remind him in a light tone.

"You did what?" he asks, sounding completely surprised. "When the hell did you promise me cuddling? I would definitely remember that."

"In your bed this morning?" I prompt, but that only makes his eyes go even wider.

"There is no way you were in my bed this morning promising to cuddle me! I would absolutely remember that."

"Maybe you were more asleep than I thought," I suggest with a shrug. "You're strong in your sleep then; it took some effort for me to untangle you from me."

Adrian has turned his whole body to face me now, and he slaps my arm lightly. "Hudson! What the fuck are you talking about?"

"Do you remember us falling asleep on the couch last night? How do you think you ended up in your bed this morning?"

"I thought I dreamed that! Did you actually carry me?" His eyes are wider than I've ever seen them, and it's kind of adorable. He almost looks like a cartoon version of himself. I want to take a picture and turn it into his contact picture on my phone, but I'm sure the second I pull my camera out, he'd change his expression, so I try to just memorize it.

"Yeah, I carried you," I confirm with a laugh. "And I promised more cuddling to get you to let go of me. So did you not actually want that? You did call me 'babe' so maybe you thought you were talking to someone else," I admit awkwardly.

He's got his hands in his hair now, and it looks like he might be pulling it. "Oh my god, I did?"

He sounds mortified, so I rush to reassure him. "Yeah, but it was no big deal, and if you were thinking of someone else, I hope you're not hesitating to invite them over because I'm here. You're being so nice letting me stay; I'd hate to find out I'm cock-blocking you."

He's shaking his head before I can even finish. "There's no one to invite. I must have been talking to some dream boyfriend in my half-asleep state. I'm so sorry if I made you uncom-fortable."

"Not at all." I laugh. "So is that a yes for more cuddling now? I do miss it. I was in a relationship for so long that it's weird to be cut off from all physical contact so abruptly…" I trail off, realizing that was probably a very weird thing to admit.

After a long moment, Adrian finally chuckles. "Alright, fuck it, let's get comfy." I settle back in the corner, scooting in so he can stretch his legs out next to mine on the wide couch while he rests his head on my chest. It's almost like I'm spooning him, but we're sitting up, and I'm holding up my phone in front of both of us.

I'm comfortable, and Adrian immediately starts commenting on the profile that's pulled up, so I assume he is too.

"Sorry for judging her, but I just don't see you dating someone who's drinking in every single picture they included. I like a fancy cocktail as much as anyone, but it seems like a red flag in every single photo."

"Yeah, I agree. Who's next." I pull up the next suggested profile and start with the basic info.

"Oh, this woman is an artist! That's fun… just kidding." He cringes when I pull up the included images. "Can you imagine having to pretend to be interested in splashed paint all the time? Every one of them looks exactly the same!"

I let out a short laugh. "Yeah, I don't think I'd be very good at pretending I like that. Okay, what about this woman?" I ask, moving on. "She's around my age, she's a teacher, so she probably likes kids. That's a good sign, right?"

"In the dislikes section, she put 'sports,'" he points out.

"Well, why the hell did it even suggest her?" I say with another laugh, trying to stay positive.

"This one has her follower count on socials, so that's a no. This one says no one under six feet—"

"But I'm taller than that."

"Yeah, but you don't want to date someone who's that judg-mental," he explains.

"Yes, because we aren't being judgmental at all," I deadpan, earning a snorted laugh from Adrian.

"Well, it's only okay when we do it," he teases. "Okay, this woman says she wants to be entertained. That doesn't sound like she's looking for a serious life partner." He moves on to another. "Hmm, this one has had too much work done; you're not looking for someone that obsessed with their image."

I smile at that comment. Adrian really has managed to get to know me so well in so little time. I wish I knew more about him.

"Careful, you're starting to sound like you don't want me to match with any of them," I tease.

Adrian sucks in a sharp breath, turning his head to look up at me. "Don't make fun of me for trying to help," he says jokingly.

"I'm not making fun of you, it's cute you're taking it so seriously, that you actually want to help," I explain, still holding his gaze.

"Of course I want to help..." he says easily. Then he goes back to teasing. "You think I'm cute?"

We're still looking right at each other, and his face is so close to mine with the way we're cuddling. I know he's only joking around, the same way I was moments ago, but for some reason his question, combined with our position, has my cheeks heating as I answer. "So cute."

Adrian's cheeks also darken with my answer, his mouth curving into a smirk. I don't think I've ever really seen his lips this close-up and my attention is snagged there, staring. Adrian has full, pink lips that look so soft I kind of want to touch them, to cup his jaw with my hand and run my thumb over his parted mouth to see if they're as smooth as they look.

"Wow, you must be really desperate for connection if you're staring at my mouth like that," Adrian jokes, reminding me of what we're actually supposed to be doing right now. "Look at your date's lips like that, and you'll be kissing them in no time."

I laugh, unsure of how else to respond to that.

Did I look like I wanted to kiss Adrian? I guess I was thinking about touching his lips quite a bit, even if I wasn't picturing actually kissing him.

Fuck. Now I am though. I wonder what his soft full lips would feel like against mine. Would it feel all that different than kissing a woman?

What the fuck is happening right now? I totally want to kiss him.

Adrian is so funny and smart and confident, and it's all so captivating, and things I'm normally drawn to in women. And cuddling was so nice. I think Adrian was right the other day, that I'm confusing myself about who he is to me. He isn't Shelby. He isn't my partner. The kissing thought is probably just because he's so pretty, and we're already cuddling. I'm obviously confused. I've never thought about another man that way before.

But I've also never met another man like Adrian.

Okay, calm down, what the hell am I even thinking? I'm just lonely. I should really meet up with one of the women on the app. I miss having someone to come home to, and I have no idea how much longer Adrian is willing to be that person for me.

I turn back to my phone, only half paying attention to the profile that's pulled up. "She seems nice. I think I'll message her."

12

ADRIAN

"I think your stovetop is clean," Jordan comments from his barstool in my kitchen.

I might have been the one who invited him over to hang out, but I haven't been able to sit still, so my glass of wine is still untouched next to his now empty one on the counter.

"So, are you ready to talk about why you're obsessively cleaning, or are we still pretending that it has nothing to do with Hudson being out on a date tonight?"

"There's nothing to talk about," I insist. "Oh! I should clean out my fridge. I haven't done that in a few weeks." Focused on my new task, I start taking everything out of it so I can do a deep clean.

And I'm not even lying. There isn't anything to talk about. Things have gone back to normal after the weird cuddling thing last week where, for a tiny second, I thought Hudson might have been thinking about kissing me. Obviously, he wasn't, and my imagination was running wild after he confirmed he'd carried me to my bed that morning. Plus all the cuddling. It was just a confusing moment that I was reading into way too much.

The night ended normally with Hudson setting up a date. For

tonight. A date that I helped him plan where to go and helped him choose what to wear.

And I was happy to help. I *love* helping my friends.

Well, normally, I really love helping my friends. I love seeing them happy and knowing that I made things easier for them, or contributed to their joy, even in some small way. I usually thrive on that. I go out of my way to solve problems for other people so I can have that moment of sharing their success.

But with Hudson? Everything is different.

As much as I do want him to be happy, and I really, really do —I want him to be happy more than anyone else I've ever met and he deserves it with how kind and positive he is, how he brings out the good in those around him—I'm still struggling. By helping him try to move on like he's asked me to, by helping him find another woman to date, I can't help but feel like I'm finding my replacement.

And I know how silly that is. Obviously, any romantic feelings between us are entirely one-sided on my part, but it's inevitable that he'll stop doing all the nice things he does for me now when he has a girlfriend to do them for instead. Whatever woman he ends up dating is who he's going to be picking up dinners for. They're the one he's going to be watching hours of TV with at night, the person he's going to go out of his way to pick up their favorite snack for. When they fall asleep on the couch, he'll carry them back to a bed they share.

And I'll still be here. Alone in my apartment, like I've always been.

Which is fine.

I love my life. I wasn't looking for it to be turned upside down when he moved in here. I'm just being dramatic right now because I've gotten so used to our routine, and now that he's on his first date, I know it's over. Once I see him with whatever girl he's dating, I'll remember that we've always only been friends.

That I have no right to feel so heartbroken right now at the thought of losing him.

Because he was never mine.

No matter how much it's felt that way since he moved in.

And I'm totally *fine*. I'm not at all jealous or freaking out, and I'm definitely not tempted to show up at the restaurant I know he's at to hide in the corner to see how his date is going.

I'm totally chill. Just cleaning out my fridge. The contents are now on the counter, and I've moved on to wiping down the shelves.

"So how have things been since the cuddling?" Jordan pushes. Obviously, the group chat with our friends heard all about that, but I don't need him bringing it up right now. Maybe I should stop telling my friends every little detail of my life?

Nah. Who am I kidding? I wouldn't last a week without that attention.

So what if I like the reminder that they all genuinely care about me and want to know about my life beyond how I can help make theirs easier? It took a long time for me to trust that they actually wanted that, and I think it's a completely typical valida-tion to crave.

"They have been perfectly normal, thank you for asking. He was in town for a few days after that night, and he was his usual ideal roommate self, walking around here shirtless, cleaning, having his chef make me food. Then he went out of town for the away games and got back late last night."

"I just don't think most straight guys platonically cuddle their gay roommates. Are you sure he isn't at least a little into you? Do you guys ever talk when he's out of town?"

"We're friends, Jordan, of course we talk. I talk to you every day too. It doesn't mean anything." His mouth is all twisted like he's fighting a smirk, so I narrow my eyes and glare at him. "I'm serious, Jordan. Stop trying to read into things that aren't there."

"Sure, sure. But one more question."

I roll my eyes. "Fine."

"Are you the one texting him first?"

Am I? I haven't really thought about it, so I pause my cleaning to pull out my phone and scroll up through our thread from the last few days. He met his date at the restaurant so he texted me a selfie when he got there and was waiting. This morning he asked if I wanted him to pick up anything on his way home after his practice. When he was out of town, I texted some comments about their game, congratulating him on his goal in the first and checking in after he took a nasty hit in the second. Earlier in the day, he told me about his lunch, and before that about how the hotel room bed was way less comfortable than the one in my apartment.

"Scrolling pretty far there," he mutters.

"Shut up. I guess he does send a lot of the first messages, but that doesn't mean he'll suddenly decide he wants more than friendship from me. That man is trying to get remarried and have kids as soon as possible. He isn't looking to have some sort of sexual awakening." I'm honestly still surprised he even wants to be as close of friends as we've become in so little time.

"You would be an excellent parent."

I let out a sigh before answering with my signature false confidence. "Obviously, I will one day. But Hudson is looking for a wife."

"If you say so."

"I do." I return to my cleaning and attempt to move on to a safer-for-me topic. "So what about you, any news on your dating life?"

Jordan snorts. "No."

Yeah, right. "But haven't you been hanging out with—"

"Don't."

"Why is the fridge empty?" Hudson asks, interrupting my

interrogation. I'm half inside the damn thing, scrubbing the back, and I bang my head into the shelf above me when I jump in surprise at the sound of his voice.

"Holy shit, are you okay?" He rushes over, arms hesitantly outstretched like he wants to touch me, but isn't sure if he should. "I'm sorry if I surprised you. I thought you would have heard me come in."

I stand up straight, rubbing the back of my head, but I wave him off. "I'm fine. Why are you back so early though?"

"The date was so awkward. At first I thought it was okay, normal small talk awkwardness, but after I mentioned my job she completely shut down."

"Did you not mention your job before tonight?" I gawk.

He shakes his head. "I didn't want to lead with what I do online because I'm trying to avoid someone only wanting to date me for the status, but maybe that was a mistake. She was so nervous after that, no matter how many questions I asked, she kept giving one word answers. And the few times she did try to say more, I ended up talking at the same time because I wasn't expecting it. I don't know, I guess I wasn't anticipating that I'd feel like a teenager on his first date again."

Be supportive, I remind myself. I should not be so fucking relieved to hear he had a bad date. "Ugh, I'm sorry it was such a waste of time. I'm sure they won't all be like that."

Jordan stands. "Sorry you had a rough night, Hudson. Thanks for having me over, A, but I have an early interview tomorrow so I'm going to head back."

"Shit, did I interrupt something?" Hudson asks, looking between Jordan and me. "Don't go on my account. You're Jordan, right? I think we've probably met, but I know Adrian's talked about you, and I feel like I've seen you around with him and Beckett Caldwell at work."

"Yeah, I'm Jordan, nice to see you again. And you didn't

interrupt anything. As exciting as watching Adrian clean has been, I really do need to go."

I'm sure it has nothing to do with his incorrect theory that Hudson might see me as more than a friend or me wanting to pry about his dating life. "Byyyye," I call out as he leaves.

I do want to give Hudson my full attention though, so I cut my cleaning short, moving things back into the fridge as quickly as I can, attempting to be the supportive friend I know he needs right now as I do. "I think the next one will go smoother; everyone is bound to have one rough date. It sounds like you got the bad one out of the way early. Have you been talking to anyone else on the app while you were out of town?"

Hudson takes Jordan's seat at the counter, slouching in the chair. "Yeah, I've sent a couple of messages to people, but I don't think I'm as excited about any of them as I'd like to be. And it's such a slow process getting to know someone entirely new. I feel like I'm so far away from having the future I want." He looks so defeated. All I want to do is hug him, but I'm also still kind of in my head about touching him after the cuddling the other night, so I stay on the other side of the counter even after I put my cleaning supplies away.

"You're only thirty-four, right? You have time."

"Yeah, I guess." He lets out a big sigh. "Have I ever told you about my dad?"

He's mentioned video calling his parents a few times since moving in, but other than that, I can't think of anything, so I shake my head.

"Growing up, I thought my dad was invincible, the perfect father. He worked hard at his job as an accountant for a local busi-ness, and numbers were never my thing so I thought that meant he was super smart. Then he'd come home and take me to hockey practice or run extra drills with me or just take me for extra time on the ice."

"He sounds really great." And like the exact opposite of my completely unsupportive parents. I'm glad he had better ones.

Hudson smiles, his whole face lighting up for the first time since he got home from the failed date. "Yeah. He was never even a huge hockey fan until I told him I wanted to play, and then he went all in, learning everything he could about the sport and getting me everything I needed. I now know hockey is really expensive, but he did it without ever complaining, and he even took me to watch professional or college games whenever he could."

I reclaim my abandoned glass of wine, silently offering one to Hudson who nods before he continues. "My mom was awesome too. She was a hairstylist at the salon in town and worked just as hard as he did. I know I was so lucky to have their support growing up, and I'm really glad that I can support them financially now, even if I do wish they lived closer."

"Where are they now?" I ask, handing him his glass.

"Minnesota. I've always wanted to follow their example, to have my own family one day too, to support my kids the way they did for me."

The way he says it, as if that future isn't possible for him, breaks my heart. I hate seeing him doubting himself like this when I know for a fact anyone would be lucky to share that family with him. "You will. Don't let a bad date discourage you. I know you'll get there. You're going to be such an amazing husband and father, you don't need to rush into it or put so much pressure on yourself."

"Thanks," he says with a small smile, his gray-blue eyes stormier than I think I've ever seen them. He takes a deep breath. "But that's not everything. Seven years ago, when my dad was only fifty-two, he got up to go to work like any other day, and what started as a seemingly innocent headache, ended up being a massive stroke."

"Oh, shit." I was not expecting that.

He nods. "He'd gone into work after complaining to my mom that he must have slept in a bad position because his arm felt a little numb. A few hours later, he'd been rushed to the hospital and couldn't move that whole side of his body. Now my family knows all about the BE FAST early warning signs of a stroke. I even try to do fundraising stuff with the team to help educate the community on stroke awareness and provide support for people who have had strokes and their families. But back then, we had no idea."

"Oh my god, was he okay?" I can't imagine how scary that must have been for his whole family.

"He's alive. We're so thankful for that. But he had seemed so young, and I was only twenty-seven at the time. No part of me was ready for that phone call. My seemingly invincible dad went from perfectly healthy to paralyzed on one side of his body, wheelchair bound, with speech and memory problems, just like that."

"Is there any treatment? I'm sorry if that's a dumb question, but I don't know much about strokes."

He shakes his head, offering me that soft smile, still so kind despite the difficult topic. "That's not dumb, I had no idea about any of it before it happened. He takes a lot of medications now, blood thinners, things to manage his cholesterol and blood pressure, and he's had good results from his physical, occupational, and speech therapies over the years. He can support himself in an electric chair, feed himself his thickened foods, and communicate with us in his own slow way."

"Wow. I'm glad he's okay, but that sounds like it must have been so hard on your whole family."

"Yeah, we've definitely had to grieve his independence, the person he was back then, but I'm so grateful that he seems to still enjoy his new quality of life. He's constantly listening to podcasts and watching documentaries. He's maintained his desire to learn, even if he doesn't retain the information like he used to. He still watches all my hockey games, and he's constantly wearing Werewolves merch. I love it. Hopefully he and my mom will be able to come to our game in Minnesota."

I smile picturing that. "Can I get his address before the game so the team can send something special?"

Hudson's smile finally reaches his eyes. "He'd love that."

I smile back, unable to look away when his gaze meets mine. "I'm glad he's okay."

"Thanks. He's still my dad, ya know." He shrugs. "Even if things have changed, his kindness and his love for his family still shine through the physical limitation his body now has. I've always idolized him, and that hasn't changed. If he can still smile, still find the joy in life even after everything he's been through, I'm not about to let a divorce hold me back."

I probably look like one of those cartoons with hearts for eyes right now as I stare at Hudson, but I can't help it. He really is amazing. Not many people would be able to remain so positive after everything he's dealing with right now. He doesn't even complain. Or bad-mouth his ex like I'm sure I would. The only thing he's really talked about with his divorce is wanting to move on and how he wants to find someone so he can start a family.

And his impatience to do that makes way more sense now that I know about his dad. He must feel like he's running out of time.

"So, is that why you're so eager to date? Are you worried that you'll have a stroke, too?"

He nods. "Having a parent who's had one does increase my risk. But it could be anything really—there's no way to know if or when you could get sick or injured. There are no guarantees in life."

I guess he's right. Why wait for what you want when tomorrow isn't promised. I try to think back on everything

Hudson has said about his hopes for his future since he moved in. He's talked about wanting to date again, sure, but it's always been tied to the fact that he wants kids. His comments are almost all about his desire to become a dad. When he was talking about how amazing his own father was growing up, his expression was as happy as I've ever seen him.

I have an idea. But I don't know if it's a selfishly motivated one, so I'm a little hesitant to voice it. "Can I ask you something?"

"Of course, Adrian. You can ask me anything."

Hopefully I'm not completely overstepping here. "Are you eager to date because you want to be in a romantic relationship again? Because you miss having a partner? Or do you feel like you *need* to date again because you want to have kids?" I think I'm asking because I want him to be happy, not because I hate the idea of him dating.

That's what I'm telling myself at least.

He crosses his arms, sitting back again with his brows furrowed as he really thinks through my question, but he doesn't seem upset by it at all; his expression is open, curious. "I'm not sure." he finally answers. "I guess I like the idea of having a partner again. I would like to share my life with someone eventually. But if I separate that from having kids... I'm in less of a hurry. The thing I want most is to be a dad."

That's what I thought he'd say. "And have you ever looked into options where you could become a parent on your own?"

He freezes for a moment before slowly shaking his head again. "No. I honestly hadn't thought to." He sits up a bit straighter. "But you're right, there are probably kids out there who need a parent, who would love to have a home. Why couldn't I do that on my own? Especially after the season ends?" He sounds more excited about the idea as he goes on, so I really hope I'm not making things up here and that he would actually qualify.

"I have no idea what the requirements are for fostering or adoption or surrogacy, but I would imagine your money would help. You'll be an amazing parent, and you don't need a wife for that to be true. I'd be happy to help you look into what your options are if that's something you're serious about pursuing." I'd do anything to keep that sad, hopeless expression off his face that he'd had while talking about his future.

Hudson doesn't hesitate; he's sitting on the edge of his chair now, gripping the counter as he tries to contain his obvious excitement, nodding eagerly. "Absolutely. Let's start now."

We spend the rest of the night looking into adoption in Illinois, and eventually he finds an agency that seems like a good fit. They have open informational meetings pretty frequently, so he plans to go to the next one he's in town for.

As I'm falling asleep, I can't help but adjust the ongoing fantasy version I have of Hudson and me, the one where we're madly in love, living together for entirely different reasons.

Tonight, we're decorating a nursery.

13

HUDSON

"*W*ho are you texting?" Ollie asks as he takes his seat next to me on the plane. He's been sitting there on our flights all season—we won again tonight against Florida—and with how many games we've won now, neither of us is going to stray from any of our routines.

"Adrian. I sent him a picture of that cute dog we saw this morning, so we've been talking about pets all day. Can you believe he's never had one?"

He nods. "I can, he doesn't seem like a pet person. Are you still living together?"

Not a pet person? Adrian would be an excellent pet parent. Ollie just doesn't know him as well as I do. That thought makes me feel a little more smug than it probably should. "Yeah, I'm still living with him," I finally answer. "But I did finally reach out to my realtor about finding my own place."

"Really? Did something happen between you two?"

I laugh at the thought of Adrian and me fighting. I don't see that ever happening. "No, nothing like that. Adrian is the perfect roommate, and I love spending my downtime with him. I'm not in a hurry to stop living together. But he did help me set some new goals for my future."

"Oh yeah? Are you going to keep playing?"

I can't help but laugh again at how hopeful he sounds. "No, you know I'm retiring."

"I know you keep saying that, but it doesn't mean I'm giving up hope you'll change your mind."

"Sorry, man, this really is my last year."

We have to pause to listen to the safety briefing before the plane takes off, but when we're settled and in the air, he continues. "So what's the new goal then?"

"Adrian and I were talking about what I want the most for my future, especially with me retiring. You know I've been trying out dating apps, and even had that one awkward date, but he helped me realize that as much as I'd like to get remarried one day, the thing I want the most is to be a parent. So I'm shifting my focus. If I meet someone, cool, but I'm going to put less pressure on myself about it and go after what I really want. I've been looking into the application process for adoption."

"No way. That's awesome! I can't imagine having kids anytime soon, but I can totally see it for you. You're going to be such a great dad."

I light up at his compliment. It's really the best one he could give me. "Thanks. I figure that I'll need to have a safe, stable home to raise kids in, so I asked my agent to try to find something with at least three bedrooms."

"Where are you looking?"

"The same neighborhood I'm in now. It's really grown on me."

Ollie smirks. "Is it the neighborhood? Or the people?"

I roll my eyes. Ollie hasn't dropped the idea that Adrian and I might be more than just friends despite our big talk about it.

"Obviously having Adrian as a neighbor will be nice, but I really do like the area too."

"Sure."

Ollie might not believe me, but I think it'll be the perfect place to raise kids. There are multiple playgrounds that are walkable, green spaces, a library, and there are a lot of families that live on his block. The restaurant we love to order from has a huge kids' menu, and I always see families eating in the dine-in area.

"Does Adrian want kids?" he asks.

I try to think if he's ever mentioned wanting them. "I'm not sure."

"Interesting."

"Why is that interesting?"

"I just thought that would come up if you guys were having a heart-to-heart about your future and how much you want to be a dad." He shrugs before he continues. "The first thing I said when you talked about adopting was that I can't imagine having kids. Adrian isn't exactly shy. It's interesting that he wouldn't have said if he wants any."

I disagree about it being out of character. Despite his very outgoing and friendly attitude, Adrian doesn't freely offer personal details about himself like that. Still, it does worry me a bit about how I've been approaching trying to get him to open up to me. Maybe I do need to be more direct.

"Are you saying I'm a shitty friend because Adrian is always so supportive of me, and I should ask him more about himself?"

Ollie laughs, then he leans in, speaking quietly enough that no one else will hear us over the loud sound of the plane. "No, I don't think you're a shitty friend. But I've seen the way you look at him, Hudson. I know you think I'm teasing you about him, and I mostly am. But my questions a few weeks ago about there being more between you two weren't just because he's gay. You always light up when you talk about him, you just said he's the perfect roommate, and you don't want to move away from him. I'm just wondering if there's a chance you might be overlooking how you feel about him because you've never been with a man before."

I shake my head, but I'm not sure how to respond. That night when we were cuddling on the couch immediately comes to mind, and how I thought about kissing him. But that was a onetime thing. And it's not like I actually kissed him. It was a passing thought. I'm surprised I even still remember having it.

"I'm just wondering if he's being careful not to make any comments that might sound like he's suggesting you want the same things in life," Ollie continues quietly. "As the openly gay man living with his assumingly straight friend, he's probably afraid to say or do anything that could sound like he's suggesting there could be more between you. If you ever did want that, *you* should be the one to say something. Don't hope that he'll make the first move. He won't."

He sits back up all the way in his seat, returning to his normal volume. "And that's all I'll say on the subject, too. Unless you ever want to talk, then I'm more than happy to."

My first instinct is to dismiss his suggestion. Laugh it off as the teasing I've been treating it as. But he sounded more serious than I think I've ever heard him be outside of hockey. Still, there's no way this guy, who's barely even allowed in a bar, would know more about my feelings than I do.

I don't want there to be more between Adrian and me.

Right?

I try to move on by pulling out my phone, but I'm blankly staring at whatever app muscle memory opened. I'm stuck on what Ollie said. How do I look at Adrian? I'm sure I look happy, the same way I do with all my friends. He's a great guy, of course I'm happy to see him. But that doesn't mean I want to date him.

Right?

Why am I not confident in my answers to these questions? Does the fact that I'm questioning it at all mean something?

"Hey, thanks? I think," I belatedly respond to Ollie, painfully aware of how awkward I'm being. "I definitely wasn't expecting the conversation to go there. But I appreciate you wanting to support me. Adrian really is just my friend, though."

Why does that sound like a lie?

"If you say so," he agrees, smirking.

Ollie pulls out his phone too, opening up the same gaming app he usually does on flights, leaving me alone with my thoughts.

Adrian is one of my favorite people, and there's no denying that. I'm always happier in his presence. He's got one of those infectious personalities where it's impossible to do anything but smile when you're near him because he makes everything more fun. Even if something bad happens, his over-the-top reaction usually gets a smile out of me, and then before there's even time to worry about whatever the problem is, he has a plan and is working to fix it.

I feel calmer when I'm with him. I know if he's around, I have nothing to worry about. We do like a lot of the same things too. And hanging out with him is so easy. Even if we're not doing anything exciting, I enjoy spending time together, being in his company.

Who wouldn't? He's confident, funny, smart, and so supportive.

Fuck.

That sounds like a pretty ideal partner. I already know I love living with him.

Do I like Adrian?

Is Ollie right? Have I been overlooking how I feel about him because he's a man? I've never been with a guy. I've never wanted to. Other than when I thought about kissing Adrian. But...

if I wanted to kiss him, that probably did mean more than I was ready to examine in the moment.

Am I ready now?

I think about what might have happened if I'd given into that thought, if I'd leaned in and brought my mouth to his. Would he have kissed me back? Would he have been surprised, maybe shy about it? If he did want to kiss me, would it have been a short, sweet moment?

No. I snort a laugh picturing Adrian being timid in any situation. He'd probably take control and show me exactly what he likes. It's easy to picture him shifting positions so he was straddling me on his couch, one hand holding my jaw so he could angle me how he wanted, the other in my hair... And I'm not hating this imagined scenario.

I'm actually enjoying it a little too much for the public plane I'm currently on. Shit, I need to stop thinking about him like that. I shift in my seat, readjusting my suddenly hard cock, pretending to be repositioning how I'm sitting so I can sleep. I know I won't be able to now that I'm having all these new realizations about Adrian, though. Well about myself, really.

I'm not sure what these new thoughts mean.

I'm not upset at all about potentially being attracted to a man. I've always tried to support the LGBTQIA+ community in any way that I can. Was there more to that than wanting to be a good ally?

I don't want to get ahead of myself though. If I actually do have more than friendship feelings about Adrian, I need to decide what to do with that information, if I even want to do anything at all. I don't want to risk losing our friendship if I decide to make a move and he doesn't feel the same way.

Or maybe I'm just lonely, and I would confuse a friendship with anyone as more because I'm so desperate for that connection right now.

I think I need to be patient, which isn't exactly a strong suit for me, but I think I need to try. I can see how things go when we're back in the same city, see if I really do like him as more than a friend after I've had some time to acknowledge it as a possibility to myself. Then if I do, I can pay more attention to how he acts around me and make a more educated guess on if he would even be interested.

Maybe I can casually ask if he wants kids.

14

ADRIAN

"I think I might actually want them to stay this time," Hudson comments from his spot on the other corner of the couch.

I'm trying to get some work done while we watch one of our favorite shows where the couple has the option to renovate their home or move. We both usually vote they should move because you can't magically create more square footage no matter how creative you get with built-ins. "Yeah, I like their backyard," I agree, even though I've been pretty distracted during this episode.

Beck has been in Montana all week, again, so I'm trying to send him a summary of what he's missed and a reminder for the short list of things I need him to sign off on or do himself in the next couple of days.

"Holy shit, look at this listing my agent just sent!" Hudson texts me the link, and my laptop and phone both ding with his message. I'm about done with the email I was working on, so I skim it again to make sure I didn't forget anything and send it before I follow the link.

Wait. I know this house. It isn't far from here, and I admire it every time I walk past. It's wildly out of my price range, but it's one of those picturesque dream homes that I can't help but imagine myself in whenever I see it. It's a gorgeous multi-level standalone with four bedrooms, five bathrooms, and it even has a fenced-in yard. I've never seen the inside before now, and it needs some updating to get the house to its full potential, but the bones are really good.

"I love this house, and the price seems way better than I would have expected for the space too. Well, for your budget at least—I could never. But with some quick upgrades, it would be a total dream home."

"And it's just down the block. We'd still be neighbors," he points out, sounding excited.

I'm trying desperately to not get my hopes up about that though. Even if we are that close, a few houses away is different than being in the next room. Our friendship right now is one of proximity; I'm sure things will change when we're no longer living together and my presence in his life is no longer required.

"Are you going to schedule a tour?" I ask, and wow, I sound so casual. Not at all like I'm desperate for him to get this house that's so close. Good for me.

"Yeah, this is for sure the best one he's sent me. When are you free?"

I blink a few times before I turn to give him my full attention. "You want me to come for the tour?" That seems like another possible overstepping moment. Something I would do with a partner.

"Obviously. I need your expertise. As much as I would like to claim I've learned a lot from watching all these shows with you, I know you'll be so much better at picturing what things could look like than I would."

Okay, when he explains it like that, it makes sense for me to come. It doesn't sound romantic; he just trusts my design opinion. "Well, if you really want me to, I'll make sure I'm free." And I'm only agreeing because I want to help my friend. I will remain impartial when we tour this house. The fact that he could be my neighbor if he did end up getting it isn't going to be a priority to him the same way it would be for me. I need to respect that and allow him to make his own decision.

"THE LOFT COULD BE A REALLY cool playroom. Depending on the ages of the kids, it's big enough to even install a rockwall or a ninja course, something for more active play if they're a little older," I suggest as we finish exploring the upper levels and head back downstairs. Hudson's real estate agent managed to get us in to see the house the next day, fitting it into his busy schedule between his morning practice and his home game tonight. We're almost done with the tour, and I love the house even more in person, but I've been trying not to sway his decision, only providing suggestions like he asked for.

And yes, I have been looking into specific design options for children, as any decent friend would in this situation. So what if I've spent hours researching different parenting methods and now know all about the different schools in the area? That's just useful knowledge. It has nothing to do with my crush on Hudson.

I definitely haven't been picturing what it would be like to live here, in my dream home, with him, helping to raise his children.

But I am picturing that exact life with some other, faceless man that vaguely looks like him who I haven't met yet. A man who's obsessed with me, because even though I can't help feeling the way I do about Hudson, I know he'll never think about me that way, and I try to remind myself that's what I deserve.

"So, have you thought about whether you'll want to try to adopt an infant or an older kid?"

"I think for my first kid, I'd really love to adopt a baby. That's what I've always pictured when I think about being a dad. But since that informational meeting the adoption agency had, I've been thinking more and more about the idea of eventually taking in older kids too. Maybe in a few years when I'm more confident as a parent, or if I'm married."

I can't help but smile at his answer. Hudson is going to be the best dad, the kind I wish I'd had growing up. "Whatever kids you end up helping will be really lucky to have you in their life."

"Alright, guys," his agent cuts in. "I'll step out on the back deck, give you some privacy to walk through on your own and really imagine what it would be like for you two to live here."

He leaves, and I turn to glare at Hudson. "Why do you keep letting him say things like that without correcting him?"

"Like what?" he asks, obviously distracted as he turns in the center of the kitchen, looking at different aspects of the room.

"Like we're a couple who will be living here together!"

"Oh. Who cares what he thinks?"

Is he joking? "Hudson, he could tell the media he sold you a house to move in with a man and adopt a bunch of kids. You just said something about being married—oh my god! Did he think you were talking about marrying me? You need to go correct him. He could be out there telling someone right now! That was the whole reason you even moved in with me—to avoid scandal. Did we just make an even bigger one?"

Fuck, how did I manage to screw things up so royally? Is this it? Is this the end of our friendship? I knew it had an expiration date, but I'm not ready.

Hudson doesn't seem to share my concern, smiling and chuckling to himself as he approaches me. He puts a hand on my shoulder. "Deep breaths, Charming. Everything is fine."

I lightly swat his perfectly sculpted chest, relieved by his touch, but still not as relaxed as he is. "Why aren't you freaking out? He obviously thinks we're together."

He just shrugs. "I've known Jason for years, and I trust him. And he'll make a lot of money selling me this house. He doesn't need to run to the media."

"You're not even a little concerned that he thinks you're with a man?"

"Nah, half the team has been giving me shit about living with you and asking when I'm going to come out and announce we're dating."

"They've been doing what?" I slap his chest harder, but he just laughs, not even pretending to be affected as he stands solidly in place. What the actual fuck? How is he not freaking out about that? "How have you not told me? Do you need me to say anything?"

"Well, maybe not half the team. It's mostly Bell, but Anderson and Martin joined in when they overheard him last week."

"Hudson! They need to be careful who they joke around in front of. God, not only would that be a pain in the ass to deal with at the end of your career when it's not even true, but Beck has been dying to have the first openly out player on our team. I'd never hear the end of it if I was the cause of rumors that got his hopes up."

Hudson finally drops his arm from my shoulder as he makes a humming sound, looking intrigued by my comment. I almost ask if he knows something I don't about any of the other players, but that is so not my place to question if he does, so I try to focus and get back to why we're really here.

"Okay, fine, if you're not worried, I will try to follow your lead." Even if I'm still internally freaking out about those comments. And only partially because I wish they were true. "So, what do you think of this place?" I ask.

"It's even better in person." His smile is as big as I've ever seen it.

"Hopefully they don't have any hidden nanny cams in here because you weren't exactly subtle during the tour. If they heard a word of what you said about how much you loved it, any hope of negotiating is completely gone," I tease. Touring the place less than twenty-four hours after they posted the listing also probably isn't helping him come across as a casually interested buyer either. I'm sure he can afford the asking price, but still.

"I definitely think you could make it into a great home." I nod as I wander the kitchen and dining area, looking around and confirming that the only thing with color in here right now is a decorative bowl full of apples. "Does it bother you that everything is pretty much white right now though?"

"Well, we'd want to change that, but I'm not in a rush to move out if you're not. Everything online says that the adoption process can take a really long time, so I think as long as I own a house, I'd be good to start applying, right?"

Did he say we? He is killing me with how much he's making it sound like I'd be living here too, so I take a deep breath and try to unpack everything he managed to fit in that comment. "First, I've already said you can stay with me as long as you'd like. That hasn't changed." Look at me sounding so casual even though I'm thrilled at the idea of him staying with me for months of renovations.

"Second, I have no idea when the ideal time to apply for adoption is, but I would agree that owning a home would probably make you a stronger candidate than someone crashing with their friend." Okay, responsible supportive comments out of the way. Question time. "But back up, Hudson. Did you say *we* would change? As in you and me? I thought I was just giving ideas today. If you do end up buying it, this would be your home to turn into whatever you want."

Hudson flashes me his biggest, most charismatic smile, managing to plead with his eyes before he even opens his mouth. "Come on, Charming, you know how much I love your design taste. The whole tour you were full of ideas for adding character and making everything more functional for kids. I know you're really busy, but would you be able to help me turn this house into the dream home you were describing? Pretty please."

Is he serious?

That's kind of a lot of pressure. Not to mention how bittersweet it will be when I've been fantasizing about this exact scenario with the dream version of him that wants me romantically.

Although… working with his money instead of my much smaller budget would be really fun. And can I actually say no to him? "Well, I was just saying what I would do, but yeah, I can help you pick things that you would like."

He walks over so he's standing right in front of me again. "I liked every suggestion you said, and you know I'm obsessed with the way your place looks. If you make it anything like that, I know I'll love it. But thinking about having to make every one of those decisions is kind of overwhelming." Then he reaches out to hold my hand as he looks right into my eyes. *What the fuck is happening.* "I know I'm asking a lot of you, and I'll obviously help if you want me to, but I'd love to not have to make every little decision. I trust you, Adrian." He gives my hand a little squeeze, and I suddenly can't remember how to breathe. "You're the best at this stuff, Charming. Can you pretty please help me do it? I promise I'll make it worth your time."

He's batting his eyelashes and smirking as he holds my hand. God, does he have any idea how suggestive that sounded? Or how hot he is?

I take a step back, forcing him to drop his hold. "Oh my god. Stop making it sound like you're offering me sexual favors," I scold with a laugh. "My body doesn't understand that the hot straight man isn't interested in me when you say things like that."

Okay, that might have been *too* honest. But he should know how he sounds right now. It isn't fair. I'm expecting him to look embarrassed, or maybe concerned at what I'm implying, but just like before with apparently not caring what his realtor thinks, he doesn't. If anything he looks… smug, maybe?

His smile only grows as he gives me a once-over. "Well, how are you so sure I'm not? I really want your help here."

What the actual fuck? Being okay with someone assuming we're together is one thing, but that comment was something else entirely. Hudson has jokingly flirted with me before, but that went much farther than anything he's said in the past.

Obviously he's still joking though. Maybe he has said things like that and it just feels like more because of where we are and everything we've been talking about. He hasn't suddenly decided after weeks of living together that now is the time for him to make an actual move. We were literally just talking about rumors, and he didn't say they could actually be true. He didn't deny it when I called him straight.

"Okay, okay. No need for the cheesy porn script," I tease, playing along with his tone. "You already know I'll help. You're basically asking me to design my dream home without worrying about it being my money I'm spending. I can't think of anything better."

"I can think of a few things," he says, and then he fucking winks. He's looking at me the same way I look at chocolate, and he needs to drop this joke before I drop to my knees.

Gathering all my strength, I chuckle awkwardly, and I know my cheeks are heating but there's nothing I can do about that. There's only so much of his pretend flirting that I can take. I need to move on before I really embarrass myself.

"So, are you going to put in an offer?"

His smile returns to his normally cheerful one, far less suggestive than moments ago.

I miss that look. But I know it wasn't real. And if it isn't real,
I don't want to see it from him. Someday I'll find someone who
actually wants me. Not someone who's asking me to help them do
something or to fix a problem they have. I have to believe it'll
happen even though a huge part of me doubts anyone will ever
see me that way.

But I really hope it does—that I'll tour a fancy house with
them, and we can really buy it together for our future family.

But I know that person isn't Hudson.

And as much as I do think we've become friends, if I wasn't
offering him a media-free place to live, if I wasn't going to help
him design this house, I'm not sure I'd have him in my life at all.

So this casual cheerfulness is better. Real. Normal.

Normal is good.

"Yeah, I'll go talk to Jason."

15

HUDSON

"Damn it," I groan as the ref blows their whistle, ending the play.

"Chicago, number 96, two minutes for tripping."

I hang my head as I enter the penalty box. I wasn't trying to trip that guy, but my stick did ended up under his skates, so I can't even complain since it was a good call. I'm not having the worst game of my career or anything. Thanks to Bell and Martin, I've actually gotten two assists tonight, but I've been distracted. I'm usually able to tune out the rest of the world and only focus on hockey when I need to, especially during a game, but tonight I've caught myself glancing up at the owner's suite more than I'd care to admit.

I know Adrian watches most of the home games from there with his friends, and despite it being about twenty rows up from the ice, it's easy for me to pick him out of the crowd. Ever since Ollie suggested I might be overlooking how I really feel about Adrian, I've been trying to have an open mind about the possibility.

I don't want to dismiss what he said, and I don't think I should, because if I'm being completely honest with myself, there has definitely been more than one moment where I've thought about kissing him and what it would be like. Or moments where I wanted to hold him in a way that I don't typically think about wrapping myself around my other friends. Now that I've given myself permission to go there, I've even wondered what it would be like to do more than just kiss him.

But I also want to be really confident in how I feel before I make any major changes. Despite how casual I might have been with Adrian when he expressed his concerns about someone assuming we're together, I do understand how big of an impact an announcement like that would have on my career, especially so close to the end of it.

There have only been a few openly queer professional hockey players, all of them in lower leagues than the NHL. If I did decide that I wanted to be in a relationship with Adrian, especially if I did so publicly, that would overshadow everything else I've accomplished as a professional hockey player. My multiple cup wins, any record I hold for the team on games played or points in a season, no one would care. All I'd ever be known for would be my sexuality. There'd be speculation about my interactions with teammates, my marriage, hell, my divorce isn't even finalized yet. No matter how cooperative I've been with Shelby's lawyers, it would probably complicate that.

And now I want to adopt. I have no idea what implications that sort of media attention would have on my chances of being approved for adoption. I meant what I said when I told Adrian becoming a parent is my priority. I don't want to do anything that might jeopardize that.

So I'm not planning to make any big changes as far as my relationship with Adrian goes anytime soon. I'm just allowing myself to think about the possibility, *eventually.* And apparently by doing so, I've become so distracted I'm earning stupid penalty minutes. We're up by two with four minutes left in the third. My penalty could shift the momentum in Toronto's favor and lose us the whole game. I need to focus. I can think about Adrian and how perfect the tour earlier today was *after* the game.

Toronto's goalie starts banging on the ice to warn them my time's almost up, and I shake my head as I stand, trying to physically rid myself of distractions. It doesn't exactly work like I'd hoped; I still don't feel as locked in as I'd like, but Anderson still manages to hold them from scoring anything else, and we get the win.

I can't be certain with how far away he is, but I'm pretty sure Adrian is already focused on me from the front row of the box when I wave up at them. He really is easy to spot with how much shorter he is than the rest of his friends, but he also stands out because he's the only one who jumps as he waves back, obviously excited about the win.

His reaction is… cute. That's the only word I can really use. I know he isn't excited that a player waved at him after the win. He's excited to be sharing the moment with me as my friend. It makes something unexpected flutter in my chest to see how happy he is for not only me but also the team that I care so much about. Adrian is just as in love with the Werewolves and even with hockey in general as I am.

That's something I've always thought would be amazing to have in a partner, but I was convinced it could never be an option for me. Could it be possible now? I can't help it; I'm thinking about the house again, about how perfectly the tour went, how happy and excited Adrian was with each new room we saw. He had a way of painting a picture for each space that was so easy to imagine. We haven't been living together for all that long, less than two months, and I've only been thinking about my feelings for him for far less time than that, and yet it was even easier to imagine sharing the home with him than it was to think about living there all alone.

By the end of the tour, I was so swept up in those thoughts that I'd pushed a little further, allowing myself to test out flirting with him again for the first time knowing that I might actually mean it.

And it was fun. Seeing him blush, joking around with him about sexual favors. I wasn't worried he might take me seriously, and I was disappointed when he didn't. I know that says a lot about my apparently obvious feelings about and for him, but today was definitely not the time to admit any of that to him.

Luckily I'm not held back for any extra press or stars tonight, so it doesn't take me long to get back to my locker. I grab my phone first thing, hoping to catch Adrian this time before he leaves.

HUDSON

Come out with us?

I leave my phone open on the shelf in front of me as I change, embarrassingly nervous about his reply. It shouldn't matter so much to me if he wants to join the team at the bar or not, but if the fluttering in my stomach is anything to go by, it obviously does. I want to see him, and not across an arena. I want to spend time actually hanging out with him.

Sure, we were together for most of the time I had off today, but it never feels like enough.

I grab the phone again as soon as it vibrates.

ADRIAN

IDK, I'm pretty tired.

HUDSON

You don't have to stay for long, it'll be fun!

ADRIAN

Hmmm… Will there be hot hockey players there for me to flirt with?

I know he's only joking. Adrian's always joked around with the whole team about how attractive they all are, how he's so lucky to work with so many hot men, that sort of thing. Everyone loves him, and I've never given it much thought, usually playing off his comments to join in on the fun.

But now that I'm thinking about him in this new light, and about the possible truth behind my own flirting... I don't love the idea of him doing that with anyone else.

HUDSON

I'll be there, so OBVIOUSLY! No need to worry about talking to anyone else ;)

Hopefully the winking emoji I sent with that makes it come across as less creepy, possessive vibes and more fun and flirty.

Because apparently that's how I want to come across to Adrian now, despite all my convictions to keep the new feelings I'm having about him to myself.

But flirting is fine. We've always flirted. It's just teasing between friends unless we actually do anything about it, and obviously we won't. I'm not ready for that.

At least I don't think I am.

16

ADRIAN

"An espresso martini, please."

Not entirely sure what the hell I'm doing out at the bar with the team right now, but I'm here instead of in bed after a long day so I need caffeine with my alcohol. I run a hand over my fitted suit jacket as I wait, thankful I went straight from the office to tonight's game. Sometimes I wear Werewolves merch to watch them, but I'm glad to not look like a random fan tonight if I'll be hanging out with the players.

"Thank you." I leave my tip and take a big swig of the drink, pretending like I'm back in my early twenties when I would have loved to be out this late with all the players. I mean, I also love it now—I'm still kind of in shock that Hudson invited me in the first place—but I'm also tired in a way I would have never admitted back then. Obviously my desire to spend time with Hudson, especially in public, won out over sleep though.

We've never actually hung out outside of my house before. I can't deny that him wanting me here with his other friends makes me feel all warm and fuzzy, even if I'm trying my best to act like it's not a big deal. I know we've spent a lot of time together since he moved in, and after everything he's shared about his dad and his dreams for the future, I would even consider us to be actual friends. But this feels like a big step in that friendship. It gives me hope that we might actually remain friends after he moves out. Maybe he truly does enjoy my company and doesn't just hang out with me out of convenience.

As much as I wish he could offer me even more, I know he can't. So remaining friends is the most I can hope for. I'm not ready to think about Hudson not being in my life, so being friends will be enough.

Drink in hand, I head to the roped off section in the back of the crowded bar where the team is.

"Adrian! What are you doing here? Is everything okay?" the team's goalie, Mathew Anderson, asks when I almost walk past him.

"Am I not allowed to sit with the cool kids?" I tease.

"Of course you can! You know we love having you around. I just haven't seen you out with us before."

"Don't worry, nothing is wrong. I just wanted to spend my night surrounded by hot athletic men, and I knew you all would be here."

Anderson is one of the guys I'm comfortable joking around with, and he laughs easily at the comment. Whenever I meet a new player, I make it clear that if I ever make them uncomfortable with my teasing, all they have to do is ask, and I'll stop. I think flirting is fun, and in my experience, teasing the players with over-the-top flirting they know isn't real actually helps make them more comfortable around me. I'm no longer one of the suits upstairs if we have that casual relationship established, and I think they feel like they can come to me if they need something because of it.

"Smart. Look no farther. Hot, athletic man right here." Matt gestures to himself.

I hum, giving him an appreciative once-over, then laugh.

"Hudson actually invited me though. I didn't randomly show up. Do you know where he is?"

He nods to the back corner. "He's probably with Bell. They've been really close this season. I think he wants the captain position when Roy retires."

"He's a little young for the C, isn't he?"

He shrugs. "Maybe alternate then. I just know they've been spending all their time together this season. Maybe he'll convince Roy to play another year."

"I doubt it." I chuckle, feeling a little smug that it seems like I know more about Hudson's future plans than some of his teammates.

"I've actually been meaning to talk to you. Do you remember that bakery you suggested for my mom's birthday last year? I can't remember the name, but she requested the same cake. Any chance you know it?"

"Oh my god, I love that place, they have the best triple fudge brownies. I'll text you the info."

"Hey! You made it," Hudson cuts in, sounding far more excited to see me than I'd expect for someone who spent a good part of their day with me already. He walks right up, wrapping me in a big hug that completely surprises me and nearly has me spilling my drink. It's a short embrace, though, and there's no time to really appreciate it before he's pulling back.

He glances at Mathew, giving him a quick nod, and instead of his usual happy expression, he seems… annoyed, maybe? Shit, I hope they aren't fighting. That's the last thing the team needs right now with how strong of a start they've had this season.

"Want to come join Ollie and me back there? I saved you a seat."

I don't want to get in the middle of whatever's happening between them, so I easily agree. "Sure. Well, it was nice chatting with you, Matt."

"You too. Don't forget to text me!"

Then Hudson takes my hand in his, and I forget all about my concern for team dynamics. It fits so nicely there, his large calloused one wrapping perfectly around my smaller, well-manicured hand. For a moment, I allow myself to pretend that he's actually holding it because he wants to, because he craves that connection to me and wants to visibly claim that we're here together in a crowded space in front of all these people.

But I know that's not what's actually happening as he uses that connection to practically drag me back to his table as we weave through the crowded bar. "Slow down, Hudson, my legs are nowhere near as long as yours."

"Right, sorry. Just eager to sit down." He still sounds a little frustrated, so I do my very best to keep up and stay right behind him until we arrive at the small round table Oliver Bell is sitting at. I take the open seat between them as Hudson sits back down in front of his drink.

"So what are you texting Anderson about?" he asks once we're settled.

"Oh, he forgot the name of the bakery I showed him last year."

Hudson hums in response, but Oliver cuts in before he can say anything else.

"So, Adrian, tell me about living with our captain."

I turn to face him, crossing my arms over my chest. "Hudson is an excellent roommate. But I have a bone to pick with you."

"What the hell did I do?" He looks to Hudson for backup, but he only shrugs.

"Apparently, you've been teasing him about us being a couple because he's living with me. I know I joke around with you guys, but that's the kind of joke that could easily turn into a rumor that could really impact his career." Oliver rolls his eyes. "I'm serious, you have to be so careful with what you're implying around who. If the media overheard—"

"Trust me, Adrian, I know." He sighs, his tone far more serious than I was expecting.

There's something in his expression, in how defeated he looks as he makes the comment that has me tilting my head and narrowing my eyes at him. Oliver has never given me any reason to suspect he might not be straight, but… "You know like you're annoyed that I'm lecturing you and want me to shut up… or you *know* like you have personal experience filtering what you say in front of the media so that rumors don't start?"

He smirks, mirroring my head tilt and squinting as he holds my gaze. "Would it really be a rumor if it's true?"

"Shut up!" I slam my hand down on the table in my excitement, all my annoyance forgotten. *Shit*, I immediately wince. I should not be drawing attention to us right now. After a quick glance around to make sure no one is looking our way, I turn back to him. "Oliver, are you saying what I think you're saying? I swear to god if you're letting me get my hopes up right now, if you're teasing me and it isn't real…"

His smile only grows. "I've been advised by my agent to not say anything. So this is me not saying anything. But I'm getting pretty tired of that plan."

I suck in a sharp breath, then I turn to Hudson and slap his chest. "Did you know about this?"

He lets out a short laugh. "Maybe."

I turn back to Oliver. "Oh my god, please let me tell Beck. We've been dreaming about having an out player for yeeeears."

He's still smirking as he bites the corner of his thumbnail, considering while he looks between Hudson and me. "Yeah, okay," he finally answers. "You can tell Mr. Caldwell. But I'm not going to tell anyone else without a plan in place to make things official."

"Oh my god, let me help you plan! When you're ready that is. I'm not trying to pressure you at all, that is a huge and very personal decision. But when you're ready, say the word, and I'll help the PR team organize the best press release you've ever seen."

"And I'll make sure the players support you, but I don't see there being any issues," Hudson adds.

Oliver's smile is as big as I've ever seen it. "Cool, thank you."

17

HUDSON

"Oh my god, and with how attractive you are, all the gay men in Chicago are going to lose it when you do announce," Adrian says to Ollie, obviously still excited to find out that the Werewolves will have their first out player.

Might not be the only queer player, I think for the tenth time since they started this conversation. Ollie is young, but he already knows who he is and is confident in his sexuality. It's been clear since he came out to me that he has no desire to remain in the closet for the entirety of his career.

His position is different than mine, I remind myself. I only have a few months left, and then I'll be out of the spotlight. Then I might have the space to figure things out. I'm still not sure if my newfound infatuation could lead to something more, and I certainly don't have the mental energy to dedicate to figuring everything out right now.

I'm in the middle of trying to purchase a home so I can apply to become an adoptive parent. That needs to be my focus.

I'm happy for Ollie that he ended up playing for a team that will obviously support him, and I'm happy for Adrian that he'll get to be a part of that significant moment for the team. I *should* be happy right now.

Even if I am feeling a little left out. I'm not sure if they even remember I'm here at this point with how intensely they're staring at each other as they quietly chat about what time of the season might be the best to bring on that sort of press attention. But it's hard for me to focus on anything other than how they're smiling at each other. Adrian just pointed out how attractive he thinks Ollie is. Does he feel the same way about Adrian?

No. I'm being ridiculous. Ollie is the one who's encouraged me to consider my real feelings for Adrian. He wouldn't make a move himself. They're just bonding over their mutual excitement. Ollie is probably thrilled that he came out to someone else and that it was met with so much enthusiastic support.

Still, these two should probably tone down the eye contact before I do something really stupid like pull Adrian onto my lap.

I've never had the urge to stake a claim like that on someone before. But between seeing him with Ollie right now, where someone could easily jump to conclusions about the two of them if they paid any attention to how into each other they look, and earlier with Anderson, overhearing their flirting and promised texting, I can't sit here and pretend like I'm not annoyed.

And let's be honest—annoyed isn't the right word.

I'm jealous. I want Adrian to be paying that much attention to me. I want to be the one he's leaning over the table to talk to, the one he can't look away from. I want to be the one he's making plans to go to bakeries with. I invited him tonight because I wanted to spend time with him, and now that's backfired as I'm forced to sit here and pretend like everything is fine while he flirts with my friends.

I don't think I've ever been a particularly jealous person before. But now that I've admitted to myself that I have complicated feelings for Adrian, I'm realizing my plan to not act on them might not have been as simple as I expected.

The thought of Adrian and Ollie sitting here laughing together, bonding, shouldn't make me jealous. I should be happy for my friends that they have other friends, other support systems in place outside of me. Being jealous is just a waste of my time and energy.

Adrian has no idea I've had any thoughts about being with him, and even if he did, even if he might want to give *more* with me a chance, he's not going to sit around and wait for me to figure out what it is I actually want.

He deserves better. Someone who has their shit together like he does, who's confident in who they are, who can proudly claim him as their partner, who knows how lucky they are to be with him.

I can't be that person right now.

So I have no right to be this jealous about him talking to other guys I don't even think are interested in him. I force a smile that hopefully looks more genuine than it feels and remind myself that I really am glad Adrian is here.

"So did Hudson tell you about the house he put in an offer on?" he asks Ollie, finally pulling my attention back to their conversation.

"No. Dude, what the fuck? That's a big deal, why didn't you say something?"

"We only toured it today. It's not like I was keeping it from you intentionally."

Adrian turns to smile at me, and the warmth in his expression finally relaxes that on-edge feeling I couldn't shake. "It was gorgeous though. I really hope you get it."

"Wait, you went on the tour?" Ollie cuts in, and I nod before Adrian can say anything. "And you guys think I'm the one who's going to start rumors about you two?" He laughs. "Look in the mirror."

"Apparently, Hudson trusts his realtor."

"I do," I insist. They both look at me skeptically, but Adrian moves onto describing the house in detail. Ollie seems interested enough, and we all spend another hour or so talking about Adrian's plans for it if they accept my offer. They should, it was well above asking. I wasn't about to risk not getting it after how much Adrian and I both loved it so much.

Adrian yawns for the third time, and I decide enough's enough. "Alright, Prince, time to get you home for your beauty sleep."

He mockingly glares at me. "I don't need beauty sleep. I always look amazing."

"That's true." I hold up my hands in surrender, he probably thinks I'm joking, but I mean it. "Even your bedhead looks better than my styled hair."

"Why do you know what his bedhead looks like?" Ollie whines. "How do you not see how much you two act like a couple?"

I laugh, shrugging, and Adrian rolls his eyes. "I am pretty tired though. Are you staying out?" he checks, and Ollie nods so we exchange quick goodbyes.

I want to take Adrian's hand again, but now that I'm less distracted by irrational jealousy, I realize that's probably not the smartest move as I leave a crowded public place with him. Still, I walk with him all the way to his car. "See you at home." I wave as he gets into it, waiting until he shuts his door to turn around and walk back toward the bar since I parked in the opposite direction.

"Did you seriously walk me to my car for no reason again?" he calls out of his open window.

"Wanting you to be safe is a pretty good reason," I call back over my shoulder with a laugh as I hear him groan.

I assume he heads home after that, so I jump a little at his voice as his big SUV pulls up next to me on the street. "I am perfectly capable of keeping myself safe."

I nod. "I know you are. But that doesn't mean you should have to do it on your own."

He grumbles something as he rolls up his window, and I can't quite hear what it is over the sounds of the city, but it makes me laugh again. Even when he's frustrated, it's so cute.

Ugh. Everything he does is cute. How does he have such a strong hold on me when I went years without thinking about him or even any other man this way? But there's no denying he does. I wouldn't say I'm suddenly really attracted to all men in general. Looking back, maybe there were some men that I was drawn to more than others, and I assumed it was in a "we'd get along well as friends" kind of way, but now that I've opened the door to my —would it be called a crush?—there's no stopping it. I'm drawn to who Adrian is as a person, and because of that, I think I'm noticing things about him physically that I wouldn't normally. I spend the walk to my car thinking about his smile, and I spend the drive home remembering how he lit up each room on the tour today. How he made the house feel like a home.

When I get back to his place, Adrian is waiting with a cup of water for me before he says goodnight and disappears into his room.

I want to follow him.

My room is before his in the hall, and I stand there, staring at the gap of his door that isn't shut all the way for longer than I'd care to admit. My imagination runs wild. What if he left it open on purpose? What if he wanted me to follow him? Would I even need to say anything, or would Adrian immediately know why

I'm there, taking my entering his space as permission to cross that line of more than friends my mind has been stuck on?

My body heats as I picture it: Adrian letting out a relieved "Finally." I'm too tall for him to kiss, but maybe he'd push me until the backs of my knees hit his bed. He couldn't actually push me around, but I'd go willingly, falling back so that he could climb into my lap, straddling me before he'd grab my face and bring our mouths together in a desperate kiss.

Fuck, that's hot. My cock is already aching, and I finally force myself to leave the hallway where I'm standing like a creep with an erection staring at his room. As I enter mine, I can't bring myself to shut the door all the way, leaving it open a couple inches, just like his was. Striping out of my clothes, I leave the lights off and give my hard dick a couple of lazy strokes, groaning at how amazing even that feels with how turned on I am right now. It's been so long since I've been with anyone, even just picturing Adrian has me far more desperate than it probably should. I grab lube from my nightstand before I climb onto the bed, not bothering to get under the duvet as I lay back and prop up on some of Adrian's endless pillows.

It's almost like I'm surrounded by him. The luxurious blanket, the comfortable bed, the mountain of decorative pillows, it all reminds me of Adrian. As if I need the reminder when he's all I seem to be able to think about tonight. I can't look away from that sliver of light coming from the hall, and I coat my hand in lube before returning it to my erection.

I honestly can't remember the last time I was this hard, this desperate for release, but I still take my time, using long, slow strokes as I stare into the hall where I know his door is also open. Logically, I know he's probably asleep by now with how tired he was. I've never heard a sound from his room, and he could have a noise machine or something that would prevent him from hearing me. But still, my cock leaks as I think about the possibility that he could hear the unmistakable sound of me jerking off.

I shouldn't be doing this. Not so openly with him on the other side of the wall, both of our doors open. But I can't stop. It only sends a jolt of pleasure down my spine as I wonder how he'd react. Back to daydreaming now, I imagine him being just as turned on as I am. That he'd want to investigate and would take the open door as the invitation that it is.

I might not be ready to make a move with him. But if the situation came up without me really making that decision…

It's easy to picture him pushing the door open and turning on the lights, catching me with my dick in my hand. In my fantasy, he wouldn't be shy about it or embarrassed. If anything, I can picture him making a comment about how big my cock is or asking if I needed any help, following a cheesy porn script like he accused me of doing when I was flirting with him.

Holy shit, I'm so close already. I don't want to stop thinking about this fake scenario, but each stroke is sending me dangerously close to the edge. I imagine him warning me against getting his bedspread dirty and offering to let me finish in his mouth to prevent any mess. The thought of his full lips wrapping around my cock, imagining how amazing his mouth would feel after so much time on my own, is too much, and I can't hold off my release any longer. My orgasm crashes into me. I come harder than I can remember from a solo session in years, and my cum coats my stomach and chest as I ride out that high. Luckily it avoids the bedding.

That was so hot.

Maybe I should be embarrassed now that I've come down from that lust-filled state of mind. But I'm not. I just lay here, mind still half in that fantasy. It wasn't anything too explicit as far as being with another man goes, but Adrian was definitely the star of it all, and I obviously enjoyed it.

I think I need to spend some time learning a bit more about what being with another man would actually be like. It's easy to picture someone else touching my dick or being on the receiving end of a blow job when those are things I've experienced before.

But if I truly want to consider a relationship with another man, I need to be all in on trying out new things that I *haven't* done before. Would I be willing to be the one with a cock in my mouth? Would I be willing to put one inside my ass? I can't say I'm begging for the opportunity, but since I haven't done either, I don't think I can say I'd hate it for sure either.

Being hypothetically willing to try has to count for something, right?

I finally sit up and grab a towel that's hung up on the back of the closet door, and pause. The cum covering me needs to be cleaned up, it's already starting to dry, but I stop myself from making any attempt and wrap the towel around my waist instead.

This is stupid. I know that. But it doesn't stop me from chasing that thrill again of knowing Adrian might catch me doing something I should be keeping private. The idea of something happening between us that would force me to confront how I'm feeling.

I step into the hallway, covered in my own release, and my heart is racing. I've never been turned on by the idea of being caught doing something sexual before, so I think it's just an Adrian thing. I take my time walking to the bathroom down the hall and am disappointed when he doesn't suddenly appear.

I don't shut the bathroom door all the way before my shower, and it's thrilling, picturing how easy it would be for him to walk in. I know I shouldn't make a habit of it, but as I walk back to my room, I don't even bother to use the towel to cover up, opting to go completely naked through the hallway.

It doesn't matter though. Adrian is probably asleep and will never know I'm suddenly desperate for him to see me naked, even if I'm still processing the rest of what being with him would look like.

ADRIAN

A Few Weeks Later–Thanksgiving

"Lincoln is such a little shit," Beck spits out as he falls into the seat across from me at the fancy gaming table set up in his grandparent's giant basement. "First whatever the hell happened with Parker and Oakley during the football game, I'm sure that's why we lost. I can't believe I have to sing at a game again this year. And now he won't shut up about how hot Jordan is during my turns playing pool. He was obviously trying to distract me."

"And it worked too," his youngest brother, Lincoln, calls out as he lines up to start the next game with their other brother, Harrison, after beating Beck.

"Are you even into guys?" Beck demands.

"Wouldn't you like to know?" Lincoln taunts back, a huge smile in place as he winks at Jordan who's sitting next to me.

He groans, covering his face with his hands, mumbling "Keep me out of this" from behind them.

Usually, the Caldwell sibling teasing amuses me. I've been friends with Beck for long enough, and his family is welcoming enough, that I even feel like one of them most of the time when we all get together. But today has been a little… *strange.*

"Anyone have any idea what had Oakley so upset during the game?" I ask, looking around to see if anyone knows.

"You know how protective he is of Parker. He probably thought Lincoln messed up his diabetes pump or something," Beck offers with a shrug.

"Should someone go check on them?" Cody, Beck's *now fiancé* asks.

"Nah, no one can get through to him better than Parker can. I'm sure they'll be fine by the time food's ready," Beck assures him.

Cody nods, and he's all smiles again as he turns his attention to Jordan. "Thanks for spending so much time with Nick while we've been in Montana. I know he's pretty lost right now, and your friendship means a lot to him. I wish he would have come today."

Jordan looks uncomfortable, glancing away before he shrugs. "Nick is cool, you don't have to thank me for being friends with him."

"What the hell am I? Chopped liver?" Lincoln calls out. I have no idea how he's following our conversation so well while it looks like he's still winning his pool game. "I spend just as much time with Nick as Jordan does. Do I get a thanks?"

Cody looks surprised, glancing at Beck with wide eyes before turning his attention to Lincoln. "I didn't realize you'd spent that much time with him. It's great to hear he has even more support."

I knew Jordan and Cody's best friend, Nick, had been hanging out since he moved here from Montana, but Jordan failed to mention Lincoln was ever with them. *Interesting.* I will absolutely be grilling him about that later.

"So how are things going in Montana?" Jordan asks, obviously trying to shift the topic, but I'm interested in Cody's answer so I don't call him out for doing it.

"They're okay given the circumstances. The psychologists and cult specialists have started talking with everyone, but there are so many people that they've had to start with large, mostly informative, sessions, and I think a lot of people are having a hard time separating that from the Kyla presentations."

"Ugh, that has to be so hard."

"Plus so many people are without work now. It's been really difficult to figure out the next steps. The donations that have been coming in from all over the world have been a huge help, and we can't thank you both enough for everything you've done to help set everything up and spread the word."

"Eh, it was mostly Jordan," I say with a shrug.

"You both have been a huge help," Beck insists. "We're trying to figure out a replacement company or not-for-profit, something that would be able to employ all the people who were displaced by Kyla's shut down, but we've only just been allowed to begin the process of acquiring the campus."

"It's a great setup. Maybe an existing company looking for new headquarters could move there?" I suggest.

"Yeah, that's one of the options we're exploring."

"What about you, Adrian?" Cody asks. "How are things going with Hudson? I feel like I haven't gotten to talk to you in person in so long."

"Oh my god, I thought you'd never ask! Things with Hudson are... annoyingly perfect," I respond with a sigh. "Other than the fact that he's straight, he has continued to be the ideal roommate, even now, months later. He also doesn't seem to own any shirts, which I'm definitely not complaining about. Honestly, the more time we spend together, the more I never want him to leave."

"Does he have a move-out date planned?"

"No, but he did finally close on that house right by me a few days ago. It needs quite a bit of work to get it how he wants it, though, so he's asked to stay with me until the remodel is done." And when it is, he'll no longer need me in his life. I sigh again. "Would it be wrong to tell him it's delayed forever so he never moves out?"

"Probably." Cody nods seriously.

"The way *he* wants it?" Jordan teases.

I glare at him. "Just because he asked me to make the design decisions, doesn't mean he doesn't agree with my choices. He's going to love it."

"He wants *you* to make all the decisions for *his* house?" Cody clarifies, and I nod.

"Wow, he really does sound like your dream man," Beck adds.

"Well, his dream is to move into this gorgeous house, adopt a bunch of kids, and meet the perfect woman to raise them with, so I won't be a part of the picture for much longer. He also officially applied to adopt now that he owns the house."

"Really? Good for him for knowing what he wants and going after it," Cody says with a huge smile.

Jordan leans over to nudge my shoulder with his. "That was all Adrian's encouragement, too."

"I just pointed out that he didn't need to wait to be happy, and he agreed. No big deal."

"It is. You're completely changing his life and whatever kids he ends up adopting." Jordan insists, and I feel my cheeks heat, but I don't know how to respond, so I just shrug again. "It's a great thing, Adrian. Even if I think you're treating him like your boyfriend without benefits."

"What's he up to today? He should have come here," Beck says, interrupting Jordan's teasing.

I roll my eyes. Obviously, I wish there were benefits, but I'm also very aware that Hudson isn't my boyfriend. "I did invite him since there's less than forty-eight hours between games, and he didn't have time to see his family, but as soon as I mentioned it was at your family's house, he turned down the offer. I think he's planning to video call his parents for their Thanksgiving meal."

"What's wrong with my family?" Beck asks, sounding offended.

"How many times do I have to tell you that the players are afraid of you?"

"Even Hudson? He's older than me! He's been on the team since I was in college. I'm not even scary," he huffs, crossing his heavily tattooed arms. Combined with his glare, he very much does look scary right now if you didn't know he was such a softy underneath the resting bitch face.

"You're still the boss," I remind him.

"Whatever. He could have come."

"It's probably for the best since he doesn't get to see his parents much. Plus, you all have given me enough shit over the past few months about us acting like a couple. I didn't need to show up today with him at my side and have your entire extended family thinking we're secretly together, too."

"Ugh, I can't wait for our player to come out. I wish it wasn't a big deal, but I know it will be. You're right though. We don't want to start speculation about the wrong person, especially when we're about to have an actual announcement."

"Don't sound so surprised that I know what I'm talking about," I tease.

"Dinner's ready," someone calls from upstairs, and everyone immediately stands, forgetting all about our conversation in favor of food. The Caldwells have a huge spread every year, and I am dying to get to dessert. Their chef always makes my very favorite fudge, and they serve it with chocolate ice cream. It's one of my top five desserts of all time.

Dinner is amazing as always, but I'm distracted. I wonder what food would be Hudson's favorite, if his chef made him something special for today, or if I should bring home any leftovers for him to try. I even catch my mind wandering to imagine a future Thanksgiving with Hudson in his new house, sitting around a table with a couple of kids saying what they're thankful for, surrounded by tasteful yet fun fall decor.

I might even put myself at the table.

But hey, it's my fantasy, so I can do what I want.

By the time everyone finishes eating and visiting, it's been dark for hours. I drove all my friends, so as much as I would have loved to leave and catch Hudson before he's asleep for the night, I'm not surprised that my place is dark when I finally get home.

It's been a long day, and I'm a little more sluggish than usual as I put away the leftovers Beck's grandparents insisted I bring home with me. I want to fall into bed and stay there for days. I typically have an elaborate nighttime skin-care routine, but there's no way that's happening tonight.

I shuffle into my room, eyes already half closed, manage to ditch the cashmere sweater I'd been wearing, and change into my silk sleep shorts when I hear it.

A moan.

A very loud moan. My pulse skyrockets and all my blood rushes south because that was *not* a sound of pain.

I spin to look at my door, suddenly very awake as I confirm that I didn't shut it all the way like I normally do before bed. Was Hudson's door closed? Are both of our doors open while he's making the most sexual noises I've ever heard in person?

I should close my door… right?

For a moment, I panic that I've interrupted an actual hookup, that he invited someone over, so I pull out my phone to quickly scan today's footage from my video doorbell app. I don't want to be a stalker, but if there's a woman in his room, I'm immediately shutting the door and running into the bathroom where I can attempt to drown out the noises of my dream man with someone else.

There's no one on the video though. The only motion, aside from me, is when Hudson went on a run this morning. He's been home alone ever since. And he was alone last night when we were watching TV; it's not like someone spent the night and is still here.

Which means he's the only one in his room, on the other side of my wall, with both of our doors open and jerking off.

He probably has no idea he isn't alone in the house. I thought he was already asleep, so I was quiet and didn't turn the hall lights on.

"Ohhhh fuuuuck," he clearly groans, and any thoughts of shutting the door are gone as my cock jerks in response to the sound.

He might hear the door if I close it, and then he'd realize I heard him.

It would be awkward, and I don't need to risk putting either of us through that.

I do, however, desperately need to get off.

I'm not strong enough to ignore the free audio performance he's providing. I ditch my shorts and grab my lube as quickly as I can. The sounds Hudson is making, combined with the taboo fact that I'm an unknown audience member for his show, that he doesn't know I can hear what he's doing as I settle onto my bed and wrap my hand around my cock, have me immediately hard as fucking stone.

My dick is already leaking, and I spread the precum around the head before I add lube. I picture Hudson's full lips hanging open as another obnoxious moan escapes his throat. I image telling him to be quiet, that I have neighbors and he needs to learn to control his moans, as much as I fucking love them, or I'll need to step in and shut him up with my cock.

In my fantasy he eagerly agrees, wrapping those perfect lips around me and sucking me into his warm mouth as deep as he can. The idea of such a stereotypically masculine man, this professional athlete with his big muscles and a full beard, submitting so easily to my pleasure has me fighting a moan of my own. Unlike him, though, I actually need to remain quiet so he never finds out I'm jerking off to the sound of him doing the same thing on the other side of the wall.

He lets out a higher noise, almost a whimper, and I adjust my fantasy. I don't want to be discouraging those sounds: I want to be the one causing them. Now he's on his hands and knees with his ass out, begging me to fuck him. I imagine taking my time stretching him open, using my mouth and tongue to really show him how amazing I can make him feel as I get him ready for my cock.

I increase the pressure of my hand as I continue to stroke myself, picturing my dick slowly sinking into Hudson's hole, so fucking tight as it practically sucks me into him as if every part of him wants us to be joined in this new way. My hips are thrusting without my permission, desperate for more, for the fantasy to be real, for the release I'm chasing, more of everything.

I must be completely delusional as pleasure consumes me, and my orgasm overwhelms my senses, because for a moment, as my eyes practically roll into the back of my head, I almost think the deep moan Hudson draws out sounds like my name.

If only.

HUDSON

December

"I know you don't normally travel with the team, but my parents were asking if there was any chance you'd go to the Minnesota game next week. I think they're sick of hearing me talk about you without meeting you."

Adrian chokes on his coffee, coughing a few times before he recovers. We're sitting on the couch, him with his laptop in front of him, while I've been watching highlights of last night's NHL games across the league. When he does finally catch his breath, he turns to me with wide eyes. "You want me to go to Minnesota to meet your parents?"

"Well, yeah, if you want to. No pressure. I just thought it would be cool if you could all meet, and my dad has a hard time traveling. Like I said, I've talked about you quite a bit since moving in here, so they'd love to meet you."

He stares at me for another long moment. "Um, let me check my calendar. That's Thursday's game, right? Do you fly in from Chicago the night before and leave back to Chicago after the game?"

"Yeah, it's between two home games, and it's a short flight, but they like us to avoid doing it all in one day if we can."

He nods, still looking at things on his computer. "I should be able to make that work. The only meetings I have Thursday can be done over video call. I can do the rest of my work from the hotel as well. I'll email Samantha about adding me to travel arrangements, but I've done it with Beck before for big games, so that shouldn't be a problem."

"Really? That isn't too big of a pain? You want to come?" I check again before I get my hopes up too much. My parents *have* been asking to meet him, and I know I could just do it over a video call, but the idea of them all together for the last game of my NHL career that my parents will be at... I don't know, it just feels right. The thought of Adrian in their box makes me feel the warm, fuzzy kind of happy that I'm always chasing. Even if my parents will have no idea how important Adrian has become to me.

Even if Adrian has no idea how important he's become to me.

I should probably tell him, I know that.

I just don't know what to say. For weeks now, I've been trying to think of how I can put my feelings into words, and I'm still struggling. It's so much easier to leave my door open at night or when I'm in the shower, to walk through the hall naked and hope he'll catch me in a situation that might give me some idea if he's even attracted to me beyond his teasing flirting. Maybe it would even force the conversation.

Approaching my newfound sexual identity questions maturely? Being vulnerable and sharing my feelings about how often I think about what it would be like to physically be with Adrian? That's so much harder.

I know Adrian is special, that I'm drawn to him, and that I want to be in his presence whenever possible. Making him smile makes me feel more accomplished than any goal I've scored this season. I'm desperate for his approval and praise. But I still don't know what to call my feelings exactly. A crush sounds so juvenile. But admitting I want to date him sounds like such a huge step when he's the first man I've ever felt this way about, and we haven't even kissed.

I know I want Adrian to continue to be in my life and not just in it peripherally as a friend. I want him front and center. I want to have some sort of claim over him beyond his title of my roommate.

I just want him to be mine.

Thoughts of sexual identify labels, words like bi, pan, queer, and even demi are all still kind of overwhelming when I've lived my entire life assuming they didn't apply to me. But after more than a month now of fantasizing about what a future with him as my partner might look like—how great a dad he would be, how I couldn't possibly find a better parent to give my future kids—I think it's safe to say this isn't a passing thought or a questioning moment.

The straight label no longer feels like my own. Even if I'm still working on claiming another. Which label I connect to the most changes almost daily. I know Adrian would be a huge help in talking me through all of it, but I don't see how I could talk about it without making it super obvious that he's the object of all my fantasies these days.

I keep circling back to my concerns that I'll fuck it up whenever he does find out. That I'll say the wrong thing, or he won't feel the same way, and I'll ruin our friendship beyond repair. So for now, I'm taking the cowardly route of not saying anything, telling myself that I'm only waiting until after I move out.

It'll be easier that way, safer. If things do blow up in my face, then he isn't stuck with me in the next room. I won't be forced to awkwardly move out before my house is ready. Maybe I'll be confident enough then to ask him on a date, to see if he would be willing to explore a romantic relationship with me.

I want to do things right, to treat him the way he deserves to be treated. I don't want him to think I'm only wanting to experiment with him because it's convenient while we're living together.

There are so many reasons for me to continue with the status quo, to wait until I've moved out before I risk changing anything between us.

But my house won't be ready for a couple of months still, and as much as I love having the excuse to continue living with Adrian, the idea of possibly having more with him after I move out is all I can think about these days. I'm tempted to tell him to cancel the contractors he's already hired so I can move in now and speed things along.

But I won't. If I'm being completely honest with myself, part of why I liked the house in the first place was because of how happy it made Adrian, how easily he was able to make it feel like a home. The optimistic—probably too cocky—part of me also keeps reminding myself that if Adrian ever does agree to date me, if there's any chance my daydream of our future family could possibly come to fruition, then Adrian could live there with me someday. I want him to have his dream house, so on the off chance he could ever want to share it, I'll keep the plans as is. He can choose exactly what he thinks it should look like, and maybe one day—if I'm not being completely delusional, and he actually gives me a chance—it could also be his.

For now, though, I'll find joy in the fact that he's just agreed to meet my parents. He's never talked about his own parents, so I had no idea what to expect when I asked him.

"I know you didn't go home for Thanksgiving, but do you ever visit any family? I don't think I've heard you mention any."

He snorts. "Fuck no. I'm from a small town in the middle of nowhere Arkansas. Even if I ever spoke to my parents, which I have zero plans to do, I wouldn't want to go back to that shitty place."

"You don't talk to them?" I gape. I can't imagine choosing to not talk to my parents. They're such a big part of my world. Even now with how far apart we are, I don't go more than a day or two without at least texting my mom.

"Nope. They were very traditional values, unaccepting, churchgoing kind of people. They knew I was different at a young age. I was one of those kids who everyone thought was gay before I even knew what that meant. They tried to get me to play sports to 'toughen me up,' and always made comments about how being gay was wrong. They didn't abuse me or anything, but by the time I was in high school, they basically ignored me as much as they could."

He shakes his head, a sad smile in place and a faraway look in his eyes. I want to comfort him, to wrap him in my arms and scold his shitty parents, but this is the most open and honest he's ever been with me. I don't want to interrupt and risk him stopping.

"The only time they would even talk to me was to make sure I was still doing my chores, a list that grew longer and longer as time went on. There was always food in the house, but I had to be the one to cook it. Probably why I prefer to eat out now. Anyway, they made it clear when I turned eighteen that they were no longer obligated to be in my life. I haven't been back since."

I can't hold back any longer. "Holy shit, they kicked you out?"

He tilts his head, maintaining a far cheerier tone than what I think the content of what he's saying calls for. "I don't know if I'd call it being kicked out when I knew it would happen. The moment I could get a job, I did, and I started saving up money to get my own place. It was a small town, and this fabulous older woman who ran the motel must have felt sorry for me because she gave me a really great rate on a room. By the time my birthday actually rolled around, I'd already moved most of my stuff there." He shrugs.

He doesn't seem too upset about it, and I'm glad he's willing to share all of this with me, but every word out of his mouth feels like another coal being added to the flames of my anger. I've never really understood the whole "blood boiling" expression until right now as I picture a teenage Adrian abandoned by the very people that are supposed to love him the most.

"Fuck, Adrian. I'm so sorry that happened to you. And neglect is still abuse. No wonder you're so strong and independent now. You were forced to be that way far too young."

His cheeks get a little red in reaction to my observation, but he continues just as confidently. "It was fine. I'd never fit in there anyway, and it's not like I wanted to stay in Arkansas. I was destined for bigger and better things than anyone in that homophobic town could even imagine," he teases, sitting up a little straighter and shaking his shoulders. "I decided a long time ago that I could let the bad things eat away at me, risk them turning me into someone bitter and full of hate, or I could choose to focus on the things I actually have some control over and work toward what makes me happy. I choose to be happy."

As if I needed more reasons to admire him. "Wow. Adrian, that's a really amazing way to look at things."

"I am pretty amazing," he agrees, and I know he's still joking, but I'm not. "Luckily I have a summer birthday, so I only lived in the motel for about a month. I had already gotten scholarships for school, so I worked my ass off earning as much money as I could before my dorm opened up. Then after college, I followed Beck and Jordan to Chicago and never looked back."

He makes it sound so simple, but I'm happy that he's finally shared more of his story with me tonight. I see how hard he works, how great he is at problem solving, and the way he lights up when people praise his efforts. Knowing how hard he had to fight to earn the life he has now, and that he's remained so positive, is truly inspiring.

I try to follow his example as I consider my response. It's obvious he's trying to keep things light, so I do my very best to hold back my anger at how he was treated. "Well, I'm really glad that you ended up here. Let me know if you ever need me to look up anyone in Arkansas though. It sounds like there are a few people there I'd like to teach a lesson to."

He snorts a laugh, and his cheeks darken even more as he holds my gaze, both of us smiling. I want to tell him how much I mean that statement. That I'm grateful not just that he ended up in Chicago, but that he ended up right here with me. That I'd gladly defend him against any and everyone who's ever caused him even a moment of pain.

But the words are stuck in my throat.

It isn't the time.

I'll keep waiting until I have my own place for those kinds of confessions. I have a feeling that, once the flood gates open, I'll never be able to stop telling him how truly amazing I think he is. How happy I am to have him in my life.

Just a few more months of this. It'll be fine.

When I'm alone in my room, unable to fall asleep as I picture what would have happened if I did make a move, I give in for what feels like the hundredth time, imagining that it's his hands on my aching cock instead of my own. I come quickly, not bothering to draw things out as I chase my release, and after I've cleaned up and gotten back in bed, I work up the courage to order a few sex toys that claim to be good for beginners.

If things ever do work out with Adrian, I don't want to mess things up because I'm inexperienced. I also don't want to promise anything I can't follow through with or won't enjoy, so probably better to figure that out on my own than in the moment with him if I'm ever that lucky.

ADRIAN

What the actual fuck am I doing here?

I mean, seriously, who flies to a different state to meet their platonic friend's parents?

Apparently me. That's who. Because I'm an idiot who's far too into my straight roommate, and every time he suggests something, I jump on it. Especially when it's a little outside of normal friendship boundaries.

Logically, I know he could never care about me the way I do him. We've become close as roommates, but it's a temporary situation. But why be rational about being just friends when I can obsess over those requests and pretend he wants me to be more?

His parents probably mentioned they'd like to meet the person he's living with in passing—this is definitely something that could have happened over a video call—and yet, here I am, after rearranging my whole work week so that I could fly to Minnesota, about to meet them in person.

And Hudson isn't even here.

He's downstairs somewhere, getting ready for the game, while I wait in this dimmed box by myself, nervously shoving M&M's into my mouth with absolutely zero sense of self-control.

Seriously, why am I so nervous?

Obviously, I want them to like me. I know how much Hudson's parents mean to him, but it shouldn't really matter if they don't. Hudson and I are just friends. This should not feel as high stakes as meeting a romantic partner's parents would be.

But that delusional part of my brain that's convinced Hudson is the perfect man for me must be in charge, because that's exactly what this feels like. The nerves dancing in my stomach right now don't seem to be calming with the chocolate like I'd hoped—which is honestly tragic because usually chocolate fixes every-thing—so I have no idea what to do as I sit here waiting. By myself.

I flew in with the team late last night, and I have a room at the same hotel they're staying at. Hudson got to see his parents briefly this morning, and he invited me to join him at their house, but I really do have a lot to get done this week with the Winter Classic coming up, so I worked from my room at the hotel while he visited them.

"Adrian, is that you, sweetie?" a woman asks, completely startling me even though I've literally been sitting here just waiting for them to arrive. I jump out of my seat and turn to face the couple that just entered the room. The man who must be Hudson's dad is using an electric wheelchair, and I'm assuming his mom is the woman at his side.

"Hi! Hello, yes! That's me. Adrian. So lovely to meet you both," I ramble, unable to stop myself. "Are you guys okay with hugs? This kind of feels like a hug moment, but that could totally just be a me thing…"

"You can call me Tina, and I would love a hug," Hudson's mom confirms warmly, cutting my nervous rambling off as she opens her arms. I rush forward to embrace her. We're about the same height, and although it doesn't last long, I'm still left with a sense of comfort as though I was momentarily wrapped in a warm blanket that could make all my troubles go away.

The first time I had a hug like that was from Beck's mom, and I immediately knew I liked her. I smile, having that same feeling now about Hudson's mom. I turn to his father next, not wanting him to feel left out, even though I'm unsure if a hug is something he can physically participate in. "And what about you, sir, would it be alright if I hugged you? I won't be offended if you want me to skip it."

Hudson warned me that his father's speech was heavily impacted by the stroke, and that it can take him a while to attempt to communicate. He suggested I give him a long time to reply, but that I didn't need to adjust my own speaking speed or volume because his stroke mostly affected the way his brain produces speech. He still has fairly good comprehension. He also suggested clear questions that didn't require long answers, so hopefully my rambling wasn't too confusing.

He nods his head slowly. I smile before I approach him and lean in for the hug. He wraps his one usable arm around me as I do, and for some reason, I have to fight back tears. I think about everything Hudson has told me about this man, how he gave him such an amazing childhood that now all Hudson wants in life is to pass that on to kids of his own. I pull back from the embrace before I really embarrass myself by crying moments after meeting them.

I clear my throat so I don't sound overly emotional. "Hudson has told me such amazing things about you guys. You both raised such an incredible man. You should be so proud."

His mom's smile grows. "Oh, sweetie, thank you for saying that. We've also heard great things about you, quite a bit actually, so we were thrilled to get to meet you. Thank you for coming all this way to do it in person."

Okay, they actually want me here. *That's a relief.* I was

worried one look at me and they'd realize I'm obsessed with their son and want me to leave.

I smile, a little more relaxed now. "Last game that you'll be at, how could I say no? I hope you got the Werewolves merch package the team sent to your house." The team, me. Same difference.

"Yes! Thank you so much. We're both wearing the jerseys now." Tina does a little spin to show off her look. I love her already. "Well, I want to know everything about you. But the game is about the start, and Robert, honey, are you still feeling alright?" He slowly nods. "So maybe we can move to the seats at the front of the box. He can't get out of the chair easily enough to go down, but there's enough room behind the stadium seats for him to park and still see the ice."

"That sounds great." I hang back and let them get settled. I know the Caldwell center has some accessibility programs in place, but seeing how limited Hudson's dad's experience is, even in the fanciest seats I'm sure money could offer, I can't help but wonder if we could improve our disability accommodations. I don't think our boxes have any special wheelchair accessibility... We have wheelchair seating but that's out in the main area where it's considerably louder than here. Hudson's mom offers Robert noise-canceling headphones, so that must be a factor for him. And the lights are off in the suite, but the arena is really bright with a lot of flashing lights, so that barely affects how light it is in the box. To watch the game, it does need to be bright, there isn't much I can think of to counteract that, but maybe offering more sensory rooms where people could excuse themselves would be an option. I think we have one, but it's a huge arena, and I wonder if we could add more...

"I don't know what Hudson told you about us to have you looking so nervous and staying so far away, but you can come join us. We don't bite, promise."

I laugh as I do just that, taking a seat next to Tina in the same row. "All good things, I promise. I was just thinking about work."

She hums knowingly. "Hudson did mention you're somewhat of a workaholic."

I laugh again, surprised. "He did?"

"Well, he didn't call it that. We were just wondering about the person he's been living with for months now, so we asked about you a bit. I hope you don't mind." I shake my head. "Hudson went on and on about how hard you work and how much you do for the team and all the players and staff who work for it. He's played professional hockey for how many years now? I've never heard him mention the behind-the-scenes operations in more than passing. But he talked for probably twenty minutes straight about all the things you've done to help the team, and how you're constantly bringing work home."

Tina turns to her husband throughout the conversation, and her chair is slightly behind his allowing me to see them both, so even though she's doing the talking, it does feel like we're all chatting together. "We know it must have taken effort to come here tonight, but it seemed important to Hudson. I'm glad you were able to." She reaches out to squeeze my hand and gives me a knowing look.

But what the hell does she know?

"Can we pretend like I'm handling this really casually and that I'm not turning the color of a tomato right now?" I ask with a big smile, only half joking. It earns a laugh from Hudson's mom, and what I think is a chuckle from his dad, so I'm fairly certain things are actually going pretty well though.

"Don't sweat it. I loved hearing all about it. He obviously has a lot of admiration and respect for you. I'm so glad he has good people to lean on when he's so far away from us. You've been so kind letting him stay with you, and he said you've been a big help with finding a house and encouraging him to adopt, too. He's talked about wanting to be a dad for as long as I can remember, and I'm just so relieved that his divorce didn't crush his spirit."

"Me too. He's been so positive the entire time. I would have definitely thrown a fit at some point, but he really has stayed so calm. He's still so full of hope for his future. It's amazing." Just like he is. Crap. Do I sound a little too impressed by him? I can't help it.

I'll choose to pretend like I'm successfully managing to maintain the supportive friend role, but I really doubt it.

"Don't underestimate your part in that, sweetie. He's never liked being alone. I think living with you has really helped him, allowed him not to focus on the bad things that have happened. Especially now that I've met you and see how positive you are too."

My smile feels permanent. I had hoped that his parents would like me, but I never expected his mom to be full of praise. "Well, he's an ideal roommate. I don't know who taught him to clean and do laundry, but I have absolutely no complaints about living with him."

"Oh, that was all Robert. Hudson has always imitated his dad. I'm glad those good qualities stuck," she says with a wink that reminds me so much of her son, her eyes the same gray-blue as Hudson's. I think both of these amazing people had a big influence on making him the man I know and adore today. It's easy to see how kind and loving his parents obviously are, and how easily they're extending that to me is such a bittersweet feeling.

On one hand, I'm eating it up, thriving as my chest feels ready to burst with the warm, fuzzy feelings they're offering. But on the other hand, this feels like a stolen moment. Another on the long list of things I've done with Hudson because he's single, and I'm the next best option while he's living with me, and I'm helping him with his house. I know I'm sitting in a temporary seat, a placeholder until he meets his future wife, and she'll be the one sharing future moments with his parents. She'll get to call these people Mom and Dad while they'll forget all about me. This is probably the one and only night I'll spend with them.

But I also know there's no use wallowing. I'm here with Hudson's amazing family, about to watch the final professional game they'll ever see him play. I'm going to focus on all the amazing parts of tonight, take some mental notes of things to look into regarding accessibility at the Werewolves' games, and have a fabulous time.

I can be sad about it being a onetime thing later.

21

HUDSON

"Thank you so much for coming with me. I have no idea why I'm this nervous," I admit.

I can't get my leg to stop bouncing as we wait for them to call me in for my interview. Hopefully this will be the first of many. The person I spoke with from the adoption agency explained this would be an initial interview to go over my application and discuss the process, and if everything goes well, I'll be approved to move forward with the next steps.

It's one of my rare no-game days in Chicago, and I'm so grateful that Adrian was able to take a few hours off as well to be here for emotional support. He's always so calm and steady, and it helps me to be that way as well. I know I'd be ten times worse if he wasn't here.

"No problem, you know I'm happy to help," he assures me with a smile. "Plus, I think it's good to be nervous. That just shows how much you care." I smile back, and I can feel my heart rate approaching a slightly more normal pace with his assurances. "Not that you have anything to worry about. You're a great applicant on paper and even more so in person. They'll see how lucky any kid will be to call you dad."

"How do you always know exactly what to say to make me feel better?"

"It's a gift," he preens, making my smile grow even more.

"Mr. Roy? You can come on in," a woman, who looks about my age, says, motioning for me to follow her into the office we've been waiting outside of.

I stand, and when Adrian doesn't follow, she turns to me. "Would you like your friend to join us?"

I perk up immediately. "Is that allowed?"

"Of course. If you'd like to, that is. But it could help if you have questions later on to have someone with you who might help you to remember everything we talk about."

I turn back to Adrian. "Would you mind?"

"Not at all." He hops out of his seat eagerly. "Can I take notes?"

The woman nods. "Yes, if Hudson is okay with it, that would be great. By the way, my name is Holly."

"It's great to meet you." We all exchange introductions and shake hands before Adrian and I settle in on a couch across from the one Holly is seated at. The whole thing feels far more casual than I was expecting. Between that and having Adrian at my side, my nerves finally turn into excitement. I can't believe this is finally happening. It all feels so real; I'm going to *hopefully* be a dad soon!

Holly offers us a warm smile. "Alright, Hudson, for this initial application interview, we'll discuss the background information you included in your application, adoption expectations, and the details of the different parts of the adoption process."

"Okay, that sounds great." Out of the corner of my eye, I can see that Adrian has already begun taking notes on his phone.

"Do you have any initial questions or concerns before we begin?"

I nod, worried about voicing my fears, but I know for this

process to work, I need to be open and honest about everything. So I take a deep breath and go for it. "Will it be a problem that I'm a single man wanting to adopt? I know legally there's nothing against it, but in practice, have you seen that be a barrier?"

Holly gives me a reassuring smile as she shakes her head, and the relief I feel is immediate. "There used to be rules and stigma against single parent adoption, and I won't lie to you, there might be some expecting women who gloss over a profile because of it, but I've seen more and more single parents successfully adopt every year. If there's no concern about emotional readiness and there's proof of a strong support network, there's no reason for concern."

I let out a huge sigh of relief. "That's great to hear. I'm really excited about the opportunity to become a father, and I definitely think I have the necessary support." I can't help but glance at Adrian as I say that, and he meets my gaze with a soft smile.

"I can see that," Holly agrees. "Okay, let's start by having you tell me a little bit about why you'd like to adopt."

"Sure." I tell her all about how amazing my parents are, about how great my childhood was, and how I've always dreamed of passing down the love I grew up with to my own children one day. Then I explain how Adrian helped me realize that I didn't need to wait to go after what will make me happy, and that led me to look into adoption. Holly nods and hums as I talk, all while maintaining her welcoming expression, so I think things are going well.

"Okay, next we'll go over your application. You're in your final year as a professional hockey player, is that correct?"

"Yes. I didn't want to wait until I was retired to start the application process, because I know it can take a long time, but as soon as the season is over, I'm hoping to dedicate my time to my family."

She nods. "And will that mean you'll no longer have any income?"

"I've saved and invested a significant portion of my income for my entire career, and I've had quite a few endorsement deals and opportunities over the years that have provided income beyond my contract with the team. I'll continue to have income from some of those investments, combined with what I have saved, it should be more than enough for a comfortable life for me and my family."

"Okay, great. I do see some information about that here in your application, but you'll need to submit official proof of all that during the home study process if you proceed."

"Of course. I've already spoken with my financial advisor about having that paperwork ready to share when needed."

"Wow, you're prepared," she says, sounding impressed. Adrian was actually the one who suggested I call and request that my advisor start that process. Adrian really thinks of everything.

"Okay, I know you attended an informational session," Holly continues, looking back down at the stack of papers in her hand. "You've indicated that you're interested in domestic infant adoption, is that still the case?"

I nod eagerly. "Yes, and I would be open to discussing any level of adoption with the birth family: closed, semi-open, open. Whatever we all think would make the most sense for the specific circumstance." She writes something down on her paper.

I turn to Adrian while I wait for her next question, and he gives me a reassuring smile. I am so grateful to have him here. From the looks of his phone, he's taking diligent notes, and knowing that we can talk about this later when I'm sure I'll be worried I said something wrong, makes me feel so much better.

"Alright, the next step of the process will require you to complete at least ten hours of training. There are required classes on prenatal substance exposure, transracial adoption, relationships with birth parents, and talking to children about adoption. The remaining hours can be on any adoption related topic of your choosing. Child and infant CPR is required in addition to those hours. General parenting classes are encouraged, and we'll provide info on where you can do all that."

"Great," I agree easily. That sounds like I'll be moving on to the next step. My excitement rises, but I try to remind myself that nothing is official yet.

"After all the required education is completed, and the necessary documents are reviewed, the next step would be a home visit and safety inspection. There will be more interviews, as well as interviews of some of your references. It's not an easy process, and everything takes time."

"I understand."

She puts down the papers to look at me, her expression more serious. "After all that is completed and approved, then you would move onto the matching stage. That can take months, even years in some cases. I know this is all very exciting now, but I want to be clear that this could be a very long process. Are you prepared for that?"

I take a moment to consider what she's saying. A lot can change in a year. I know that firsthand. I feel like a completely different person than I did even six months ago, when I was married and hoping to get Shelby pregnant. Now I'm desperately hoping that the man sitting next to me might consider dating me, might eventually want to be the hypothetical kid I'm talking about adopting's other parent.

But I like the person I am today. And everything about this process has felt right, as if I were exactly where I'm meant to be. So I answer easily.

"Yes. I know that it might take years, but I feel like I'm meant to do this. I'd like to think it'll take however long it needs to, and

I'll end up being the parent of whatever child is meant to be in my life."

Adrian puts his hand on my knee, giving it a supportive squeeze that has my heart racing. *Would he want to be a part of that, too?*

But those thoughts can't be my focus right now, so after a quick smile at him, I turn back to Holly. Her encouraging expression is still there. "Alright, Hudson, if you don't have any other questions, I'll be in touch soon."

We all exchange goodbyes, and I manage to maintain my composure until Adrian and I are alone in the elevator. "Okay, am I too confident, or did that go really well? I don't know why I thought it would be more of an interrogation, but I feel good about it."

His grin lights up the small space. "It was perfect! I'm so glad they let me come in with you. I took notes on everything, and I already shared the document with you so you can refer to it if you have questions, but you did a great job. Everything came across as so genuine. I'm sure they'll approve you."

Before I even consider what I'm doing, I have my arms wrapped around Adrian, lifting him slightly off the ground with how enthusiastic my hug is. I know I should pull back… but I don't want to. Today feels like one of those days that I'll never forget, and I know it's been so much better because he was at my side.

"Thanks for being here," I murmur into the top of his head. "I don't know what I'd do without you." He hasn't pulled away, sinking into my hold and resting his head against my chest, tucking it under mine as he squeezes just a little, hugging me back. *He fits so perfectly against me.*

"Of course, Hudson. Don't worry about it. I'm not going anywhere."

I really hope he means that.

This stolen moment where we're all alone, holding each other, hidden away from the world in this elevator, almost feels frozen in time. It's so easy to picture the future that we could have together, and his smaller frame surrounded by mine, his hard body pressed against me, feels way too good. I know I'm only seconds away from him noticing the physical reaction my dick is having to our contact, so I give him a final squeeze before I finally force myself to step back.

Adrian doesn't need to find out I'm attracted to him because my erection grinds into him in an elevator. That's creepy. It doesn't exactly scream "I want to date you. Give me a chance, and I'll do everything I can to make you happy."

"So, should we go out to dinner tonight? Celebrate how well that went?" he suggests, completely unaware of where my thoughts have strayed. "Or do you need to eat at home?"

"Let's go out. That's a great idea."

We end up at our favorite restaurant, dining in for once. I spend the entire meal reminding myself that it's not a date, no matter how much it feels like one.

Maybe one day.

Maybe just a few more months.

Later, when I'm alone in my room, I decided tonight's the night I should use the toys I ordered, no more hesitating. I wanted to kiss Adrian in that elevator.

I want to kiss him every time I see him.

I want to know what I'll want to do with him if ever given the chance.

The toys were delivered in discreet packaging, and for some reason, that disappointed me. Probably the same reason I keep leaving my door open at night. I'd kind of hoped Adrian would see what I ordered and it would lead to more. That he would offer to help me use them, or ask why I'd want to use silicone when he has the real thing.

I've been doing a lot of research on bottoming. I don't know what Adrian's preference is, but I figure either way, it's info I should know if I'm planning to have sex with another man. I've also learned that some couples don't actually have anal sex, that not everyone enjoys it. I'm going to try not to put too much pressure on myself if it doesn't end up being something I like, but I would like to find out.

As physical as my relationship with Shelby was, I've had the time now to look back and realize that's pretty much *all* it ever was. We never bonded the way Adrian and I have as friends, and we obviously didn't want the same things or share the same values. But Adrian and I already have that connection. If I'm right that we could use that foundation to build a romantic relationship, I think it would be so much stronger than any other I've had.

And I already enjoy spending time with him more than I do anyone else. I'm sure that adding anything sexual would only increase our bond. Whether that means penetrative sex, or blow jobs, or even if we just end up making out like teenagers, I think that it would be enough for me to be happy.

All that being said, the idea of being inside of Adrian, or hell, even him being inside of me, sounds really fucking hot. And I have the beginners kit I ordered… so I might as well use it.

I had already opened up the kit and cleaned everything when it was first delivered, but as I pull it out of my nightstand, I realize I might need to relocate.

One of the things included in the kit is a douche, and if I'm going to do this, I want to commit. During my research, I learned I already follow a pretty bottom-friendly diet, but I still like the idea of feeling clean if I'm putting anything up my ass.

The instructions that came with it warn that you'll need some time between the clean and any fun activities, so I only bring the bulb with me to the bathroom, holding it under an extra towel but not exactly hiding it as I walk through the hall with only a towel around my waist.

It doesn't matter though. It never does. Adrian always stays in his room for the night once he's in there.

I brought my phone, too, and do a quick internet search, again, to make sure I don't mess this up. *I got this*. Don't use water that's too warm. Do use lube to make inserting it easier. Relax. I'm so used to putting my body through hell for hockey, pushing myself through injuries, fights, illness, whatever I need to, to play. It's all a mind game. This is just another thing to add to the list of potentially uncomfortable things I'll go through to get what I want.

Checking that the water seems okay, I fill up the bulb, grab the lube from my shower, and position myself with one leg up on the toilet seat. Kind of an odd position but better than trying to stick my hand in the toilet.

I take some deep breaths, and then some more, just in case. I do feel pretty relaxed, so I carefully push the tip in. I'm not preparing for a colonoscopy here, so everything I saw online said not to go in too far, but even the smallest bit feels strange. Not bad, so I think the breathing and lube did their jobs, but definitely a new sensation for me. I'm very aware of it, so that's probably in far enough.

The water is an even stranger sensation, but I continue following the instructions, holding it in until my body is clearly done. It said to repeat that a few times, but after one more round, I'm no longer feeling like this was a sexy, fun new experience for me, and I think it did what it was supposed to. My ass feels cleaner than ever. The rest of me though? Well, I'm ready to wash my entire body after being so focused on the toilet.

I'm supposed to wait anyway, so after cleaning the douche, I opt for a full-body shower, really taking my time to wash everything, even doing some light manscaping while I'm at it.

Feeling way more confident than I was before I got in the shower, I finally focus on why I was doing any of this in the first place. I want to be with Adrian, and I want to not seem like the completely inexperienced thought-he-was-straight-a-few-months-ago man that I am.

I don't think he would judge me or anything, but I already feel like I'm waiting long enough with my plan to hold off until we're no longer roommates. If the time comes, I want to be ready.

Thinking about physically being with Adrian has blood rushing to my dick again, and I finally feel like I'm back in the right headspace to use the other, hopefully more fun, toys that I got.

Back in my room, I lay down on my bed with everything out next to me and decide to start simple with my finger. I saw someone online recommend you begin with breathing exercises while working your finger in, then as you continue the breathing, to apply pressure rotating around your hole as you do to stretch out the different areas.

My dick is still hard, so I give it a few strokes as I start my deep breathing, feeling like I'm relaxing into the bed. I bend my legs up for easier access to my freshly cleaned hole, and lube up my finger. After teasing my hole for a few moments, spreading the lube around, on a deep exhale, I slowly push the tip of my finger in without any resistance and work on the rotating stretching out technique, glad that I have a plan and didn't jump into shoving things inside of myself blindly.

Again, this isn't some magical, new experience for me, but it's fine, nothing uncomfortable. I continue to stretch myself as much as I can with my finger, going deeper as I do, until the whole thing is comfortably inside me. I could probably repeat that process with two fingers, but I think I'm ready for the first toy.

There are three silicone plugs, all different sizes to work my way up to the biggest one that's almost as wide as my dick.

Starting with the smallest, I add more lube, and I'm impressed to find my finger did its job because it goes in easily. I take a moment to evaluate how I'm feeling, continuing with my breathing, clenching and unclenching a few times.

It's a good feeling, I think. I'm very aware of my ass, and nerves I've never really paid attention to are suddenly all I can think of. The feeling of being full is pleasant, and I quickly find myself wishing there were more. I wrap my left hand around my cock, tugging a few times while I try to focus on the dual sensation of jerking off while also having something inside me. The combination is surprisingly hot, the pleasure of both combining to have me already climbing toward release.

Fuck, not yet.

I back off from my dick, and add lube to the middle-sized plug before I remove the first. My hole clenches around nothing, and I'm immediately disappointed by the sensation of feeling empty. This plug is a little more work to get in, but I take my time, continuing with my breaths, and before long I'm enjoying a more intense fullness.

I definitely like this. My dick is really fucking hard now, straining toward my abs, but I continue to ignore it in favor of the plug. This one sits deeper inside of me, and as I shift my hips, mostly involuntarily at this point, I think my prostate is finally involved as the pleasure intensifies with each movement. There's another plug to try out, but I don't think I can wait—there's another toy, a prostate massager that suddenly has all my attention.

It's curved and rounded, and a few minutes ago, it seemed very intimidating, but now that the plug is inside of me, teasing me with random jolts of *holy fuck that feels amazing,* I think I'm ready.

Feeling even more empty after removing this plug, my hips are constantly moving now, desperate for something to fill me up or touch my cock. It takes a second to figure out the curve, but having something back in my ass is a huge relief. I know there's even more this can do for me now though, and I adjust the angle until I'm moaning loudly with how fucking good it feels when it finally rubs over that perfect spot.

How have I never done this before? I'm clearly in the group of people who enjoy having something up their ass, because this is the best solo session I've ever experienced, and I haven't even finished. I'm being so obnoxious with the loud moans and whimpers escaping my throat right now, but I can't find it in myself to care. I want Adrian to hear me. I want my sex sounds to be all he can think about as he falls asleep.

I finally grab my leaking dick, spreading the precum around the head before stroking the shaft as I picture what would happen if he came to investigate. Would he want to watch? Would he drop his pants and offer to show me what a real dick feels like? I'd be ready for him and more than willing.

My orgasm hits so intensely that I swear I black out for a moment, completely consumed by the euphoria.

My breathing is more labored than during any hockey game as I wait to calm down from that high. The whole sexuality label might still be confusing to me, but right now, as I think about how great that felt, the label of "bottom" is feeling like one I could easily embrace.

22

ADRIAN

January

"I know you said you'd help however you can—and I so appreciate it—but are you sure you're willing to take all the classes with me?" Hudson asks again as we're walking up to the building where today's class is being held. "The CPR one was great, definitely important knowledge, but I'm less convinced you'll enjoy *The Basics of Baby Care.*"

I grab his arm, stopping him in his tracks. "Hudson! You're the one who asked me to come."

He glances down at his feet sheepishly, his cheeks pinkening above his beard even more than they already were from the cold. It's kind of adorable to see such a masculine man, looking extra big today in his puffy coat and beanie, look bashful. But Hudson literally always looks good, so I shouldn't be surprised.

"I know, and I do think that it'll be way more fun having you here! I just feel bad that I keep dragging you to this stuff with me."

"Don't feel bad! It's not your fault so many of these classes are designed for couples—not that we're a couple, obviously," I add with a nervous laugh. "Plus, I always have a good time hanging out with you. And who knows when I might need to babysit for you. Or maybe I'll even have my own kids one day. It'll be good for me to know this stuff, too."

He perks up; I think at the mention of me babysitting. I've been slowly starting to believe that he actually will want to remain friends even after he moves out, and it's probably a relief for him to know he won't lose my support, that I won't disappear when he does become a parent. I know some people drift apart from friends when they have kids, but Hudson has nothing to worry about. He's stuck with me in his life until he tells me otherwise.

"So, you do want kids?" he asks, sounding excited.

I nod, laughing. "How have we not talked about that?"

I know it can take me a while to really open up and talk about anything real, especially about myself. I can ramble about unimportant things with the best of them, and my inner circle is used to hearing every detail of my life, but I guess I've been afraid to scare Hudson away. I might have overcorrected there, though. "But yeah, I'd like to be a dad one day. I don't have any retirement plans like you do, so I haven't been quite as eager timeline wise, but I hope it happens for me."

He smiles. He's such a softie sometimes. I just want to wrap myself around him like a koala and never let go. I'm still daydreaming about the elevator hug and that was nearly a month ago now.

Time has honestly flown since Hudson's interview. The contractors have made great progress on his house even though it's nowhere near being done. He took a quick trip to see his parents for Christmas, and missed all the drama in my friend group—not that he really knows Oakley and Parker. But still, I wish he had been there when it all happened.

Thank God they gave me permission to tell Hudson, though.

So he got to hear all about how I was totally right all along and how I've always known those two should end up together with how much tension has been between them. *Now if only my straight roommate and I could have the same outcome.*

I know I shouldn't entertain thoughts like that. But lately… I don't know… Maybe it's just how much I've been helping him with all the things required for the adoption, but sometimes it's so easy to picture, with the way he teases and flirts, something that could actually mean more. With the way he looks at me sometimes… it just feels so real. Even if I know that's all wishful thinking.

He hasn't gone on any more dates since he started the adoption process, though, so he's spent all his nights in town with me. It's so easy to pretend we could be a couple when we live together and do all the perfectly normal, domestic things that make me so happy.

Who knows what he does on the road, though. He could be hooking up with different women every away game. God, I really should hook up with someone too. It's been so long.

I just can't really picture going out to find someone when the person I want has a bed in the next room. I've tried to be so good about not taking advantage of the proximity and try to remember to shut my door and respect roommate boundaries. But every once and awhile, I hear Hudson obviously jerking off, and I'm never strong enough to resist touching myself while I enjoy the erotic sounds he makes.

Obviously, he can never find out about that, though.

Maybe when Hudson moves out, I'll force myself to go on a date or even just go out and meet someone for the night, but for now, I'm more than content with the way things are.

"Well then, I guess it is good you take the classes with me," he concedes, pulling my attention back to him. "Let's go learn how to change a diaper!"

HUDSON

*A*drian really is good at everything. He had no trouble with the diaper, he picked up swaddling in no time, and now he's mastered, like, four different burping positions while I'm still worried about hurting the fake baby doll they have us using.

It just seems so tiny in my giant hands even though I know newborns are even smaller. Still, I'm used to throwing my body into another grown man's as we fight over the puck, being aggressive and physical. I'm definitely not used to being so delicate.

"Hudson, don't look so afraid of it," Adrian teases, carefully placing his baby in front of him. He reaches out to cover my hands with his, maneuvering me slightly until I have a better angle. "See, you were so close."

I know he's just trying to help, and I appreciate it, but touching me is far too distracting to be productive while I'm trying to learn this.

"I don't know. I'm worried about what will happen if you're not there to help me when it's the real deal," I admit.

He laughs like I'm joking. "I can be there if you want. We'll still be neighbors, right?"

Right. Neighbors. That's fine. Good even.

But I still want him closer than that.

Like on the other side of my bed.

Chill. It's good that he seems so eager to still be around after I become a parent. That's a great sign for all the dates I'm planning with him on the off chance there will also be an infant joining us.

Just need Adrian to agree to them first.

Details.

"Great job. everyone. Now let's practice the transition from burping to feeding. Remember, you'll want to offer the feeding break to burp every couple of ounces if you're using a bottle, or every time you switch sides while breastfeeding," the instructor says as they walk through the classroom we're in.

I look over at Adrian, who effortlessly cradles the fake baby in one arm, rocking slowly back and forth, and soothing the child as he pretends to feed it. "God, you're a natural. You really are good at everything."

He smirks. "Glad you finally caught on."

So am I. I can't believe I've known Adrian for years and never realized just how much I like him. Granted, we weren't as close as we are now, and I wasn't single for most of that time, and I also assumed I was straight. But now, I can't imagine looking at Adrian, with how warm his blue eyes are, how soft his styled hair looks, and not wanting to stake some sort of claim over him.

"It might help if you actually try to feed the baby," Adrian teases. Right. I should focus on the class, not how incredibly distracting Adrian is in the best way.

I try my hardest to position the doll to feed, yet I still feel like I'm risking crushing it with how giant I am in comparison. But the instructor comes around and confirms I'm doing well, so maybe I just need to be more confident and channel some of Adrian's energy. The rest of the class passes by pretty quickly, but I find that I'm not eager for it to be over.

I'm happy to be learning this stuff, and joking around with Adrian while doing it makes it really fun. I assume he won't want to come to the adoption-specific classes with me, but ask anyway.

And he keeps coming with me. To all of them.

Luckily, we're able to find multiple classes on the days I'm free and in town, some days doing back-to-back info sessions to fit it all in.

His steady presence combined with his charm and positivity makes each one so much better than if I'd gone alone.

Having Adrian at my side makes anything better.

February

BEFORE I KNOW IT, I've managed to complete all the required education and paperwork, and I'm following Adrian around my house as he explains to the person inspecting it exactly how much time is left on the current projects.

All the structural projects are completed, and now it seems like every room is being re-painted or wallpapered, or molding is being added. They agreed to come for the inspection even though I'm not living there yet since the next phase of the process can take so long actually matching with someone. They said it would be alright to do a first inspection now, and another if and when the match happens, as long as they also inspect Adrian's house since that's where I'm currently living. Adrian was fine with that, and that tour went well last week. He's also already been interviewed as one of my references and even agreed to the requested background check since we're currently living together.

"Alright, guys. That seems like everything," the inspector says, tucking his clipboard under his arm as he heads to the front door. "I was told this was the final step, so someone will contact you shortly with more information. Have a great night."

"Thank you so much." I wait until he leaves and sink against the back of the door as I close it with a relieved sigh. "We did it! That was the last thing I needed to do before I could be approved to make my adoptive parent profile."

Adrian chuckles. "*You* did it! Congrats, Hudson. I bet you'll be a parent in no time."

"Thank you. And thank you for all your help. It probably would have taken me twice as long to finish everything if I'd been doing it on my own."

He smiles, dimples popping, drawing my attention like they always do. "Don't mention it."

"We should celebrate!"

"Right now?" he asks with a chuckle.

"Yeah, we can pick up some champagne on the way home and celebrate finishing the home study phase, and my divorce being finalized."

"I thought we celebrated that yesterday by going to that fancy place for dinner?" he challenges.

"I think it deserves an extended celebration."

"Would you even have any? You barely ever drink."

"It's the NHL break; I can have a glass or two," I say with a smirk. "Plus I know you like it, so I don't think it'll go to waste."

He grins conspiratorially. "Alright. Just don't tell your trainers I'm a bad influence or anything."

I wink. "Never."

We lock up and head down the block to the liquor store. I've been so focused on being on our league's break that it isn't until we're inside that I realize what week it is for everyone else.

"Holy shit, what day is it?" I ask, looking around at all the decorations.

"Uh, Thursday," Adrian answers absentmindedly as he searched the sparkling wine section.

"No, like the date," I clarify as I take my phone out to check for myself. "Charming, did you know tomorrow is Valentine's Day?"

That gets his attention, and he turns to face me fully. "Why would I care about Valentine's Day?"

"Oh come on, you love holidays!" I insist. "I've lived with you through the multiple Halloween costumes in one night. I got to hear you sing a Christmas carol on the ice before a game because you lost the game of football on Thanksgiving. You got yourself three different advent calendars to count down to Christmas."

"Yes, well, those were fun holidays about spreading joy." He rolls his eyes and crosses his arms. "Valentine's Day is for people in relationships to rub it in the faces of single people. I feel like I'm back in school, and I'm the last to get chosen in gym class. I get it, I'm no one's favorite person, but I don't need it shoved in my face with heart decor."

"But that's not true," I blurt out, heart aching at how sad he sounds.

He raises a brow at me skeptically. "Which part?"

I know I should be casual right now. I'm not ready to tell him everything.

But he seems so defeated. I never want him to look like that. Adrian is strong and independent. I had no idea his lack of romantic relationship made him feel so alone.

I might not be able to tell him everything yet, but I can give him something. "You're my favorite person," I answer honestly.

He rolls his eyes again. "No, I'm not."

"But you are."

He uncrossed his arms. "Hudson, there's just no way."

"Then who the hell am I forgetting? Because I say it's you."

"I don't know! Maybe your parents?"

I can't help but chuckle. "They don't count. We're related, we have to love each other. You're looking for someone who doesn't have to be in your life but chooses you as their favorite person anyway. That's me."

He stares at me for a moment, jaw hanging open, brows furrowed in confusion. Finally, he clears his throat. "Well, that's very kind of you to say, but it's still different. You're my roommate, not my valentine."

I spin and walk away toward the register where there's an elaborate candy display set up for the holiday. I pick up the box of chocolate hearts and head back to Adrian.

He still looks confused, but he's laughing now as I approach. "What the hell are you doing?"

I give him my biggest smile, the one I save for when I'm really desperate for his help with something. "Adrian, will you be my valentine?"

His eyes are wider than I've ever seen them as his gaze flickers between me and the chocolate.

"Seriously, what the actual fuck is happening right now?"

"I thought I was pretty clear." I hold the chocolates out toward him. "Just waiting for your answer."

He shakes his head, but he's smiling so I don't think I completely fucked this up if that defeated expression he had is gone.

"Fine," he finally agrees. "If you're buying me champagne and chocolates, then I guess you're a pretty good valentine."

"Just pretty good? I need to step up my game."

He glances down at the wine again. "Maybe a fancier bottle?"

"You can pick out whatever one you want, Valentine."

"If you insist," he says with a smirk before he picks up one of the more expensive ones.

Whatever keeps him smiling.

When we're back home, I pour us glasses and make a toast. "To my valentine." Adrian laughs, completely unaware of how much I want this night to be for real. But we're also celebrating moving onto the next step in the adoption process, and I know I need to focus on that and stick to my plan. I'm so close to moving out, and I still think that it's for the best to wait until we're no longer living together to ask him out. There are too many ways it could go wrong otherwise.

I can wait a few more weeks to offer him what he deserves.

I think.

ADRIAN

"*A*m I completely insane to think he might actually be into me?" I ask my friends after spending the entire break between the first and second period telling them all about our Valentine's moment.

It's a Tuesday game, one of the first back after the break, and we've pretty much secured our playoff spot, so the Caldwell box we're watching the game from is fairly empty. Beck and Cody aren't even here. They've been meeting closely with a company they're hoping to help take over the old Kyla headquarters, so they're back in Montana. Before this season, Beck almost never missed a game, but after everything that happened last summer, he's only made it to about half of the home games this year.

He acts like he's doing it all to make Cody happy, but I know him better than that. He found out firsthand how easy it was to fall into Kyla's trap, and he cares about helping the other cult victims. The people there are lucky to have him fighting for them.

Jordan, Oakley, and Parker are all here, though, staring at me with varying levels of amusement.

"Well?" I prompt again "Give me something! Am I being delusional? What completely straight man would ask me to be his valentine with champagne and a chocolate heart, and then spend the night watching romcoms with me?"

"Hudson?" Jordan deadpans.

I playfully smack his arm. "That isn't helpful! I have no idea if I'm reading into things that aren't there or if there's a chance he's slowly working up the courage to tell me that he's madly in love with me," I say, only half joking.

"Madly in love might be kind of a strong thing to start with," Oakley cautiously points out.

"Yeah, well, you're not exactly the best person to be giving advice on this," I remind him. "How long were you into your best friend before you guys did anything about it?"

He smirks. "Well, we *did something about it* way before we ever talked about it."

"Are you saying I should make a move? There is absolutely zero chance of that happening. I'm not throwing myself at a straight man, no matter how many times I trick myself into thinking I've caught him checking me out."

"That's a good point," Parker says, putting his hand on Oakley's knee. "Don't be like us. You should talk about it instead of potentially wasting months that you could be together."

I take a deep breath as I imagine all the ways *that* could play out. "See, that sounds great and all, but what about the very real possibility this is all in my head and I ruin an amazing friendship? He could move out early because he's so uncomfortable. He could ask me to stop helping with his house! I'm not risking that. His future children deserve the perfect home."

Jordan nods along as I'm talking, so I assume he agrees. But then he opens his mouth. "And does any part of you also want them to be your future children, too? Because correct me if I'm wrong, but haven't you gone to every meeting and class with him? Didn't they even inspect *your* house?"

I sink back all the way in my chair, letting out a big sigh. "Yes, they did. And I have."

"Are you sure you aren't applying with him?"

I roll my eyes. "Yes, I'm sure. They always inspect all the residences of the applicant, and those classes are open to public enrollment. I was there for moral support."

"Uh-huh." Jordan sarcastically agrees. "I still think you two are acting way too much like a couple for him to not be into you. Even if he's never claimed a rainbow label."

"Maybe it's new for him, and he's still processing his attraction for you," Parker suggests.

"Ugh, if that's the case, I'd like him to process things a lot faster."

"Faster than asking you to fly across the country to meet his parents?" Jordan asks.

"Minnesota is hardly across the country."

"You hear yourself talking, right?" he teases. "You flew to meet his family. You helped him buy a house that he asked you to renovate. You've been at his side for the entire adoption process. And he has been the one asking for you to do all of that. There is no way that man isn't into you. He might not have said the words, but the actions are speaking very loudly."

The horn sounds, drawing our attention back down to the game as the starting line takes the ice for the second period.

"But what if we're wrong? Or what if there's a tiny chance of that possibly being true, but I manage to fuck it all up because I rush him?" I ask Jordan.

"I really doubt that's possible... but I do understand your concerns. Maybe give it a little more time, follow his lead. But also trust your gut. You know him way better than any of us do. I hope it works out for you though. He's a great guy, and you deserve a great one."

"Thanks." I can feel my cheeks heating as I focus my attention on the ice, watching as Joshua Martin gains possession and successfully crosses the blue line. Hudson and Oliver race after him. Oliver is faster, going straight toward the goal, while Hudson effortlessly accepts a pass from Joshua who hadn't even looked his way.

God, losing Hudson really is going to be a blow for the team. I know I'm going to miss watching him play, but hopefully I'll still get off-ice time to see him. Oliver and Joshua are going to have a really hard time replacing him on their line though.

Hudson is able to avoid New Jersey's defenseman, passing to Oliver at the last second. He fakes out the goalie, getting him to shift right, the wrong direction, and manages to send the puck in on his left side.

No one would think it's a chill weekday game with how loud the Caldwell Center is after the horn sounds and the goal music starts playing. My friends and I are all right there with the rest of the fans, on our feet, shouting the goal song.

I really am so lucky to have ended up where I'm at. I love my job and the team I work for. I'm surrounded by a great group of friends who feel more like family. I know that I'm where I'm meant to be, living my best life.

And if that life eventually involves Hudson as my person, then I'll be thrilled. But I doubt it could even be a possibility, so if it doesn't, and I was only the side character in his story who encouraged him to adopt, well, that's still really fucking cool.

As much as I pride myself in being a person who takes action and goes for what I want, as much as I hate waiting around, my gut is telling me that it's what I need to do. I can't pressure him into anything. And with our roommate arrangement right now, I don't think I could even trust that he wanted anything long term. I've seen the romcoms, I know a forced proximity situation for what it is. Maybe my friends are right and living with a gay man has led to Hudson questioning things about himself. But while we're living together, if he actually did make a move physically, I don't think I would be able to trust that I was anything more than an experiment.

Maybe the wait will be worth it. Maybe I should focus more on the journey I'm already on and the time I get to share with Hudson now instead of wondering how our story will end. If it could ever even be our story at all. I wouldn't have dreamed of our current friendship a year ago, though, and I'm so grateful for it.

I'm happy, and I'm going to continue to choose to focus on the good things, to be happy whenever I can.

Does that mean I'm suddenly not desperate for him? No. Does that mean my heart doesn't stop every time he's thrown into the boards? Absolutely not.

But I'm not willing to risk what we do have for the slim possibility of more. So I'm not going to make any major changes any time soon.

HUDSON

March

I've just finished changing after our morning skate when my phone rings from its place still inside of my locker. We've officially secured our spot in the playoffs this year, so the mood in the locker room is a little more relaxed and happy than it's been at other times during the season.

Still, my anxiety spikes when the ringtone sounds, because who the hell is calling me? My mom and Adrian always text first… unless something is wrong…

"Hello?" I quickly answer without even glancing at the caller ID.

"Good afternoon, can I confirm who I'm speaking with?" a woman asks, using a very pleasant tone.

"Hudson Roy," I respond, still a bit concerned.

"Hello, Hudson, this is Holly from the adoption agency. I know we haven't spoken in a few months, but I'm very happy to inform you that a local expectant mother has requested a meeting with you!"

"Oh my god! Already?" I practically shout into the phone,

earning questioning looks from my teammates that are still here. My giant smile must prevent any of them from actually saying anything though.

Holly chuckles. "Yes. It's certainly not a guarantee of anything, though. Many people meet with multiple prospective parents to see who they think will be the best fit before they actually match for the adoption."

"That makes sense. I understand," I assure her, but her warning doesn't dim my mood.

"She would like to schedule a meeting as soon as possible. I know your current schedule might be busier than most. Do you have any availability this week?"

"Absolutely. I'm off tomorrow, then I'll be out of town for four days. I'll be off again on Sunday, and then we're in town for another four days, so I could find time then as long as it isn't during a game."

"I'll reach out and see if tomorrow or Sunday would work."

"Great. Wow, I can't believe this is happening already. Thank you so much."

"I'll send you an invitation via email to confirm the time. Do you have any restrictions on where you'd like the meeting to take place?"

"No, whatever they think is best, I'll be there."

"Alright, Hudson, have a great evening, and we'll talk soon!"

"You too! Thank you!"

She ends the call, and I immediately dial Adrian's number. He picks up after the second ring. "What's wrong? Why the hell are you calling without texting first?"

I chuckle. "Nothing is wrong. I was too excited to text this! A local expectant mother liked my profile enough to request a meeting!"

"Holy shit! Already?"

I'm nodding even though I know he can't see me. "Right?

That's what I said too. Nothing is promised, but I'm so excited; I'm shaking right now."

"Oh my god! I'm so excited too. Even if this first meeting isn't the final match, that has to be a good sign that someone already wants to meet you! Did they say when?"

"I gave the woman from the agency, Holly, my schedule for the week, so hopefully I'll hear back from her soon!" Shit, I hope the time works for him too, I should have asked. "Do you think you'll be able to come?"

"You want me to?" he asks, sounding completely surprised by the request.

"Yeah, Charming, I'd love for you to be there if you can. I'm sure I'll be a mess of nerves and you always know how to make me feel better. Also, when are you going to stop being so shocked that I want to spend time with you?"

He laughs again. "Probably never. But if you want me there, I'm there."

Always. I'll always want him there.

But that's an inside thought, so I force it to stay there.

"Is it bad I've never been here?" I whisper to Adrian as we walk through the public library. The expecting mother requested the location for our meeting as neutral territory, and we've reserved a conference room to have some privacy.

"Depends. Have you been in any library before? Or is this your first time?" Adrian asks with a cocky grin.

I smirk tilting my head to the side. "Just because I'm athletic doesn't mean I'm an idiot."

"Obviously."

"That being said… I'll admit it's been a while."

Adrian's grin grows, his dimples that I've become obsessed with making an appearance. "Don't worry, I haven't been here either." We walk past shelf after shelf until we finally reach a wall of doors, each with a sign next to them. "Okay, this is it, room B," Adrian says, already knocking, not giving me even a moment to panic.

"Come in," a feminine voice calls out. Adrian swings the door open, motioning for me to enter first.

A young woman with dark curly hair pulled into a messy bun is sitting at the conference table, her laptop open in front of her with what I'm assuming is a textbook open on one side of it and a notebook on the other. She stands, one hand casually resting on her stomach, the other outstretched to me. "Hello, Hudson, it's great to meet you. I'm Emily."

Her warm smile melts some of my nerves as I shake her hand. "It's great to meet you, Emily. I'm sorry if we were late."

She waves a hand at the busy table in front of her. "You weren't late. I was just studying."

"You're a student?"

Her face lights up. "Yeah! I'm finishing up my third year of medical school."

"Wow, congrats, that's amazing."

"Thanks." She turns her attention to Adrian. "I'm sorry, the agency only gave me Hudson's profile. Are you a couple?"

Adrian starts cough-choking in response to her question. I'm not sure how I should interpret that… but I'll have to obsess over it later; this is potentially the most important meeting of my entire life. I step in with a smirk. "No, Adrian is my best friend. He's here for moral support."

She nods. "That's nice. Okay, should we all sit down?" When we're settled, she smiles right at me. "So, I've thought a lot about this meeting and how it should go, and I think the best thing to do is just blurt out all the awkward-but-important information first, and then we can actually chat afterward. Would that work for you?"

I chuckle. "That sounds great. Who should start?"

Emily takes a deep breath. "Me. I think the biggest question you probably have is why I'm interested in adoption, so I'll start there. I have never wanted to be a mom. Nothing against my own mother, she was amazing, but I've just never had that desire. I think every kid deserves to feel wanted, like they're the most important thing in their parent's world, and I just don't think I'm capable of providing that."

I'm kind of shocked that she's being so blunt, but I am absolutely loving the honesty.

"Which leads to the next thing. I'm finishing my seventh year of higher education. I still have another year before I start my residency, which is at least another three years depending on what specialty I match with. I don't think that schedule is ideal for a child to put up with when I have no support, and to be honest, I have no intention of giving up my plan to become a doctor now."

I'm nodding along, trying not to seem too excited about her interest in adoption and how I might fit in with that.

"This was obviously unplanned, and the father has zero interest in parental rights," she continues. "But I think that some things happen for a reason, so from the beginning, I knew I wanted to have this child. I just didn't think I should be the one to raise them."

"That all makes a lot of sense to me, but you don't need to justify your choices," I assure her. "It sounds like you're doing what you think is best for you and for the baby. That's all I really want to know."

She smiles. "And what do you think I should know about you?"

Okay. *Moment of truth, I can do this.* "Well, I'm thirty-four years old, and I'm recently divorced, but more than anything, I've always wanted to become a father. To go with the total honesty thing, I'm worried about being a single parent applying for adoption, especially with what you said about not being able to give the child an ideal schedule or the feeling of being the priority. I'm concerned that it'll scare you away or make you think I'm not the best option to become a father for your child when there's only one of me, and you might be comparing me to couples, but I think I could be a really great dad."

I can't help but look at Adrian as I go to explain his involvement in my decision, and his encouraging smile gives me a confidence boost. "My ex-wife filed for divorce about eight months ago because she didn't want children. I was far more upset about the idea of losing the future kids I'd wanted us to have than I was about losing her, though. So obviously, we were not meant to be." That earns a soft laugh from both Adrian and Emily, so I go on in the same light tone, but it does nothing to conceal my nerves.

"I moved in with Adrian while I was house hunting, and he helped me realize that I didn't need to rush back into dating. I'd been trying to meet someone new to settle down with quickly, hoping to have kids right away. I know becoming a parent is my priority, and I finally realized that I don't necessarily need a partner to do that. So, I've spent the last few months doing everything I needed to in order to qualify to adopt. I'm sure you saw in my profile, but I'm about to retire from the NHL, so I will have plenty of time to dedicate to my family. Even with it being the middle of the hockey season, I've been able to complete all the inspections and trainings and paperwork that was required before I could even create a profile. So hopefully you'll believe me when I say how important this is to me. That I would happily and easily make my child the center of my world."

Emily is still smiling, but I'm so nervous right now, I honestly don't think I could repeat what I just said. Hopefully it made sense.

"I'm not concerned about you being a single parent," Emily reassures me, and the anxiety that's consumed me for months about if anyone could ever think I'm good enough to raise their child, finally eases.

"Thank you."

"No need to thank me. I was raised by a single parent, and like I said, my mom was amazing. I'd much rather my kid have one great parent than two not-so-great ones."

I smile fully now. Does that mean she thinks that *I* could be a great parent?

"I have one more thing to get out of the way," she warns.

"Okay."

"I feel like I need to admit that I selected your profile mostly because I recognized you."

"Oh." My heart sinks. All the anxiety that had been fading moments ago comes rushing back. Meeting fans is always great, but I don't want someone to match with me because I have a cool career. I want them to think I'll be the best person to raise their baby.

Still, I force a smile. "Big Werewolves fan?"

"Nope!" she says confidently, completely throwing me off. "I didn't even know what NHL stood for until I looked it up while reading your profile."

Okay, that's definitely not what I was expecting. "So, how did you recognize me?"

"You spoke at a fundraising event last year at the hospital where I was doing clinicals. You talked about your dad having a CVA and how important you think stroke education is in the community. The way you spoke about your parents and your family was really moving. I guess it stuck with me, because when I saw your profile, I instantly recognized you."

"Wow. What a small world," I say with a sigh of relief. That's so much better than her saying she was my waitress once upon a time or recognized me from the dating app or any other potentially awkward scenario that started running through my head when she said she wasn't into hockey.

I'm trying so hard right now not to read into that chance encounter, to not feel like there was a reason our paths crossed before today. But I desperately want it to mean something. Emily seems really great, and despite every logical part of my brain warning me against it, I can't help but picture a little toddler version of her running around my house.

I know that I'm getting ahead of myself here, though, so I force myself to focus on the conversation. That daydream will never happen if she thinks I'm unfit because I spend the meeting spaced out and distracted.

I can fantasize about that later.

ADRIAN

"Is there anything else you'd like to hear from me? Something that maybe wasn't in my profile?" Hudson asks.

I knew he would be great in this meeting; he's so charismatic and kind. Plus his desire to become a parent is so sweet. I've never worried about any of the interviews during this process.

Despite all of that, though, I am so fucking nervous for him right now.

This entire process of applying to adopt has been so extensive, and throughout every new step, they've warned about how long it can take, if it ever even happens at all. Those warnings made the actual matching part of the whole thing seem so distant, almost like a daydream that you revisit again and again but never expect to actually happen.

But this is happening. And the idea that Hudson could be a father *really freaking soon*, feels so real! We're sitting across from a woman who is already pregnant! Hudson's future child could be in the room with us at this very moment!

I have no idea how he's staying so calm when I'm freaking out, and I'm not even the one hoping to adopt her baby.

I mean... Okay, I'm not going to read into that claim too closely, because obviously if Hudson decided to take a page out of the fantasy version of our lives I fall asleep picturing every night, then yes, I would also be wishing for her to choose *us* to adopt her child, not just Hudson.

I honestly really like Emily, too. She's got a chill vibe and is kind of quirky with how blunt she is—I'm so here for it. She knows exactly what she wants and isn't apologizing. Truly a modern queen thriving in her independence. *And she wants to be a doctor on top of that?* She's going to be amazing if this meeting is anything to base her bedside manner on.

"It said that you were open to all forms of adoption," she says confidently. "An open adoption would be my preference. As much as possible, I'd like to keep the communication option open so that if they ever have questions for me, I'll be available. I don't want them feeling unwanted, and I think knowing me might help with that." Hudson is nodding along and smiling as she talks, but he's doing a good job of having that come across as agreeable and not desperate like I'm sure he's feeling right now.

"I don't think we would need to establish a visitation schedule or anything," Emily continues. "Life can be so unpredictable, and I don't want to feel like I'm breaking promises, but I wouldn't mind being invited to a holiday or birthday party if everyone agreed that it would be appropriate. As they get older, and can voice their own preferences, I also like the idea of letting them decide when I would or wouldn't be a part of things."

"Honestly, that all sounds perfect," Hudson responds easily. "On my application, I put that I was alright with any level of interaction, and I really am, as long as I think it's in the child's best interest, but what you're describing sounds like it would be great for them. I love the idea of seeing what makes the most sense as time goes on, following their lead as they grow up but never keeping them in the dark."

They're both all smiles. God, I really hope that this works out for him. Emily seems like such a perfect person to navigate an adoption with, and I don't know if I've seen Hudson look this hopeful since he started the process.

They chat a bit more about their lives and places they've traveled. Hudson tells us about his family road trips growing up to national parks, and how he's always wanted to take his own kids to them one day.

"Adrian has the perfect roadtrip car, one of those big SUVs that could easily fit a couple of weeks' worth of suitcases," he tells Emily. "I've been debating getting one like his or just embracing the minivan."

I can't help it; I burst out laughing. I've been trying so hard not to insert myself in their very important discussions, but now that he's pulled me in, I'm unable to stop myself from saying something.

"You're going to trade in your fancy sports car for a minivan?" I gawk.

"What's wrong with a minivan?" he challenges with a smirk. "They're rated very well for safety. Plus, the parenting blogs I've been reading about the best cars for parents mentioned that little kids sometimes swing the side doors of SUVs into the cars parked next to them."

"Huh, I never thought of that, maybe minivans can be cool after all," Emily adds before she pulls out a notecard full of what I'd refer to as "politically divisive" questions. "What would you do if your child told you they were transgender or asked to sleepover at a friend's house when you've never met the family?" She runs through the questions quickly, like a pop quiz.

Each answer Hudson gives makes me fall for him just a little bit more. Emily seems to agree, because after we've been here for about an hour and a half, she puts the notecards down and glances between Hudson and I. "Alright, I think that's all the time we have scheduled. Plus, I really do need to study." She motions to all the course material surrounding her. I am so glad that I'm done with my grad school days. I don't miss studying one bit.

"The person who works for the adoption agency warned me not to make any promises in a meeting with a prospective family and that I should at least sleep on any big decisions. So I'll let them handle the communication for the next step. But it was so lovely to meet you both."

"You too, and thank you so much for even considering me," Hudson says, taking her outstretched hand to shake over the table. I do the same.

"It was great to meet you too, Adrian. I'm glad you were able to come today, even if you were pretty quiet during the meeting part."

"Don't worry, if, and hopefully when, we meet again, I'll let my fabulous side out a bit more," I promise with a smirk. "I just didn't want to distract you from meeting Hudson. He really is one of the best men I've ever met. I know that I'm biased when he's throwing around titles like best friend, but I truly believe that he will make an excellent father."

"Adrian, you don't need to…" Hudson trails off, obviously embarrassed.

"I love that he's so supportive," Emily assures him before turning back to me. "Hudson is lucky to have you."

And he could be even luckier if he asked. I smirk to myself even though I know that isn't going to happen.

HUDSON

I hop over the boards, claiming a spot on the bench after my shift ends as I fight to catch my breath. Seattle is not messing around, and I'm struggling to keep up. Not only that, but they're far more aggressive than I remember our last game with them being. Every possession has felt like a complete battle, and I've been thrown against the boards more tonight than any other game this season.

I'm struggling, we're tied, and there's still five minutes left.

It also doesn't help that I'm really fucking distracted. It's been days, and I still haven't heard anything from the adoption agency regarding Emily's decision. I finally broke down yesterday and called Holly, who assured me that whenever someone matches with Emily, I'll be notified so I won't be left wondering.

I know it's a huge decision for her, and she's got her own busy life to work around… but that doesn't stop me from stressing about what's taking her so long. Did I mess up something during our meeting? Did she change her mind entirely? I doubt it; she seems very confident in her choices. Still, the anxiety is very real as I await her decision.

So, I'm trying my very best to stay focused on hockey, but again, I'm struggling.

Ollie nudges my shoulder with his from his spot on the crowded bench next to me. "Let's go out tonight."

I chuckle dismissively. "No thanks. I'm not in the mood."

"That's exactly why we're going to do it," he insists. "We don't need to go out to a bar, we can grab a late dinner, but I'm not going to let you sit alone all night in your hotel room staring at your phone again. A watched pot never boils or whatever."

Now I actually laugh. "Yeah, alright."

The rest of the game goes the same way, a whole lot of work with nothing to show for it. We have to go into overtime, as if I wasn't tired enough, and they manage to psych out Anderson, slipping the puck into our net with only thirty seconds left.

At least we didn't have to go into a shootout.

Reluctantly, I keep my promise to grab a late dinner with Ollie.

"You're going to need to do a lot of the talking tonight. Sorry, I'm too drained," I apologize after we've ordered.

"And are you really expecting a call from the adoption agency when it's after midnight in Chicago?" he teases, pointedly looking at my phone that I just checked again where it's face up on the table.

"No," I sigh. "I just hate the uncertainty and all the waiting. I feel like that's all I'm doing these days."

"What else are you waiting for?"

"Mostly my house to be ready."

He gives me a questioning look. "I thought that you liked living with Adrian?"

"I do..." I trail off. As influential as Ollie has been this year on me coming to terms with my feelings for Adrian, I haven't actually shared them with him, or anyone else. I'm not ashamed that I'm into a man, I just have no idea how things will play out.

If I finally make a move, and it doesn't work out, I'd rather less people know I was rejected. Still, the longer the waiting goes on, the closer I feel to blurting out everything, and it's probably better that I do it to Ollie than Adrian himself

"But...?" Ollie prompts when I don't say anything else.

"But... you were right. I want to be with Adrian, and I've decided that I should wait to tell him that until we're no longer roommates."

His jaw drops open. "Are you fucking kidding me?" I shrug, shaking my head. "Why the hell are you waiting? You're already living together! You could be hooking up every night and no one would know. Why are you wasting that opportunity?"

"Because I want to do more than 'hook up' with him. I think we could be really good together, and I don't want to rush into things. Adrian deserves better than that."

Ollie shudders. "God, I didn't realize you were such a romantic."

"I'd also like to avoid the awkwardness of still sleeping on the other side of the same wall if he rejects me," I add.

"Okay, first off, there's no way Adrian rejects you. Second, sleeping on the other side of the wall sounds hot. Do you ever hear him, ya know?" He raises his eyebrows suggestively.

I immediately think of all the nights I've left the door open just a crack, hoping to hear something, hoping he'll hear me as I jerk off thinking of him.

He's all I think about these days.

I clear my throat and shake my head again, but I know I'm blushing, and Ollie's smug expression makes it clear he doesn't believe me.

"Well, then I hope your house is ready soon."

"You and me both."

MY RINGTONE WAKES me up the next morning instead of my normal alarm, and I bolt upright, sitting on the edge of the bed as I glance at the clock on the hotel's nightstand. Six a.m.—who the hell is calling me?

Any grogginess is gone when I see it's Holly's name on the caller ID. *Fuck. This is it.* I have no idea if it will be good news or bad, but I think the period of uncertainty might finally be over.

"Hello?"

"Hello, Hudson. Do you have a moment?"

"Of course," I agree on a heavy exhale.

"Well, I am very excited to inform you that Emily would like to move forward with you adopting her child!"

My heart stops, and I jump up out of bed. "Oh my god, really?" I need to hear it again to confirm it's real.

She chuckles. "Yes, really. Congratulations, Mr. Roy. It sounds like you two really hit it off."

I'm going to be a dad. It's real.

"I... I can't believe it. Everything said it would take so long. I didn't want to get my hopes up of course, but obviously I did. I'm so excited! I have to tell Adrian. I have to tell my parents. What happens now?" I ramble.

"Well, you've both indicated that you would like an open adoption, and our agency believes in supporting as much independent communication as possible from the beginning to help establish a healthy relationship between all parties involved. We have you both come in and fill out paperwork regarding your intentions. The finalization of your parental rights won't happen until after the child has already been living with you for at least six months, though. The agency will remain very involved with post placement requirements, more visits, interviews, and paperwork."

That all sounds familiar from those early meetings, but at the time it had seemed so far away. I can't believe this is all actually happening already. "Okay! That sounds great."

"Emily is in the office now filling out her paperwork with one of my colleagues," Holly continues. "She requested to talk with you. Would that be alright?"

"That would be amazing!"

"Okay, I'll put you on a brief hold while I find her." Waiting music starts to play, and I want to scream with how excited I am. I want to run around the hotel and wake up the whole team so we can all celebrate. But I know I only have a few moments where they can't hear me, so I opt for a silent happy dance instead.

"Hudson, thank you for holding," Holly says, pulling my attention back to the call. "I've got you on speaker here with both Emily and one of my coworkers who was helping her with her paperwork."

"Hello!" I greet them all eagerly.

"Hey, Hudson!" Emily says. "I was wondering if you wanted to be included in the rest of my OB appointments?"

I gasp, and apparently it's loud enough for everyone on the other side of the line to hear because there are a few chuckles in response. "If that would be alright, I would love to!"

"Awesome! I actually have one this afternoon at twelve thirty. I'm sorry I didn't plan this sooner; this past week was a really busy one with school and today is the first day I've had off to come down here."

I deflate. I have a flight in a few hours and another game tonight. "Wow, I so wish that I could come. But I'm in Seattle right now. There's no way I'd make it back in time even if I did get approval from the team to miss tonight's game."

"No worries," Emily responds easily. "Hopefully you can

make it to the next one. Or hey, if Adrian wanted to come and take pictures or call you or whatever works, he'd be welcome to join me too."

I perk up again. "If you wouldn't mind, I can see if Adrian is available. That would be amazing."

"Cool. I'll be here for a while filling stuff out if you want to call us back."

"Perfect! I'll call him now, talk soon!" After quick goodbyes, I hang up and immediately dial Adrian while I pace the room, far too excited to even attempt to sit still.

"What's wrong?" he answers on the second ring. "Isn't it like six a.m. for you?"

"Emily agreed to move forward with me adopting her child!" I practically scream into the phone.

"Holy fuck! Congratulations!" he shouts back. If my smile wasn't already the biggest it's probably ever been, his level of immediate excitement would have it growing even more.

"I mean, obviously she made the right choice! No one else could be a better fit. But still, it's so exciting to have it official and confirmed! Oh my god! We have to start getting the nursery together! You should make a registry! Ohhhh, do you think she would want to be at a baby shower? Obviously the team is going to throw one. I wonder if I could get your mom to fly out for a few hours, if I set up backup, on-call nursing staff to be available for your dad. He wouldn't want to come, would he? I could set up a wheelchair van with medical staff to drive him, even across states if he wanted. I've looked into it, and it's a little pricey, but it's an option," he rambles.

I have to take a few moments to process everything he just said. He's researched ways to get my dad to Chicago? That's probably the most thoughtful thing anyone's ever done for me, and he just said it so casually. I'm actually a little choked up thinking about it.

"So what happens now?" he asks when I'm unable to respond quickly enough, and his question reminds me of the reason I was calling.

"She offered to have me go to her doctor's appointments with her."

"That's amazing!"

"There's actually one today, and when I said I was out of town, she asked if you'd want to go and call me, or take a picture and tell me all about it later, whatever makes the most sense. If you're free that is. No pressure, I know how busy you are."

"Oh my god, Hudson! Of course I'll go! What an honor. Send me the details, and I'm there."

I sigh in relief. I was so excited about the opportunity to participate in the prenatal appointments, and I know I'll be able to go to another, but having Adrian help me be a part of the one today, so soon after I found out that the baby will be mine, is a huge relief. "Thanks, Charming. You're the very best."

"I'm honestly happy to do it, Hudson. I'm so excited for you! You're going to be a dad! Congratulations!"

There's another part of me that's excited to have him involved for more selfish reasons. I want him to be a part of everything in my life, including this adoption. And hearing Adrian say those words, that I'm going to be a dad, somehow makes them feel even more real.

My dreams are coming true. Maybe Adrian will even want to continue to be a part of things after I move out, too.

All my goals for becoming a parent are happening… Why not the ones about Adrian and I?

ADRIAN

"Hello, I'm meeting my friend Emily here for her appointment at twelve thirty. She isn't already back there, is she?" I ask the person in cute pink scrubs sitting behind the counter in the OBGYN lobby Hudson passed on the info for.

The office is in a hospital, which I thought would be kind of intimidating at first, but I guess would be super convenient for the doctor who needs to be delivering babies. Now that I'm inside, it feels like any other doctor's office, except I never really thought I would be in an OBGYN appointment, so I'm far more nervous than I'd care to admit.

"No, she hasn't checked in yet," the woman confirms. "Feel free to sit wherever you'd like."

"Thanks."

I might be a little early, so I'm not surprised that she isn't here yet. *Okay, I'm really early.* But Hudson asked me to come to this appointment in his place. This is a huge fucking deal! He's officially going to be a dad, and he asked me to be a part of today. I know he's had me come to a lot of stuff with him during the adoption process, but this is different. This is actually his baby. He's trusting me to represent him with the mother of his child.

Realistically, I have another half an hour or so before Emily will probably get here, so I decide to spend that time planning the nursery. I've done research on them already over the last few months, but Hudson and I agreed that preparing a room for a baby before he matched with anyone felt like it could jinx his chances. Now that Emily has chosen him, it's time. Should he get a convertible crib so he can upgrade it whenever the baby is ready? Or maybe something more traditional? There are so many things to consider for the nursery itself. I also start a list of suggestions for other typical baby registry items.

"Hey, Adrian! You made it," Emily says, pulling me out of my deep-dive into the best type of humidifiers.

I immediately stand but catch myself before touching her. "Hello! Are you a hugger? I don't want to overstep."

"Thank you for asking. You have no idea how many people think they can touch my stomach just because I'm pregnant." She shudders, but then stretches her arms out. "We can hug though. I think we're going to be good friends."

I beam at her prediction as we embrace. "I would love that." I sit back down, and she takes the spot next to me. "So, what should I expect? Believe it or not, this is my first time at an OBGYN appointment."

She chuckles. "Well, they usually check my vital signs, measure my stomach, ask if I'm having any new symptoms and warn me about what to expect. They also check the baby's heartbeat. I thought that would be what Hudson would want to hear."

"Absolutely! He'll be so excited."

"Emily, we're ready for you," another person in scrubs interrupts, and we head down a hallway. Emily has me hold her bag while she stands on a scale, and then they lead us into the room. The nurse pulls a curtain and asks for Emily to change into a hospital gown. "Wow, this is kind of intense," I whisper when she's changed, with a sheet over her lap to cover her legs, and it's just the two of us.

"Pregnancy is pretty intense," she confirms easily. "There are so many things that can go wrong for mom or baby. They have to monitor everything they can to try to catch anything out of the ordinary." The nurse comes back in and checks her blood pressure and other vitals while asking her a million questions about how she's been feeling. Before I know it, an older woman is knocking on the door.

"Good afternoon, Emily. Oh! You brought a friend, how lovely. Or are you the father?"

"Oh god, no. Very gay," I blurt out, holding my hands up like I'm innocent, and Emily laughs.

"Adrian is living with the man I've chosen to adopt the baby," Emily explains.

"Well, congratulations! I'm Kathy, the midwife. And now that you're officially in your third trimester, Emily, we'll all be spending a lot of time together. Appointments will be every two weeks for the next two months and switch to weekly after that."

"Nice to meet you." We shake hands, and then her attention is all on Emily as they run through exactly what she told me about. "The fundal height is right on track at twenty-eight centimeters," Kathy announces after measuring her stomach. *No idea what that means, but I'm not interrupting.*

"Baby should be shifting to a head down position soon, and as they grow, you'll likely have less energy than the previous trimester. Start doing kick counts daily if you haven't already. Call me if you think anything is off, okay? Don't hesitate."

Emily smiles. "Of course."

"Okay, let me grab my doppler, and we'll listen to baby!"

"Adrian, did you want to call Hudson?"

"Yes, absolutely! Sorry, I was so distracted by all the words I didn't know. I'm way out of my depth here."

"I can go through it all with you later," Emily promises as I dial Hudson. He answers right away.

"Oh my god, is it happening?"

"Yup! The midwife just got out the machine to hear the baby!"

"Okay, I'll stop talking!" he promises, making my smile somehow grow. His unfiltered joy and excitement at becoming a dad make me so happy.

I hold my breath as Kathy squeezes out some gel onto Emily's stomach, and then moves the wand over it. She quickly finds a good spot and a steady *whoosh whoosh* sound echoes out.

"Is that it?" Hudson quietly asks, and I turn to Emily and Kathy with big eyes, unable to voice the question myself with how tight my throat is. I knew that this appointment would be emotional, mostly because of how excited Hudson is and how happy I am for him, but I hadn't expected to feel like my heart is ready to burst with the love I already feel for this child.

And it isn't even mine! I can't imagine what Hudson must be feeling right now. My vision blurs as I fight back tears. I know how much Hudson has wanted this, how he's dreamed of this moment. Even if he isn't here in person, he's hearing his child's heartbeat for the first time. I selfishly love that I'm a part of this special moment that he'll never forget.

After a few more long moments of us all appreciating the rhythm of their heartbeat, Kathy asks if we're ready.

"I could listen to that all day," Hudson says with a chuckle. "But yes, thank you all so much for letting me be a part of today. I know you didn't have to invite me. And thanks again, Adrian, for dropping everything to be there. I'd love to go to an appointment in person sometime, too."

"I'll try to schedule the rest of the appointments while I'm here today, if they'll let me, so I can give you more notice," Emily promises.

"And don't be silly, Hudson, no need to thank me. There's no place I'd rather be!" I assure him before we all exchange good-byes and hang up.

Emily and Kathy finish up the rest of the appointment, and I try to pay attention to ask Emily questions later on so I can report everything back to Hudson. When Kathy leaves, she closes the curtain again for Emily to change.

While she's getting dressed, Emily calls out, "I think it's so sweet that you've kept your relationship a secret, but I see how much you and Hudson care for each other. You'll make great parents."

And my heart fucking stops.

Did she just say our relationship? As in, a romantic one…? She must if she thinks I'm also going to be this baby's parent.

My jaw is on the floor.

My eyes are trying to jump out of my head with how wide they are.

Does she honestly think we're a couple?

Fuck. Is that why she picked him?

This can't seriously be happening.

I have to tell her though. Even if that risks fucking things up for Hudson, and even though I desperately wish what she's assuming was true—it isn't—she can't pick him to adopt her child because of a lie.

I have no idea if it's a good thing or not that she can't see my devastated expression as I awkwardly laugh, painfully aware that I might be risking Hudson's dream as I correct her. "Oh, no. We really are just friends!"

She joins in laughing, but I can't see her either as she's still behind the privacy divider, so I have no idea what her expression is.

"Right. Don't worry, Adrian, your secret is safe with me."

Fuck. Fuck. Fuck.

"No secret. Unfortunately for me, Hudson is straight," I explain desperately, offering a bit more of my truth.

She finally pushes the curtain to the side, back in her own clothes.

"Whatever you say," she says with a wink, opening the door and stepping into the hallway. "I have a study session to get to soon, but if you want to stick around for a little longer, I can try to get those other appointments scheduled."

I'm frozen in place. I don't really want to turn this into a bigger thing in the middle of the hallway, and based on how dismissive she was of what I was saying, I'm not sure anything I tell her right now is going to convince her that Hudson and I aren't together.

I have no idea what to do. Maybe she'd believe Hudson?

I don't think I have any choice but to pause this discussion for now as she starts down the hall, forcing me to trail after her.

This is just a pause though, because there is no way in hell Hudson can adopt her baby if she only picked him assuming we were covering up a relationship. That wouldn't be fair to anyone involved, and I won't let it happen.

Even if it means ruining the man of my dream's dream in the process.

HUDSON

Our game had an earlier start time than most at six p.m., so the team flew back afterward to give us a true day off tomorrow, even if that's already technically today since midnight has come and gone.

After being gone for four days, I'm glad to be back, even if I am exhausted. Maybe Adrian would grab lunch with me so I can see him before tomorrow night. I'm sure he's already asleep by now.

Except when I try to silently open the door to his place and sneak inside, I hear the TV on in the main living space. That's really weird. Adrian is never up this late, especially with work tomorrow.

Fuck, does he have someone over? Maybe he didn't realize I'd be back tonight… Does he have men over when I'm out of town often? Have I been a complete fool waiting to make a move and someone else has already swooped in?

I know I should give him privacy, but I'm so tired, I think the rational part of my brain checked out a while ago. No part of me wants to catch him with someone else, but I can't stop my feet from advancing down the hall into the main living space.

Where Adrian is alone, *thank god*.

But he's in his pajamas, staring blankly at the TV with a bag of blueberry acai flavored dark chocolates in his lap. He isn't even eating any.

"What's wrong?" I blurt out before he's even noticed I'm here, and he jumps up, standing and spinning to face me at the question.

"Holy shit! You scared me. How do you always sneak in here so quietly?"

I shrug. "Why are you still awake? What's wrong?"

"I'm sorry, I know I should have probably called, but I didn't want to fuck up your game when there was nothing you could do about it, and then I almost called afterward, but I didn't know if there would be any media around, or even teammates you didn't want overhearing," he rambles, not actually saying what's the matter, though something clearly is.

I walk up to him, putting a hand on each of his shoulders before I demonstrate a deep inhale. "Hey, Charming. I need you to take a big breath for me, and tell me what's going on so we can fix it."

He does what I ask, looking more nervous than I've ever seen him.

"Emily thinks we're together," he finally spits out quickly, and my nerves that had been climbing quickly settle.

"Okay… is that it?" I ask, confused and maybe even a little hurt that he seems so distraught over the incorrect assumption. "Why do you seem so upset about that? Would dating me really be that awful?"

I try to say it lightly, but now I'm worried for a whole new reason. I've been holding on to hope that there might have been some truth behind Adrian's flirting all this time. That maybe he's wanted to be so involved in the adoption process because there's a part of him that wants to be involved as more than my friend.

But if he's this panicked over Emily thinking we're together… There's no way he'd want to actually date me.

Fuck.

"You don't get it!" he insists. "She made a comment about how we will both be such great parents, together, as a couple, and when I told her she had misunderstood, that we really are just friends, she fucking winked at me! She promised our secret is safe with her!"

"That sounds nice," I point out, still failing to see the reason for him being so freaked out.

"Hudson! You were the one who was so nervous about being passed over because you'll be a single parent. What if she only agreed to match with you because she thought we were really a couple? You're a professional athlete living with a gay male roommate. It's not exactly the biggest leap to take that we would be claiming to just be friends for the media's sake."

Fuck.

What is happening right now? Moments ago, I was excited to finally be home, to sleep in Adrian's comfy guest bed. Now my too-tired brain is being forced to process not just my hopes for Adrian and I falling apart, but potentially the adoption match ending as well.

And why? Because the woman who already picked me agrees with me that Adrian and I would be a great couple? Because she correctly assumed that I'm into him and want to be dating him?

That's bullshit.

Why should I lose my chance to be a father because of that?

I've been waiting, trying to be patient and do things right, but what if that was a mistake that ends up costing me everything?

Does the idea of being with me really sound so awful to Adrian?

This isn't at all what I had planned, but I can't wait any longer to find out.

"What if we weren't just friends?" I blurt out, still standing right in front of him, hands still on his shoulders as I look down into his confused gaze.

"Hudson, you can't lie to her! Do you know how fucked up that would be? How unethical? You're straight, you can't just—"

Okay, maybe that's the issue. It isn't that being with me sounds awful; he needs proof that I'm not straight. I shift my hands from his shoulders up to hold his face, angling it up as I lean down and cut off his rambling by bringing my mouth to his.

This isn't how I pictured our first kiss going.

But I'm so tired, and Adrian seemed so convinced that I couldn't be into him, and we were already standing so close together. I've wanted to kiss him for months, and all the excuses I've used to hold myself back seem pointless now when I feel like I could lose everything I've been hoping for.

Adrian needs me to convince him that I'm not straight. What better way to do it than with my lips on his?

He's frozen, obviously shocked by my move, but I want to show him what I'm too exhausted to explain with words. I pour the months of questions and longing into the kiss as I move my mouth against his. I step even closer, bringing my body as close to his as I can while still leaning down enough to accommodate our height differences.

Just when I begin to worry that our connection really has all been in my head, he relaxes, sinking into my hold, and finally kisses me back. The feel of his soft lips moving against mine lights me up from the inside. Was I tired before? I'm completely awake now as Adrian's tongue teases the seam of my lips, every motion feeling even better than the last. I immediately open for him, deepening the kiss, and I shift us slightly so that the back of my legs hit the couch.

Still holding his face, unwilling to break free from our connection for even a moment, I slowly pull him down with me as I sit. He climbs into my lap, just like I'd hoped, pushing me to rest against the back of the couch as he takes complete control of the kiss, just like he's done in so many of my fantasies of him.

My dick is rock hard as all those nights of leaving my door cracked, all the times I've used the toys, every time I've pictured this happening, collides with this moment. I'm finally kissing Adrian, and somehow, it's so much better than I'd imagined. I wasn't sure how different it would be kissing a man, but as I finally run a hand down the length of his torso, following the hard curves of his toned muscles obvious through the thin, silky fabric of his matching pajamas, I'm even more desperate for him. Adrian is smaller than me, both in height and in his build, but there's no mistaking the fact that he is a man.

And I'm loving every second of it.

I knew I wasn't making up our connection. All the hope I've been holding on to wasn't for nothing.

I move both hands to his hips now, unable to stop myself from positioning him over my aching cock as I grind into him, desperate for relief. It's been so long since I got off with another person, sure. But I know the level of need I'm feeling right now is specific to Adrian. I can't remember the last time I was this excited about the idea of being with someone. A loud moan escapes my throat as I shift my hips up into him again, and even the slight friction feels like it could be enough to get me off with how good everything he's doing feels.

But then he's pulling back, scrambling off my lap, looking even more confused than he did before I kissed him. His pajamas are doing nothing to hide his erection, so I have no idea why he's stopping when we were both clearly enjoying that so much.

"What's wrong?" I ask through labored breaths. He shakes his head, mouth open, but no words come out for a long moment. "Why did you stop?" I repeat.

"Because!" He throws his arms out to the sides defeatedly.

"We're not doing this! You're not going to finally kiss me after all these years because you want to lie to a pregnant woman to convince her we're together to let you adopt her baby!" He sounds as devastated as I feel as I realize how much I fucked up if he thinks that's why I wanted to kiss him.

I'm the one shaking my head now, unable to find the words to explain. "I—" He cuts me off before I can say anything.

"You're better than that! I deserve better than that! And if any of that was real, because that was a damn good kiss, but if you ever want to kiss me again, then you're going to need to ask me nicely and fucking apologize for even thinking that you could use me to manipulate an innocent woman like that."

He storms away to his room where the sound of his door firmly shutting echoes throughout the condo.

Obviously, this is really bad.

I'd been waiting to make a move for a reason. I was worried he would think I was just experimenting, or I was just horny and confusing him with a partner because we're living together like he used to accuse me of when I moved in.

Him thinking I only wanted to kiss him to lie to Emily is worse than all of that, and in no way is it true.

But there's also a part of me that's stuck on how fucking hot Adrian standing up for himself and putting me in my place was. Bossy Adrian scolding me for being bad is apparently now at the top of my list of fantasies.

I need to make things right between us as soon as possible. But when I knock on his door, he doesn't respond.

Fuck.

I also seriously need to talk to Emily. For some reason, I'm less convinced than Adrian seemed to be that she only picked me assuming we were together. We had a whole big talk about how she was raised by a single parent after she reassured me that my being single wasn't something she was against when considering prospective families for her child. We bonded over my speech at the fundraiser. I'm not giving up hope that she'll still want to continue as planned when I clarify that Adrian and I are not together.

But I'm also really hoping I can clarify things with him so, eventually, that won't be the case.

ADRIAN

HUDSON

I'm really sorry about how last night played out.
I tried to knock on your door, but I'm not sure if
you heard me.

HUDSON

I'd love the chance to talk about it in person.
Are you free for lunch today?

HUDSON

I'm going to meet Emily for dinner at that Italian
place on Greene after her clinicals today at
seven. I'd really love it if you could join us. I'm
going to clarify everything with her.

HUDSON

I understand if you don't want to be a part of
that… Is it still okay if I stay with you? Or do you
need space?

ADRIAN

OMG you don't need to move out, let me be the
dramatic one.

ADRIAN

I'll come to the dinner.

ork was crazy today, despite the players having the day off. It didn't help that everything I did took way longer than it should have with my mind still very distracted by the events of last night.

Talk about an emotional rollercoaster. I spent hours freaking out about telling Hudson that Emily thought we were a couple, anticipating his own panic when I did tell him, and then he just… didn't freak out. He didn't seem concerned about that at all.

The last thing I was expecting, though, was for him to run with the suggestion. And even if he was so desperate for her approval that he wanted to pretend to be together in front of her, which obviously I wouldn't agree to, he didn't need to kiss me! Why the fuck did he do that?

And it wasn't just a quick kiss to show he would kiss a man to prove a point or something—he was all in.

After I got over the shock and gave in, that was easily the best first kiss of my life. Probably even the best kiss, period. I wanted it to lead to so much more, and with how hard Hudson was, grinding up into me, it seemed like maybe he did too.

But as I started to think about more, to question how far he would be willing to go, I remembered why he'd even kissed me in the first place. I stand by what I said last night. He's better than that. He isn't a manipulative liar, and his first parenting act shouldn't be one of deceit.

I know I deserve better than someone who only wants to be with me for appearances—an easy option for their own personal gain. Even if that person happens to be my dream man. It's what I was worried about when my friends were trying to say Hudson was into me; he's my roommate, and I want to be more than a convenient hookup or an easy first man for him to try things with sexually. As real as it felt in the moment, as disappointed as Hudson seemed when I pulled away… There were way too many layers to what happened last night for me to know if any part of him was kissing me simply because he wanted to.

And unless I'm one hundred percent confident the only reason he kisses me is because he wants to, it can't happen again. I'm not strong enough for that.

A onetime confused moment, we can move on from. And we will. I'm not going to let him move out or change our friendship over it. I just needed some time today to process things, so responding to his texts earlier seemed like too much.

He knocked on my door last night? No, I definitely didn't hear that over the sound of my shower that I was desperately jerking off in after that fucking kiss. *Meet for lunch to talk about that kiss?* Where other people could overhear us? No, thank you.

I'll have dinner with Emily, though, because that will be us talking about *not* being together. Anyone can hear that when it's the truth. And I think it'll be easier for her to believe us if we're both there.

Plus, I don't hate the idea of having her as a buffer when I see him for the first time since last night. I need some time to stare at his perfect face where I can't throw away all my morals and jump him, or try to convince him that kissing me was a great idea, even if his motivation was all wrong.

If we're in public, though, and Emily is there, I know it'll be easier for me to stick with my convictions.

I made sure I was the last one to get here. I didn't want there to be any chance of Hudson attempting a conversation about last night before Emily showed up. They're seated in a round booth, Hudson already claiming the middle, so I slide in next to him, across from Emily.

"Hello," I greet them awkwardly with a small smile. I have no idea what Hudson told her to get her to agree to see him in person again so quickly.

"Hi, Adrian! I brought some of the copies I had of the earlier ultrasounds, so I just gave them to Hudson if you want to see them too."

Hudson turns to me with a big, hopeful smile. Hoping for what exactly? I can't be sure, but those pleading puppy dog eyes I can never say no to are certainly in use. "Want to see?" He holds them out toward me.

"Obviously," I say lightly, rolling my eyes, even as my stomach twists into knots, unsure if Hudson and Emily's arrangement is about to blow up in our faces. I take the picture, and the too-full feeling in my chest that I felt while listening to the heartbeat is back.

"What if we weren't just friends?" Hudson's question from last night replays over in my head for the hundredth time today. God, I wish he'd said that under different circumstances. I wish that he meant it because he really wanted there to be more between us, not because he's so desperate to become a dad that he'd agree to almost anything to do it.

I hand the image back to Hudson. "They're perfect," I manage to get out, unable to hide how choked up I am with all the conflicting emotions running through my mind right now.

Ugh, he lights up even more at my comment. That man's smile really will be the death of me.

"So, as lovely as it is to see you both again, you mentioned wanting to talk about something?" Emily prompts, obviously curious as she looks between us with a raised brow.

Hudson doesn't hesitate. "Adrian was concerned that you thought we might be a romantic couple, and we're hiding a relationship because of my job. As lucky as I would be to be linked to someone as great as he is—" He pauses to look at me, and what the fuck am I supposed to do with a comment like that? As lucky as he would be? Is there any chance he means any of this? That he isn't just trying to soften the blow for Emily, make sure she understands he isn't homophobic?

If he really wanted to be with me, why the hell would he wait until there was the excuse of Emily thinking we were already together?

"We wanted to make sure you understand that we are just close friends, and that I'm currently only living with him until the remodel is complete at my house," Hudson continues, and I try to focus on the conversation instead of the same mental spiral I've been falling into all day.

Emily looks between us with a smirk. "Alright, if you insist. But I stand by the fact that I think you would make a great couple."

Hudson continues to smile at her, like that's the end of the conversation, but I need to hear her actually say it.

"So to be perfectly clear—because, honestly, I've been freaking out since you made the comment—you still want Hudson to be the person adopting your child. You didn't choose him assuming we were a package deal?"

Emily laughs, and I feel like I can breathe for the first time since we left that appointment room. "Yes, I still am confident in my choice matching with Hudson. I'm sorry I worried you so much. I like that he has you, that he's someone other people care about enough to support, but I meant what I said about one great parent being worth more than two less than great ones."

"Thank you," Hudson replies, but he doesn't look as relieved as I'm expecting.

"Besides," Emily says, turning to me. "In Illinois at least, you always have to choose the primary person to adopt. Just in case there's any changes during the process—if a couple splits or one of them passes. When you waive your parental rights, you're doing so without condition. They make you understand that before you even look at applications."

"Oh" is all that comes out of my mouth. I'm so relieved that nothing has changed, but after being so stressed for the last day and a half, dealing with such a variety of emotions, I feel like I'm crashing hard. I let out a deep breath. "Will anyone judge me if I start with dessert? I think I need some chocolate to regulate my system."

It's a very serious comment, but they both laugh, and whatever tension that had still been there is effectively broken.

Hudson gives me an indulgent smile. "I'd be concerned if you didn't order chocolate right now."

HUDSON

"Oh my god! You have to see pictures of the playroom!" Adrian gushes, showing only some of the hundreds of pictures he's taken of my house. "Obviously, they'll grow into it, but it's got a whole obstacle course set up that can adjust as they get bigger, starting out with short things to help them pull to standing, a small ball pit, that sort of thing. But eventually, everything is in place for a rock-climbing wall and monkey bars!"

Now that things are settled with Emily, it's hard to focus on anything other than Adrian. My grilled chicken is practically untouched in front of me because I don't want to look away. He's so expressive, telling her about the research he's been doing for the nursery and talking about the other renovations he's been in charge of at my house. I love seeing how passionate he is about everything.

But I'm also realizing that the way he expresses his excitement is different when we're with other people than if it's just the two of us. It's not like he's a different person when we're alone or anything, more like he's less… performative, maybe? I'd like to think it means something, that he's more comfortable with me, that he knows he doesn't have to put in any extra effort to impress me. Or maybe he's nervous, and his projection of over-the-top confidence is an attempt to cover that up.

Whatever the reason, I'm glad I get to see that other side of him.

Or at least I did.

I have no idea where we stand after last night.

I loved every moment of our kiss. I've replayed it over and over again in my mind all day. And I've thought about what he said afterward, and about how hot he was standing up for himself as he scolded me, just as much. I definitely confirmed everything I'd guessed about our potential physical connection.

I just need to make up for the fact that he thinks I only kissed him because I was desperate for Emily's approval. Now that we've already kissed, now that I know how amazing it was to kiss him, I know I won't be able to wait for my initial timeline. I want to be with Adrian. I want to date him and claim him as mine. No hesitation.

Well, other than the fact that I am still a professional hockey player, and claiming Adrian publicly as my boyfriend would be a pretty big deal for my career. I can't even imagine Ollie's reaction.

But before I worry about any of that, I need to get him to agree to be my boyfriend in the first place.

When the dinner ends, and we're all saying our goodbyes, I plan to follow Adrian to where he parked like I normally would, but he stops me before I can even try. "Why don't you walk Emily to her car? I'll see you at home."

Obviously, I can't refuse that, so I agree and hope like hell he won't be locked away in his room when I get back.

To my extreme relief, he's waiting for me at the kitchen table, a glass of water set for both of us.

"Hey," I greet with my best attempt at a flirty grin as I sit down. Not sure how well I manage, though, with how nervous I am. His unreadable expression doesn't shift. He'd said I didn't need to move out earlier, but what if he changed his mind? "Oh god, are you kicking me out?" I blurt.

He chuckles. "No. But I think we need to talk about what happened."

"Yes, definitely!" I rush to speak first. "I'm so sorry that my actions last night hurt you and made you feel used. I respect you so much, and I would never intend to do either of those things."

"I know you wouldn't, Hudson," he agrees, finally smiling just a little. "And I appreciate you saying that. I'm sorry if my reaction in the moment was overly harsh."

"Nah," I tease. "That was actually really hot. Feel free to scold me or put me in my place whenever you'd like."

He clearly wasn't expecting that reaction. His eyebrows scrunch together, and he looks deep in thought for a moment before he shakes his head. "Okay, after last night, I think we need to stop jokingly flirting with each other. It's too confusing."

My stomach feels like it drops right through the floor. That's the opposite of what I want. I don't want to stop flirting; I want to do it more. I want us to know that the other person really means it when we tease and flirt. I want us to cuddle and not have him think it's weird.

But he doesn't know any of that, and I'm the only one to blame.

"I wasn't joking," I assure him. "And I don't want to stop flirting with you."

He shakes his head again. "I don't understand." I stand up and walk over to him, picking up his hand in mine. "What are you doing?"

"Trying to get you to stand up."

He rolls his eyes but follows my lead, not dropping my hand. "What now?"

"Now I'm going to ask you nicely," I say, smiling at how cute his confused expression is as he looks up at me.

"What the fuck are you talking about?"

I take a steadying breath, really hoping I'm not about to fuck everything up. Again. But I know I need to do this. I'll never forgive myself if I don't try. "You said if any of it was real, if I ever wanted to kiss you again, I would need to apologize and ask you nicely. You accepted my apology, so, please, Adrian, can I kiss you?"

He doesn't respond right away, his gaze shifting from my eyes to my mouth and back again. I feel like my heart is in my throat as I wait for his answer.

Finally, on an exhale, he asks, "Is this a fucking joke?"

"No," I insist, squeezing his hand. "Why would I joke about wanting to kiss you? Last night was incredible, even better than I'd imagined. I want to do it again. I want to do so much more if I'm being honest."

"Than you imagined? More? But... but you're straight!" he practically shouts.

"No, I'm not." And even though that's still a new concept to me, one I haven't talked about out loud much, I don't hesitate. I know it's true, even if the specifics are less certain.

I'm not sure if it's all in my head, if I just want to see it, but Adrian's confused expression looks more hopeful. "Since when?"

I had hoped this would involve more kissing and less talking, but I guess we're getting into it. "I think I had just assumed I was straight. Looking back, I guess there have been other men that I was drawn to, who I had an instant connection with. I assumed that meant I wanted to be friends with them, and it never led to anything more," I explain for the first time. "But with you, just being friends isn't enough. I want more."

"You want to kiss me?" he repeats.

"Very much."

ADRIAN

*H*udson wants to kiss me. Again.

And even though it sounds like this could still be some sort of experiment for him, the first time he's worked up the courage, or maybe had the opportunity to act on being attracted to a man, I'm not strong enough to refuse him when he sounds so confident about it. I just wish he'd brought all this up on his own instead of waiting for the stress of Emily thinking we were together to push him to it.

My biggest concern last night was that he didn't actually want to kiss me. That he was only doing it to prove that he could be convincing enough if we needed to pretend in front of Emily.

Or at least, I'm pretty sure that's what my stressed-out, over-tired concern was. Now that I've spent the entire day obsessing over how amazing the kiss was… I'm not really looking for any reason not to do it again.

Done with overthinking everything, I mutter "Fuck it" and step even closer to him, reaching up to cup his face with my hand as I go up on my toes to reach him. Hudson eagerly leans down, wrapping his hands around my waist to grip my hips and pull me into him as our lips meet.

There's no quiet buildup this time. We both want this, and the exact details of his motivation don't matter right now. He wants to kiss me, and I can worry about what this all means later.

There's no hesitation as we immediately open up for each other. I should probably attempt to chill out, to hold back a little and let him lead since this is so new for him. But that's just not who I am, and I've been fantasizing about this man for months—years honestly, if I count the time before he moved in and showed me firsthand that he was even more perfect than I could have imagined.

The kiss is desperate as we explore each other. His lips are soft, full, and feel amazing moving against mine. He's gripping my hips hard enough to bruise, probably afraid I'll end the kiss again, but there's no way in hell that's happening. He said "better than he'd imagined." That he'd thought about kissing me before. Could that be true? And then he basically begged me to kiss him. That has to be one of the greatest moments of my life.

Why the fuck didn't he say something sooner though? But if I'm being completely honest with myself, I know that even if he only wants to be with me because of how convenient it is with us living together, I'll go along with it. If he's wanted to have sex with a man, I've been on the other side of the wall this entire time. Sure, I had hoped that the longing glances I thought I'd caught weren't all in my head. I've fantasized about his flirting having a deeper meaning. But there was never any actual indication that he could be into me before last night.

I run my hands over his chest where he's wearing a shirt for once, a fancy button up that looks so good on him, but I absolutely hate it. I want to feel the muscles I've been drooling over. I want to trace his tattoos with my tongue. Does he have any hidden ones I don't know about?

I quickly undo the buttons on his shirt, push it off his shoulders, while continuing to kiss him the whole time. He easily follows my lead, not jumping in to do it for me or moving to take off anything else, just shifting exactly as I guide him.

Does he have any idea how fucking hot that is? How much of a high it gives me to feel like this big, athletic man who has six inches on me is so willing to let me be the one in charge? It's not like he isn't participating: he's kissing me back just as passionately as I'm kissing him. His hands haven't left my body, but he isn't fighting for control.

I love everything about this.

Except for how many clothes we're still wearing. I undo the buttons on my dress shirt, ditching it quickly. His hands move to roam over my torso, skimming up to my chest. For a second, I worry this will be the moment he realizes he's making out with a man, or he'll realize even if he was attracted to men in the past, I look nothing like the other professional athletes he's used to being surrounded by.

But if anything, Hudson is only more desperate after my shirt is gone. He lets out a deep moan, trying to step in even closer to me as if he hates that there's any space between us at all. I agree.

I finally pull back just a bit, letting my head fall to the side as Hudson continues to kiss down my jaw and neck. His beard is rough against my clean-shaven face in the most enticing way. I wrap my arms around his neck, and when I've caught my breath a bit, I mutter, "Stand up, all the way."

He does without hesitation. *So hot.* "Why?"

"So you can catch me," I answer with a smirk, jumping up to wrap my legs around his waist.

He laughs as he easily adjusts to hold me. Now I'm at a much better angle to kiss him, and there's no space between us. It's also just really fucking sexy that he can hold me so effortlessly while we make out. My dick is rock hard where it's trapped between us, and I can't resist grinding into him even more. He shifts his hips in response, probably seeking his own relief.

I have no idea how long we stay like this, making out in the middle of my kitchen while Hudson holds me, my legs wrapped around him. I wish I had a way to capture this moment; one of those people who paints the first kiss at a wedding on hand so I could hang it up and stare at this kiss for the rest of my life and know that, at least for this brief moment, everything was perfect. Kissing Hudson without any of the concern for his motives that I'd had yesterday is amazing. I could kiss him like this all night and be happy.

But I want more. And he said that he did too.

I have no idea what "more" he was referring to, but I'm going to find out. I don't know if tonight will be a onetime thing, so I plan to take full advantage, to do whatever Hudson is willing to try.

Before I let my fantasies run completely wild, I need to figure out what his expectation is. I try to pull back again, and he chases my mouth, a sexy-as-fuck whimper leaving his throat when I put a hand firmly on his chest to hold him back.

"Why do you keep stopping?" he whines, and his impatience makes a smug grin stretch across my face.

"What did you mean by wanting to do more?"

Without hesitation, he answers, "I want to have sex with you."

I'm glad he's so confident, but I'm concerned about what his expectation for that might be.

Physically, I'm pretty much exactly what most people would picture when they hear the word "twink," even if I'm a little old for the label according to some people. At five foot six inches, I'm on the shorter side. I'm fairly slim, and I happen to prefer the clean-shaven look. I have an expensive hairstyle, and take time to focus on looking and feeling good about my appearance every day. I also have a big personality and enjoy attention. Some might even describe me as dramatic.

And for some reason, most people associate those things with wanting to bottom.

But I don't.

Been there, done that. I don't enjoy it, the sensation of something in my ass or feeling like I'm less in control. And as much as I believe Hudson is the definition of my dream man, I'm not going to compromise what I enjoy to have sex with him. There are plenty of ways we can get off together where he isn't topping me, if he's willing.

I let out a big sigh. "As much as I really don't want you to put me down, you probably should."

He squeezes his grip on my thighs. "Why?"

"So we can talk about that."

He also sighs, leaning in for another kiss that was probably meant to be quick, but neither of us is in a hurry to end. Finally, we break apart, and he gently sets me back on the floor, his hands back on my hips like he doesn't want to let go. I don't either, so I rest mine on his pecs, trying not to get distracted over how firm his muscles are.

"So, what do we need to talk about?" he asks, gaze still dropping down from my eyes to my mouth every few seconds.

"What having sex with me would look like. More specifically, who would be doing the fucking."

He nods. "Okay. What are you saying?"

"I don't bottom. But there are other ways we could get off together," I hurry to add. "Sex doesn't always mean penetration."

He looks at me for a moment before repeating, "Adrian, I want to have sex with you." It's as though he didn't hear me at all.

"Hudson, did you understand what I said? I only top," I rephrase, hoping to clarify so we can move on to what he *would* be willing to do with me.

"Okay. And?"

"Okay?" I echo back, completely not expecting that answer

and needing to make sure I actually heard him correctly and my mind hasn't run away with fantasies again.

"Yeah," he replies, smirking now. "I said that I want to have sex with you, and you let me know your preference, so I said 'okay.' I know I'm new to the whole sex with another man thing, but that seemed pretty clear to me. Did I do something wrong already? Am I supposed to know a secret code word? Because you'll have to teach me that sort of thing."

He sounds so casual as he jokes around with me, that for a moment, I almost forget what we're talking about. That this man, who I was still fairly certain was straight less than twenty-four hours ago, is now agreeing to bottom like I just asked if he'd rather have Coke or Pepsi, and he has no preference.

But how can he possibly *know* if he has no preference if he's never tried one of the brands?

"But… but you're—"

"Don't say straight. I am definitely not. I very desperately want to have sex with you right now. That isn't straight."

I can't help it. A laugh escapes from my throat at how different his reaction is to the one I was expecting. "Are you sure? Have you ever done that?" I ask. I know some straight men are into ass play, pegging, that sort of thing. This conversation is making it very clear that I have no idea what he's into, and that I shouldn't assume.

His cheeks darken as he bites his lip, still smirking at me. It's the most captivating mix of embarrassed and playful, almost mischievous even. Whatever the word is, I love that I'm the one he's looking at that way. As though he wants to share all his secrets with me. I want to wrap my arms around him, to hold him as he does, and learn every little detail there is to know about him.

That's pretty intense for what is, in all likelihood, just a hookup situation though. He hasn't said anything about wanting to be with me, just that he wants to have sex with me.

And that's fine. Even if I wish it could be more.

Honestly, something casual is what makes the most sense for us both right now. He might be my roommate at the moment, where this can be an easy arrangement kept between us, but his house is so close to being ready. Truth be told, he could already be living there with how trivial the improvements that are still happening are.

Plus, he's still a professional hockey player. For the team I work for.

And on top of all that, he's about to adopt a baby. He doesn't need to worry about starting an actual relationship when he has all that going on.

And I'm really busy, too. I mean, I'm sure I could make the time, but... not the point! Casual is good. Hooking up with Hudson is a very logical, mature decision on my part.

If he wants someone to get off with, I'm more than willing to volunteer.

"Well?" I tease. "Have you? If we're going to do this, you need to get really comfortable with me, really quickly. No holding back."

His smile lights up his face as he chuckles. "I guess that's true. Well, I got a few toys a couple of months ago. That was my first experience with anything going into my ass."

My cheeks hurt from how big my smile is.

Oh my god. Hudson got sex toys to play with his ass after moving in with me? The thought of that is both the greatest thing ever, and also such a disappointment. *Because hello?* That's so fucking hot to think about him doing in my guest room, but also, I could have been helping him do that this whole time.

"So what toys did you get?" I can't help but ask.

"Umm. Well, it was a whole kit for beginners sort of thing. There are some plugs, a prostate massager..." he trails off, quietly mumbling what sounds like "a douche."

My eyes go wide, and I playfully slap his chest. "Hudson Roy! Are you telling me that you used a douche, while in my condo, to experiment with prostate toys, and I had no idea?"

"Total honesty?" he asks skeptically, only making me even more curious.

I quickly nod. "Tell me!"

"I never locked the door. Sometimes I wouldn't even bother to close it. I was kind of hoping you'd catch me doing something, and maybe you'd want to join in." His cheeks are really red now. But as he shifts closer to me, his erection is obviously straining his pants, and it's clear his embarrassment isn't getting in the way of his arousal.

I gasp, practically shrieking "I can't believe you were doing that on purpose!" as I playfully slap his pecs again. "I did notice you leave the door open a few times, but I had no idea what you were doing. Ugh, I wish that I had walked in on something, that sounds so hot. And did you like it?"

Because that's really the million-dollar question, isn't it?

Is there really a chance that my dream man and I are actually compatible?

"I love it," he says, no hesitation as he shifts his hips more solidly into me. "Have I convinced you I'm ready to bottom?"

I give him a quick, assessing once over. He doesn't seem nervous in any way. He's confident in everything he's said and asked for. But still, I have to ask one more thing. "So this will be your very first experience with a man ever?" He nods. "Are you sure you don't want to ease into things? Maybe a blow job?"

He's shaking his head before I even finish asking the question. "I want you to fuck me. I've been on the receiving end of a blow job plenty of times. If you want me to attempt to blow you before that happens, I'd be willing to try. But I just—I really need you inside me right now. I actually took a pretty thorough shower right before dinner, just in case you were willing to talk things through with me, hoping we might end up here."

Holy fuck. Is manifesting real? Did I will this situation into fruition with the amount of times I fantasized about it?

I grab his hand and drag him after me as I lead us out of the kitchen.

"Is that a yes?" he asks, chuckling as he follows me down the hall. "You want to?"

"This is a hell-fucking-yes. Of course I want to."

HUDSON

I can't believe that this is actually happening.

Adrian opens the door to his bedroom, and I step inside with all the lights on for the first time. Everything is drenched in a deep green color. Wainscoting, a word I didn't even know before moving in here, makes it feel elegant, while the abundance of pillows on his giant bed and the built-in bookcases taking up an entire wall, displaying an array of both books and trinkets, manage to make it feel cozy and lived-in.

I love it. But I only have a moment to take it all in before Adrian pulls me back to why I'm in here in the first place, asking, "Can I take off the rest of your clothes?"

I quickly nod, stepping out of my pants and underwear as he pushes them down too slowly for my liking. When I'm completely naked, he stays in the kneeling position he'd ended up in, and it's like he can't look away from my dick.

"Fuck. I knew you'd have a nice cock, but it's even better than I'd imagined," he says dreamily. "I know that I said we'd skip blow jobs, but can I play with it for just a second?"

I laugh. "Like I'm going to say no to that? Go ahead."

"Yay! Okay, on the bed. I'm not fucking up my knees when I probably can't even reach you properly with how short I am."

I do as he says, moving to lay down on the bed, and somehow it's even more comfortable than mine is in his guest room. My head has barely hit the pillow when my soul momentarily leaves my body.

Apparently, when Adrian said "play with it for a second," he meant that he was going to immediately attempt to deepthroat my entire dick in one motion. I hadn't even realized he was starting, and it already feels so fucking incredible as he swallows around me.

"Oh fuck! Charming, you're so good at that. Oh my god." I let out a deep moan, even more turned on thinking about all the sounds I've made over the last couple of months, hoping that he'd hear me, that eventually we'd end up together. And now, here we are, where every sound is because of him.

He pulls off as quickly as he started, and I groan again.

He laughs, teasing me. "I thought you said you'd rather skip blow jobs?"

"I did. I just hadn't realized you'd be that amazing."

"Don't worry, we're just getting started. Roll over. Go on your hands and knees, or prop some pillows under you so you're comfortable with your ass up in the air toward me," he instructs, and my anticipation grows. It's actually happening. Adrian is going to fuck me.

Excited is an understatement.

"Do you know what rimming is?" he asks, and I forget how to breathe. I nod, unsure if my voice would even work right now. "Can I eat you out?"

I've been enjoying a lot of porn featuring men having sex with other men, and I have really been into scenes with rimming. It always looks so hot, and I know they could just be acting, but the person on the receiving end usually seems like they're having a great time.

The thought of Adrian having his tongue inside my ass is still a little hard to wrap my head around, but I think about what he said earlier about getting comfortable with each other, being honest. And as intimidating as it might seem, I am curious. So I nod. "Go ahead."

He doesn't hesitate, he grips my ass with a hand on either side, and licks right over my hole. Sensation wise, it's such a sensitive area, and his warm, wet tongue feels absolutely amazing as he moves it around. He lets out a moan, and for a second, I wonder if it could be possible he's enjoying this as much as I am. For a while, I'm consumed by how spectacular it feels as he continues licking me, relaxing as I let the pleasure remain my focus.

"I'm going to start to open you up now, okay? You seem pretty relaxed, but let me know if I need to stop or change what I'm doing. If anything hurts, tell me right away."

"Okay." I already sound breathy, and Adrian has still only used his mouth on me.

He moves back to my hole, licking and kissing, giving it plenty of attention. Honestly, I feel like I could eventually get off just from this. I try to focus on calming my breathing, and on a deep exhale, Adrian slides his tongue inside me.

"Oh, fuuuuuck," I moan, and he continues to fuck his tongue into my hole. Then he adds a finger and slowly stretches me out even more with that. An embarrassingly high-pitched whimper escapes my throat when he pulls out. "Why did you stop?"

"To get supplies. We need more than spit."

"Fair." I stay in the same position with my ass in the air, exposed for Adrian as he undresses and adds lube to his fingers, spreading it all over my hole. He starts again with one finger inside me, making sure I'm appropriately stretched before adding a second, and eventually, a third finger with even more lube, which I appreciate.

I love how full I already feel from his fingers, and I know if I was using my toys right now, I'd be close to finishing already. But, obviously, I don't want to do that. I want Adrian inside me. I think he's avoiding my prostate as much as possible while he stretches me out to continue to tease me, and it's absolutely working. Each time his finger brushes against that spot, I want to cry out and beg him to do it again and again. To never stop because it feels so fucking good.

"God, you really are good at this already, huh? I can't believe you've been practicing," Adrian praises. "You seem pretty prepared to me. How are you feeling?"

I shift my hips, squirming a little. No pain. "I feel like I needed you inside of me, like, five minutes ago."

He laughs, running his hands appreciatively over my ass, moving to the top of my thighs and back up to my hips "Are you ready then?"

I want to say yes, to beg him to stop teasing me, because I want him inside of me as soon as possible. But as I think about that moment, I realize that I don't want to have my face buried in a pillow. I would much rather be looking at him, to share that moment. "Wait, not yet." I turn my head so I can look at his face. "Would it be alright if I get on my back? I want to see you while you fuck me."

Adrian doesn't respond for a moment, and I'm worried I did something wrong, again. That maybe I broke some unwritten role or boundary of his that I was unaware of. But eventually, he responds. "Of course you can. Whatever you think you'll be the most comfortable doing."

I roll over so I'm on my back, taking a second to prop a pillow under my hips. My head is leaning against some pillows, and this is already so much better than before because now I can see Adrian in all his naked glory as he stares down at me adoringly. His dick is bigger than I was expecting given his frame, and it's more curved than mine. Right now, it's jutting out toward me, long and so hard. The tip is even leaking. A few months ago, I would have never thought another man's dick could be so erotic, but staring at Adrian's cock somehow has me even more desperate for him.

"Is that better?" he asks, and I finally tear my gaze away from his dick to smile at him.

"So much. Now come here, I want to kiss you again." He smirks and leans over me to oblige. His lips on mine are just as heady as before. They're so soft and full, and the way he controls the kiss, licking into my mouth, sucking my bottom lip between his after nipping it, is so hot. I don't think I'll ever get over the fact that I waited so long to kiss him. I'm so glad I get to do it now.

I get lost in the sensation of our kiss, which has quickly turned into a full-blown make-out session as we continue to explore each other's mouths. Adrian is the first to break our connection. Pulling back, he rests on his knees between my bent legs.

"Okay, are you ready now?" I nod. I'm much more comfortable in this position as I pull my legs back, and he opens the condom he must've grabbed and placed on the bed next to us. He puts it on, adding more lube to both his dick and my hole before lining up with my entrance. At first, he just teases me, tapping against it, making no effort to actually push in.

"Adriaaaan," I whine, and he chuckles.

"Alright, alright. Big inhale," he instructs. On my exhale, he slowly advances until his tip is inside of me, pausing to allow me to adjust to the new sensation. His dick is a little wider than the biggest plug I have and definitely longer.

"Fuck, you're so tight, Hudson," he says breathlessly. "I can't believe you're letting me be the first man inside you."

That makes me smile, and I relax even more. I love his praise, knowing that he seems to be enjoying this just as much as I am. I want this to be just as good for him as it already is for me. I don't want him to just be the first man inside me, I want him to be the only one. But I don't think now is the time for those sort of declarations, so I stick with encouraging him to continue. "You can go further. I'm doing fine."

He nods, muttering, "Okay. Yeah, me too. So fine. Not freaking out about how unbelievable this is." His reaction is everything. I never want this to end. Then he's pushing in a bit further, stretching me with so much care that it makes me feel cherished, as though my comfort and pleasure are the most important thing in the world to him. He waits again before slowly pulling out, and then advancing even more. Every extra inch lights me up, pleasure building at the base of my spine as he continues to stretch me out and fill me up in a way I can't even describe.

This might be a new experience for me, but nothing about it is awkward or uncomfortable. This feels like the natural progression of our relationship, like exactly what Adrian and I should have been doing this whole time.

Looking up at his blissed-out expression, I feel so connected to him in a way that I don't remember with any of my previous partners, and I'm so grateful I get to experience this with another person. Maybe it's different because he's fucking me, or maybe it's because he's a man, but I think it's just that we spent so long as friends, supporting and admiring each other without the motivation of a physical relationship. He's been there for me through so much already, simply because he wanted to help. That level of friendship being added to this physical one only amplifies everything I'm feeling.

I'm so glad we finally got here.

He lets out another groan as he bottoms out inside of me.

"Hudson, you feel so incredible. I still can't believe you've been practicing with toys, hoping this might happen."

He's slowly pulling back and thrusting back into me as he talks. The pace is torturous, every shift of his hips has his cock dragging against my prostate sending me closer and closer to my climax. "This... is so... much better," I get out between my ragged breaths.

I'm trying to hold back, not ready for this to end. All I can hope is that this is only the beginning for us, that we can do this again and again. Being with Adrian has been my fantasy for months, and now that I know what being with him is actually like, somehow so much better than I'd hoped, I never want to go back.

As he continues to fuck me, it's clear Adrian not only has a nice dick but he also knows how to use it. He isn't just pounding into me, chasing his own pleasure. Each roll of his hips has me making more desperate, uncontrollable sounds, and when Adrian moves his hand to my leaking cock, spreading the precum around the head to tease me, I blurt out, "Fucking-holy-mother-of-fuck!" My hips thrust up into his hand on instinct, seeking more friction. The movement throws off his rhythm, and he chuckles at my outburst, but the sensation of him inside me while also touching my dick has me seeing stars.

He grabs the lube, adding some to his hand.

"I think your cock is perfectly curved to rub against my prostate every time you grind into me like that. If you touch my dick while you do that, it's over," I warn him.

He smiles, and those fucking dimples that I'm obsessed with are on display, tugging at something in my chest. "Good, that's kind of the point."

"Well, are you close, too?"

He's looking at me like he does his favorite triple chocolate fudge brownie, and the adoration mixed with longing has that feeling in my chest threatening to consume me before he pulls me back to the moment. "Hudson, I've been close this entire time."

"Thank fuck," I say on an exhale.

He resumes that perfect motion with his hips as he wraps his lubed hand around my dick, twisting up and down as he does, and I have no idea what noise I make, too overwhelmed with the euphoric feeling of my orgasm as I finally come all over my stomach and chest.

Adrian cries out a moment later, hand still working me through my release during his own. We both take a moment to catch our breath before he slowly pulls out of me and removes the condom.

I hate how empty I feel at the loss of him, but when he leans over to kiss me again, that sensation seems like more of a reminder of how great being together was, rather than the lonely one it had moments before.

I'm not ready when he pulls away, whispering, "I'll be right back, don't move."

I don't think I could even if I wanted to. My limbs feel boneless as I float on the cloud of Adrian's bed.

Seriously, how is this so comfortable?

ADRIAN

I think Hudson might have fallen asleep while I was in my bathroom getting cleaned up and grabbing a warm washcloth. I'd wanted to draw a bath for him, but maybe not. I plug in my phone and move his to a wireless charger on my night-stand before climbing back onto the bed with him.

He doesn't stir. I think he'd appreciate not waking up with dried cum in his chest hair, though, so I gently clean him up. When I'm done, I realize he's blinking up at me with hooded eyes, looking like he's still half asleep with a big smile on his face.

"Hey, Charming."

I've always loved his silly nicknames for me, but right now, after that, I'm even happier to hear him use it. "Hey, Hudson."

"That was amazing," he says in a dreamy tone that has my heart aching even more for this perfect man. I can't help myself, and I lean down for another kiss that he eagerly accepts.

I have no idea what his expectations for the rest of the night are, but he seems pretty blissed out, and if there's any chance he's going to crash after this, I hope he isn't alone. Maybe I can convince him to sleep in here tonight. That's totally a thing hookups do, right?

Friends with benefits can definitely include cuddle benefits in my opinion.

"Do you want to stay in here? Or…?" I trail off as he tugs me closer to him.

"Shhh. Come to bed."

Well, I'm not arguing with that. I pull the duvet over us, and Hudson wraps his arms around me as I settle in next to him. "Do you need me to set an alarm for you?" I ask before I let myself completely give in to just how comfortable I am, how perfect this moment is.

"Nah, it's set," he mumbles into my hair.

His strong arm around my waist settles something inside me that I didn't even realize was on alert. I always feel so comfortable in his presence, but this is a whole new level. Usually, I spend quite a lot of time fantasizing about a dream version of my life to help me relax my mind enough to sleep, but tonight, reality is even better. And with the star of my fantasies in my bed, I'm asleep in no time at all.

HUDSON MUST HAVE BEEN EXHAUSTED, because he sleeps through my alarm, me slipping out of his hold where he was still wrapped around me, and my entire morning routine. I'm usually the first person in the office, and as much as I would have loved to hit the snooze button to stay with Hudson this morning, I knew that would only make things harder.

We didn't get a chance to set any boundaries last night about what either of us is expecting going forward. I didn't need to pretend like us cuddling meant more than it did. Hudson and I have cuddled in the past without it meaning anything, and that was way before anything ever happened between us.

Although, now that I know he isn't as straight as I'd previously assumed, I guess I have no idea what it meant to him…

We definitely need to talk as soon as possible. I have meetings all day, and even though I know Hudson is in the building for his practice and workouts and a whole lot of other things throughout the day, our paths don't cross.

Hudson has a PR photoshoot scheduled late in the afternoon that I know will take a while, so I actually beat him home. I'm glad to have some time to consider everything that I'd like to say to him. All day I've been thinking about what last night could have meant. I've tried to focus on all the reasons Hudson and I have to not be together as a reminder to not let my fantasies take control.

I want to stay busy as I'm thinking things through, so I start to cook some of the chicken that Hudson's chef prepared for us. Some of the meals he makes are meant to be reheated quickly, but others have short cooking instructions, and I opt for one that requires me to grill the chicken.

There's a possibility he wanted it to be a onetime thing, that he wanted someone safe to have his first time with, and as much as I would be disappointed if that were the case, I think we could still move on from that as friends. I could be happy that I got to be that person for him.

I'm having a harder time wrapping my mind around what else it could mean though, what his expectations are if he wants to do it again. What I would even want it to mean. I've been fantasizing about Hudson for so long as someone I could never have, and now that I've had him, a very big part of me feels like it isn't even real. How do I shift those fantasy thoughts to reality when I've been telling myself for so long that there was no possibility of us ever being together?

As much as I want to be prepared for the conversation, it was clear last night that I can't predict what Hudson wants, so it's probably best to just wait and see what he actually says when he gets home soon.

I try to focus on cooking, flipping the chicken when I'm supposed to. I jump, nearly throwing the tongs I was using as Hudson wraps his arms around me from behind and places a kiss on my neck.

"Oh my god! I need to put a bell on you or something!" I shriek.

He chuckles right into my ear, placing another kiss on my neck before he says, "Sorry, I wasn't trying to be quiet." One of his hands moves under my shirt, pushing it up to splay his hand over my stomach, moving up to my chest like he wants to touch all of me and can't decide where to focus.

He goes back to kissing my neck, moving up and down, across my jawline, before focusing on my pulse point and sucking lightly.

"What are you doing?" I ask, already sounding breathy.

"Kissing you." He places another kiss on my neck. "Touching you." His other hand moves lower to cup my growing erection over my pants. "Is that okay?"

Is it? I know I had been set on us talking… but that was before his hand was on my dick.

Ugh, but he's probably never touched another man's cock before either, and we do really need to talk about what this means if we're going to keep doing it.

We should be responsible, even if the voice in my head is chanting that we should get off together again first.

"Wait," I groan, gently pulling his hands away.

"Shit, is that not okay?" he asks, immediately stepping back and sounding horrified. "I thought that after last night..." He trails off, so I step in.

"Exactly. We need to talk about last night before we do anything else."

He looks a little worried, but agrees. "Okay."

"It isn't a bad thing," I assure him. "I just want to make sure we're on the same page. I made us both food. We can eat and talk if that works for you?"

"Sure."

Hudson sets the table and gets us both water while I finish preparing dinner. It isn't long before we're seated across from each other, Hudson staring at me expectantly, completely ignoring his food.

It seems like he's waiting for me, so I go for it. "So, I was going to start by asking if you wanted to have anything happen between us again, but based on that greeting, I'm guessing you were thinking it wasn't a onetime thing?"

He looks a little embarrassed. "Can I be totally honest?"

I snort a laugh. "I really hope so. That's kind of the point of this conversation."

That gets him to smile, and he rolls his eyes. "Okay. If we're being completely honest, I was kind of hoping that last night meant we were together now."

My jaw drops open; I can't help it. I know Hudson has been a bit codependent since he moved in, and he was going through so much, so I was happy to go along with it. But still, I wasn't expecting him to think one hookup somehow meant we were, what? Boyfriends?

"Like together, together? Like you want to date me?" I check, not sure if I understood that correctly.

"Yes, I want to date you. But I wasn't expecting you to look so horrified by that idea. Can you please keep talking?" he anxiously asks.

"Oh, shit, sorry. Not horrified," I rush to assure him. "I'm just surprised. I mean, last night was the first time you ever did anything with a man, right?" He nods. All the reasons I've been focused on today about why Hudson and I shouldn't be together as I was trying to prepare myself for his rejection flash through my mind once more, and maybe I was a little too focused on them, because I can't seem to move past it. I've fantasized about this man for so long. I should be thrilled right now, jumping at the opportunity to really be with him... But when things seem to be too good to be true, in my experience, they are.

"I guess with everything else going on, I had just assumed this conversation would be about setting up boundaries for some sort of friends-with-benefits situation where you could have your first experiences with a man, not a relationship..." I trail off, unsure of what I really want anymore.

"Everything else going on?" he repeats as a question.

"Well, you're still in the NHL. A public relationship with a man would be a huge deal for your career," I remind him. "And even if you ignore that, you're fresh off a divorce, and you haven't even had a chance to live on your own yet."

"Is that a bad thing?"

"I don't know," I admit, thinking through our time together, all the lines that were blurred when I thought he was straight. "I joked around with you about treating me like I was Shelby's replacement, but there was some truth in that. From the very beginning, we've basically acted like a couple, minus the physical benefits, at least when we were alone together. It was one thing when I thought you were straight, but now you're saying you want us to be together, I don't know..."

He shakes his head. "What does Shelby have to do with us? I'm saying that I want to be with *you*, Adrian."

I groan. "Fuck. Hudson, you have no idea how many times

I've thought about being with you. Believe me, I am furious with myself right now for not jumping at the opportunity, but—"

"So don't say 'but.' Jump at the opportunity," he suggests with his pleading charismatic smile that I can never say no to.

But I need to stay strong. I smile back at him, really hoping I'm not about to fuck everything up. "Fuck. I so want to. But I can't move past what I said the other day, about how I deserve to be with someone who wants to be with me, period. Not because it's convenient or because I'm the first man they're with. If I'm being perfectly honest, I think we'd be setting ourselves up for failure if we started dating right now. I think a part of me would always be wondering if you actually wanted to be with me or if I was just the convenient option because we're roommates."

Hudson hangs his head back against the chair groaning. "Yeah, I was worried you might think that," he admits. "That's why I'd been trying to wait until after I moved out to ask you out."

"You've been planning to ask me out?" I repeat. This conversation is giving me emotional whiplash.

"Yeah, does that change anything?" he asks hopefully, staring at me with those damn puppy-dog eyes.

Does it? I wish it did. But fuck, it still doesn't change the fact that I've been basically acting as a pseudo-partner for months. I still have no idea if Hudson would want to date me once we're no longer living together. If he had time alone to consider if I was really who he wanted to date or if our proximity was why he thought that.

I shake my head. "I don't think so."

We both sit there in silence for a moment. I have no idea where to go from here.

Then Hudson sits up straighter in his chair. "But you were willing to talk about boundaries for a hook up situation? Would you still be willing to do that?" he asks, still sounding so hopeful.

I take a second to consider it. "I don't want to stop if there's an option where we get to keep having sex. That hasn't changed," I admit. "I like the idea of being your first for everything, I just don't want you to feel like that means we need to be together."

A smile lights up his face now. "Okay. So let's do that. We don't need to label anything right now. I think you're saying that you'd be willing to date me if I could prove to you that you're my number one choice, right? Not the convenient one?" he checks.

I nod, continuing with full transparency. "Yeah. I really like you, Hudson, that isn't the problem. I just don't think it would be fair to either of us to start a relationship with me already insecure about it."

He nods, his smile softer now. "Thank you for being so honest." I'm glad he's being so understanding, that I haven't completely offended him.

"So, what if we keep hooking up while I'm here," he continues, sounding more excited, "I want you to be all my firsts, too. That's not why I want to date you, but I understand your concern. Then when I move out in a couple of weeks, we agree to stop hooking up, and when we're no longer together during all my free time out of convenience, I can start to work on convincing you that you're still my number one choice."

I can't hold back my smile as what he's suggesting sinks in. He isn't giving up on the idea of us being together, even when I tried to dismiss it. Even if that's because of our current situation, I think it's a good sign that he's already planning for the long term and not just what makes sense right now. I know if we continue to hook up, I'll probably fall even harder for him, be even more screwed if he does decide we're better off as friends when he has his own space... But I'm probably already far too gone for him now, anyway, for it to really make a difference.

If we go along with that plan, we can reassess when those excuses to be together no longer exist, and with them gone... I do think we'd be starting in a much healthier place, or at least I would be more confident about us.

Plus, we'd get to keep hooking up. And I'm not strong enough to say no to that.

Is it the most mature plan in the world? Absolutely not.

But can I twist it enough to justify it? Would I feel better about it than I would if he called me his boyfriend right now, and I spent the next few weeks terrified that it would end the moment he moved out?

I think so.

"I also think that this plan could be good with the baby coming so soon. I don't know how that would affect us if we were in a real relationship. I know asking you to date me is more complicated with me becoming a parent, and I would hate for either of us to feel like we weren't committed if we were together."

I nod again. "You know I want to be a parent. I'm not against dating someone with kids, and I think you know that I already love this baby from a fun uncle standpoint. But I agree, I think because I already love this baby, it'll be even more important that we don't rush into anything. Right now, I am very clearly not that child's parent, but if we started dating, that might blur the lines even more, and I think we would both need to know that we are all in before we did that."

"That sounds mature," he says lightly.

"Yes. I think we can at least pretend we're being responsible," I agree in a similar teasing tone.

"Soooo, does that mean we get to keep having sex?"

I smile conspiratorially at him. "Fuck it. Let's do it."

HUDSON

"*O*kay, I think your ass probably needs a break after last night, but if we're checking off your other first times, how do you feel about blow jobs? You seemed pretty willing last night, but no pressure if you want to try something else?"

"I want to do everything with you," I admit. "But you mentioned talking about boundaries. Do we need to do that?"

"Right, yes! We should. Sorry, I got distracted by the thought of touching your dick again." He laughs. "Okay. I already told you I don't bottom. Is there anything you don't want to do? Obviously, if something comes up you can just say no, but right off the bat, is there anything?"

I've got nothing.

"I want to take this seriously, I really do," I tell him. "But I'm also really distracted by the thought of touching you again, so I can't think of anything."

He smiles, dimples distracting me even further. "Okay, maybe we hook up and then finish the conversation?"

I nod quickly. "Yes, that option." I stand from the table, the dinner he so kindly made for me completely ignored. "Does that mean I can kiss you now?" I check.

He laughs, also standing. "Umm, maybe only kissing during a hookup? That way it isn't too much like a relationship?"

Ugh. I don't like the idea of filtering when I'll get to kiss him, but it's not like I'll be able to kiss him in public anyway, so if we're only kissing in private anyway, I can probably still do it whenever I want and just turn that into a hookup. Sounds like a win-win situation to me. "Deal," I agree.

"Okay, let's go back to my room."

I'm very pleasantly surprised when he grabs my hand to drag me there, that he seems as eager for this as I am, even if he's struggling with the idea of me actually wanting to date him.

Since learning more about his life growing up, that his parents only really paid attention to him when he was doing chores or other things for them, I've wondered if his overly helpful nature might be in response to some insecurity about not feeling wanted, that he feels like he needs to prove himself as useful in order for people to want him around. I hadn't considered his insecurities might go beyond that, that it could also translate into him not believing that I want to date him, but I'm proud of him for being so honest, for standing up for what he knows he deserves.

I hate that he questions my motives, but I get it. He has done so much to help me, but those things aren't why I want to be with him. I've wanted him by my side through everything the last few months because his presence makes everything better, because being around him in general makes me happier. I hope he hasn't felt like I was taking advantage of his kindness. I'm determined to prove to him that I want him without him having to do anything to earn that.

"I won't know what I'm doing," I warn him when we get into his room.

He smirks. "Do you want me to go first? I can blow you, and then if you still want to try it, you can copy me."

As nice as that sounds, I think I need to start proving to him that he doesn't need to give in order to receive, so I shake my head. "No, I want to blow you. You can talk me through it if I do something wrong or if I can do something better, but I didn't get to touch your dick at all last night. I want to do it now, if that's alright."

He's still smiling. "During this arrangement, you don't need to ask to touch my dick. I give you full permission."

"Same with mine."

"And if you want my cock in your mouth, I'm sure whatever you do will be great," he assures me as he takes off his clothes.

"Perfect," I say on an exhale, half in response to his comment, half in reaction to his naked body on display for me. How did I go so long without realizing I'm attracted to him? To the male body in general, I guess. His toned muscles on his slim frame are fascinating. The curve of his dick is something I'll be fantasizing about for the rest of my life. I'm already uncomfortably hard just from staring at him, but I could do it all day. I want to memorize every little detail that makes up the man who has quickly become my favorite person.

Last night was absolutely perfect, but I'm excited I get to actually touch his dick this time. I've spent the last few months wondering what it would be like to be with another man, to hold someone else's cock in my hand. Yesterday confirmed that the real deal is so much better than I'd even imagined, way more enjoyable than any of the toys I've tried. It only made me more eager to do other things too.

He lays down on the bed, lounging back against the pillows.

I'm still fully dressed, too distracted by him being naked to have removed anything. "Should I get naked first?" I ask him, unsure why it feels like I need his permission, but I kind of like it, so I go with it.

"No," he replies firmly. "I don't want you to be able to touch yourself. I want to be the one to make you come."

My dick jerks a little at that, and I don't argue. I climb onto the bed so I'm kneeling next to his waist. His cock is swollen, and now that he's laying back, that damn curve is pointing up toward his abs in the most enticing way. I try to channel some of Adrian's confidence as I reach out and run my finger along his shaft, loving the silky smooth feel of him. It's so easy to imagine what each motion would feel like on my own dick as I wrap my fingers around him, twisting as I move up and down, and thinking about what I like makes this even hotter.

I spit in my hand before bringing it back to his tip, slowly spreading it down and back up, adding more until the entire thing is coated with it so I can easily twist and squeeze as I enjoy the feel of him in my hand.

"Fuck, Hudson, that feels really fucking good. And the look on your face right now is so hot. If you don't want me in your mouth tonight, just keep doing that and I'll come soon," he warns.

"No, I do!" I let go, and he groans. "Sorry, I just got a little distracted playing."

He smiles indulgently at me, dimples driving me wild. "Don't apologize. Like I said, you can play whenever you'd like."

"Thanks," I say with a wink before I turn back to his erection. The tip is leaking now, and I go for it. Using one hand to steady the base, I lean in and suck the head of his cock into my mouth. The taste isn't unpleasant, and the soft texture as I suck surprises me in the best way.

I don't want to get ahead of myself, so I pull off to lick up and down his shaft, around the head, exploring each part to see what earns the biggest reaction from him. Each noise he makes feels like praise, turning me on even more. I suck him into my mouth again, fitting more of him in on this attempt, and his hips shift up so he bumps the back of my throat, making me gag a little around him, but even that was really hot, thinking about how far he must be inside of me to get that reaction.

"Fuck, sorry, I didn't mean to do that!" he apologizes. "That feels so good. It's really hard to remember you haven't done this."

I pull off to respond, a huge smile on my face. "That's awesome! Don't remember, do whatever you want. It's so hot when you take control, and I don't have to think about if I'm doing everything right."

He eyes me skeptically. "You didn't mind gagging?"

I shake my head enthusiastically, working him in my hand while we talk. "That was hot too. I'm pretty sure my pants are going to be ruined with how much I'm already leaking."

"Do you really want me to take over? To fuck your face?"

I don't even need to think about it as my dick jerks again. "Yes. That, please."

"Well, if you're going to ask me so nicely…" he teases, grabbing my hair and guiding my mouth back onto his cock. "But make a fist and put it on my thigh. If your hand relaxes, or you tap me or move it at all, I'll stop, okay? Show me."

I do as he says, putting my fist on his thigh, tapping, and returning it to that same spot. "God, you're perfect," he mutters under his breath so lowly that I don't know if he meant for me to hear. But I did.

And I fucking loved it.

Adrian can think this is casual all he wants, but I have big plans to convince him otherwise.

"Try to relax your throat, and breathe through your nose when you can," he instructs. Then he uses his grip in my hair to push me further down on his cock, guiding me to bob up and down the full length of him. I try to suck and lick as much as I can manage, but every once and a while, he holds me down, forcing me to gag around him before pulling me off to catch my breath. Every time, I worry I'm going to finish in my pants because of how sexy it is, but he told me not to come, and I don't want to disappoint him. Thinking about him scolding me for it is almost hot enough for me to say "fuck it" and stop holding back, but I really do want his mouth back on me, so I fight off my climax.

"Fuck. Hudson, I can't..." he mutters between panting breaths. "Going to come... Tap my leg twice if I can finish in your mouth."

I hurry to double tap, desperate for the full experience, and as soon as I do, my mouth is flooded with his release. On instinct, I swallow as much as I can, and only a little gets past my lips, dripping down my chin as he continues to thrust into me through his orgasm.

Adrian finally lets go of my hair, and I pull off him, smiling. "That was awesome!"

He laughs, showing off his dimples as he sits up to hold my face in his hands before desperately kissing me. I know he can taste himself on me, and the thought has me moaning into his mouth as he makes out with me.

He palms my leaking cock, squeezing me through my pants before shifting his hands to my chest to guide me back to lay on the bed. Still kissing me, he pushes my shirt up, tracing his fingers over each of my abs before finally breaking away to pull my underwear and pants off me.

He doesn't waste any time teasing me, and I'm grateful as he sucks me deep into the back of his throat. "I'm already so close," I warn, and he hums around me, earning another loud moan from me. His mouth feels incredible, so warm and tight as he swallows around me. He pulls back just a little, using his hand to cover what doesn't comfortably fit in his mouth, twisting and moving up and down with his motions as he continues to suck my dick like it's his favorite thing in the world.

His tongue swirls around the head of my cock before teasing the slit, and I'm sure he can already taste me. The thought of both of us tasting like each other lights up something primal inside me, the part that desperately wants to claim him. I want that, all the time. We might not be officially dating yet, but tasting like each other's cum sounds like a great option for now. I wonder if there are other subtle ways that we could claim each other. Would he be willing to give me a hickey? Would that raise too many questions? Maybe something more subtle. I could borrow some of his cologne? Maybe one of his fancy watches. I love the idea of having some part of him with me all the time.

As much as I want to live in this moment forever, with the taste of Adrian's release fresh on my lips and his wrapped around my cock, everything feels way too good, and I know I'm close. "I'm going to—" I try to warn him, but it's too late as I come in his mouth. He continues to lick and suck at my tip as I enjoy the high, though, so I don't think he minds.

My orgasm is so intense after so much build up while blowing him that I worry I won't be able to move after it's finally over. I lay there, trying to catch my breath.

He shifts to lie next to me, cuddling up to my side. "This is going to be fun."

I laugh. "Yeah, it is." Then I remember we agreed to talk after. Is he about to ask me to go back to my own bed? "Can I stay in here? Is that a boundary thing?"

He's quiet for a minute, thinking about his answer. I appreciate when he does that, when he takes the time to consider what he actually wants instead of jumping to agree with me about everything. It makes me feel like he's invested in us, in doing things right even if we're approaching things physically before we agree to anything more.

"Yeah, if you're okay with it, I'd like the option to cuddle or sleep together after we hook up. Otherwise, I'm worried one of us might end up feeling neglected or used. That isn't what this is. We both care about each other. We just need to figure out our timing, if it really makes sense for the long term."

I let out a sigh in relief. "Good. I'm definitely okay with that."

And I like his confirmation that we care about each other, that he might be referring to this as an arrangement, but he hasn't completely dismissed the possibility of more.

Being with Adrian physically has only made it more obvious that I want there to be a long term for us.

I won't give up, and I'm ready to prove to him that he is my future and to fight for us until he believes me.

ADRIAN

April

"Hey! I brought your favorite coffee. Have you been going through withdrawals when I'm out of town?"

I startle a little at the sound of Beck's voice. I guess I've gotten pretty used to being alone here with how often he's been gone. Even with the Werewolves in the playoffs now, this is the first I've seen him in the office in over a month.

"I am perfectly capable of buying my own coffee." I gesture to the almost empty cup sitting on my desk. Beck doesn't need to know that Hudson bought it for me, or that he's been showing up earlier than he needs to for his morning weight sessions so we can leave and get here at the same time.

One of the boundaries we did agree on was not carpooling to work, even if our schedules happened to match up. It seemed like a good idea to not have people seeing us driving together. I certainly wasn't expecting Hudson to rearrange his schedule to match mine as much as possible anyway, or for him to always buy my favorite coffee for me when he is here.

Beck laughs. "See, why am I even here? You don't need me."

I roll my eyes, smiling as I assure him, "I always like to see you though."

"Thanks, A. Are you free now? I wanted to talk to you about something, and I thought it would be better to do it in person."

I glance at my computer screen and save the email I'd been typing as a draft, since it isn't urgent, then I log out and follow him into his office, sitting in one of the chairs across from him at his desk. "So, what's up?"

He looks at me seriously, takes a deep breath, and for the first time, maybe ever since I started working with Beck, I'm nervous.

"You're overqualified to be my assistant."

I laugh nervously. "That's been true for years."

He nods. "None of my siblings' assistants have master's degrees. I have one. You somehow earned two while working full time."

"You know I like to stay busy, and they've both been useful." I shrug, trying not to let my nerves show and failing miserably. "I'm sorry, but what is happening right now? Are you about to fire me? Because honestly, that would just be stupid unless you're planning to come back full time. No one else is going to be able to cover for you like I have."

Beck laughs, and I relax a little. "I'm not trying to fire you. I'm trying to give you my job. You've basically been doing it this season anyway."

"Your job?" I repeat back in shock. His job has never even been on my vision board with how unattainable I considered it to be. For one thing, Beck is my best friend, and I would never want to take it away from him. But for another, the Werewolves are very much a family-owned team. Beck's dad ran it before him, and his father before that. I had assumed Beck planned to run the team until he and Cody eventually had a child to pass it down to.

And if they don't end up having kids, certainly one of his brothers would.

But me? I am not a Caldwell, and as far as I know, all the brothers who are interested in men, have no interest in me.

Not that I'd want to be with any of them anyway. I am perfectly content with my situationship with a very attractive hockey captain. Thank you very much.

Oh fuck.

I'm sleeping with the team captain. I can't be the team's president.

"It's not like I'd be stepping away entirely, this team is a huge part of my life, but I'd like to transition to more of the ownership role and give up my current position as president," he continues, completely unaware of the internal spiral I've fallen into.

"Things are going really well in Montana. We've found investors for all the individual businesses that temporarily had to shut down after the government seized Kyla's assets for their investigation. So the banks, healthcare, fitness, childcare centers, all of those are operational again. And that documentary that some of the ex-members have been filming was picked up by the major streaming companies. A lot of people have wanted to participate, share their story, so that's helped people stay positive. Some of them have been able to find jobs in whatever they were doing before joining Kyla, but I'm really hoping this deal will go through with that startup I was telling you about, so that they can take over the old headquarters and hire more people."

"Look at you, all excited about helping others." I can't help but tease him.

"Shut up," he says with absolutely no heat. "So you'll do it? My dad obviously agrees that you're the best person to take over, and he's happy to have me assume the owner role. That was always the plan eventually, so it shouldn't be a problem to get everyone's approval."

"I would love to take over in July!" I say confidently, hoping that maybe he intended for the transition to happen between seasons anyway.

"July? What? No, I was hoping we could start everything as soon as possible. It shouldn't take long to get the approvals."

I laugh nervously again. "Um, yeah, it's just that, well, there might be a conflict of interest if I was promoted this season," I finally blurt out.

With Beck out of town so much recently, we haven't been as in tune with each other's day-to-day life. Even Jordan has been so busy with everything that he isn't telling me about the men in his life, and Oakley and Parker have been so busy after their big surprise a few weeks ago that I haven't actually told any of my friends that I've been sleeping with Hudson for the last month.

Both meanings of the word. He hasn't spent a single night in the guest room since that first night together.

I know they'll be shocked to find out I've kept literally anything from them, especially something so important, but what Hudson and I have right now feels fragile. We aren't really together, we agreed that it made sense to wait to see how we were both feeling after he moved out, which I'm really trying not to think about as that date quickly approaches. Anything I do to change the status quo feels like it could make what we do have all fall apart.

And telling my best friend, who happens to be both of our bosses, feels like it could definitely disrupt things.

"A conflict of interest?" he repeats slowly.

I nod, a falsely confident smile plastered to my face as I nod. "But I think that should be cleared up after the season so I would love to take over then. Plus, you should officially finish out the season! We could go all the way, and you should get the credit."

"I don't deserve the credit," he insists. "I haven't been here.

You have. Now what the fuck conflict of interest exists that would affect my title and not yours? And why the hell don't I already know about it?"

Right. Okay, I guess we're doing this.

"So funny story," I start with a cheery tone that Beck obviously isn't buying as he glares at me. "At the beginning of the season, when I filled out the HR forms saying I was living with Hudson, they specifically said that your role couldn't date a player."

"You're dating a player?" he whisper-yells, obviously not wanting anyone outside of his office to hear us.

"No! I'm not dating one," I assure him. "But I am sleeping—"

"Shut up," Beck interrupts, no room to argue in his tone this time. He stands. "We are *not* talking about this here. Let's go."

He walks out of the office, leaving the door open. "Where are we going?" I ask as I trail after him, and he doesn't respond as we ride the elevator down to the main lobby and out onto the street. It isn't busy. Tonight's game isn't for almost nine hours.

Beck storms across the street, leading us away from the Caldwell Center. "Seriously, Beck, where the hell are we going?"

"Somewhere that I'm not your boss. We need to have this conversation as best friends."

Okay. That doesn't sound so bad.

After a few more blocks he turns, holding open the door to a tiny pub. "Why here?" I can't help but ask.

"I feel like I'm going to need a drink for this conversation, and I didn't want to pick a sports bar. This place doesn't even have any TVs," he points out as we approach the bar.

"I'll have a pint of Guiness, and do you have an espresso martini?" Beck asks, and the bartender snorts a laugh.

"I'll take a cider," I try instead.

Drinks in hand, Beck leads us to the booth in the back corner, not that there are many people here to begin with. One table was full near the front window, and there's a man seated at the bar, but I don't think anyone is going to overhear us.

Beck takes a large sip from his drink. Actually, I don't know if "sip" is the right word when he finishes half of the glass in one go.

"Okay, we're going to pretend like we don't work together for this conversation, and I'm officially drinking so I can reasonably claim I forget anything you tell me, anyway. Who are you sleeping with?"

My jaw falls open, partially at his theatrics dragging me here, because honestly, I appreciate the effort, but also because the answer should be obvious.

"Hudson! Who the fuck else would I be sleeping with?"

"Oh thank god," Beck says on a heavy exhale. "That makes way more sense. For a moment, I panicked with Ollie's whole coming out campaign—"

"Oliver is, like, ten years younger than me, and not at all my type. Honestly, Beck, you claim to be my best friend! Have you forgotten the player I've been drooling over for years?"

He shakes his head laughing. "Not at all. I just didn't know that player wasn't straight."

"I honestly don't know if he's claimed a different orientation label," I admit, realizing that we haven't actually talked about it. Maybe he doesn't need a label. He was so confident when we first hooked up that he wasn't straight that I haven't questioned it again.

"But I have been fucking him for about a month now, so the conflict of interest is there," I mutter before taking a big sip of my cider.

Beck looks even more surprised than I'd anticipated. "A whole month? Are we in a fight I didn't know about? Are you mad at me? How did I not know about this?"

"No fight!" I quickly promise. "I just—I don't know. Talking about it felt like I was going to jinx the situation, and it's already complicated enough as it is."

"Complicated how?"

"Well, for one, he said he wanted to date me, but I don't believe him. I think he's just excited about being with a man for the first time, and while we're living together, everything feels so easy that he thinks he wants to be with me."

Beck is squinting at me like he's having a hard time understanding what I said. "Things feel too easy living together and sleeping together, so you think he doesn't actually want to date you?" he repeats as a question. I nod. "A, relationships are supposed to feel easy. That's a good thing."

I roll my eyes. "That's not the point. I meant that, right now, I'm the convenient option, but when he has space and his own place, he'll remember that other options exist, and he won't actually want to be with me."

Beck continues to stare at me incredulously. "Do you know why Hudson has been the captain for as long as he has?" he finally asks.

"Because he's a great player and a good example for the young guys." I shrug, keeping my answer short so I don't break out into a monologue about how amazing Hudson is.

"Both on *and* off the ice," Beck emphasizes. "He has never been a PR concern before this season. He has never ended up on a puckbunny site or a gossip blog."

"He was married."

"Even before then. And he's been on the team longer than anyone. He's turned down higher paying contracts to stay with the team who believed in him when he was first coming up in the AHL. That man is loyal. If he says he wants to date you, I don't think he's going to suddenly change his mind."

I blink at him, unsure how to respond.

"What was the other thing?" he asks.

"What?" I blink at him, mind still reeling after Beck's little Hudson speech.

"You said 'for one,' what's the other thing?"

"Oh. Well, he's about to become a father. Emily is in her final trimester. If we started dating, I'd basically be signing up to be a dad."

Beck nods. "You've always talked about wanting kids. Is that a bad thing?"

"Well, no," I splutter. "I just don't know that I'm ready, and that baby deserves the absolute world."

"Is anyone ever ready to become a parent? You went to all those classes with Hudson, though, right?" I nod. "So you're probably more ready than a lot of people. And thinking that the baby deserves the world seems like a pretty good starting point."

"Okay, who are you and what have you done with my grumpy best friend?" I demand. "When did you turn into this?" I flail my hand around in front of him. "You're all wise and calm and shit. It's weird."

He laughs, taking another sip of his beer. "Being in love does weird things to you."

"Apparently," I agree. "You're over here, trying to save a whole city, giving sage advice."

He shrugs. "And you would be an excellent parent. You didn't need to have good ones to be a good one, Adrian."

I don't know what to say to that, so I go back to his previous statement wanting to clarify. "And who said anything about love?" I scoff, chugging the rest of my drink.

Beck smirks knowingly before finishing his as well. "We should get back to work. I'll miss working with you when I officially resign in July."

I smile, my excitement growing as I realize what he's saying.

I had almost forgotten what started this whole whirlwind of a conversation. "Thank you."

"No need to thank me when you've earned it. You deserve it, A. You deserve all of the good things. Don't let your head get in the way."

If only it was that simple.

HUDSON

ADRIAN

I'm going to be working late tonight so I'll be getting home after you.

HUDSON

Damn. Okay, thanks for the heads up. Do you want me to have your dinner ready when you get home?

ADRIAN

That's sweet, thank you. But I actually had another idea.

HUDSON

For dinner?

ADRIAN

For when I get home. Remember how you said you used to leave your door open during solo time, hoping I would catch you...

HUDSON

FUCK YES

ADRIAN

I'll be home at seven p.m. sharp.

HUDSON

Best. Idea. Ever.

I glance at the time: six fifty. Perfect. I'm already showered and naked on my bed with some toys and lube laid out next to me. I considered just jerking off because I'm impatient and I want to address my aching cock, but I want to really live out the fantasy I had countless times of Adrian catching me with a toy up my ass.

I can't believe he suggested this. I'm already desperate even thinking about him walking in. I don't know if he's going to pretend like he's just surprised I'm having fun without him or if he'll really play into the fantasy and act like he has no idea that I'm not straight, but either option sounds hot as fuck.

I decide that a butt plug is probably my best option. I can prep myself for him without getting myself so worked up that the fun ends before he can even begin. I've become far more accustomed to this process over the last few months, relaxing is easy, and I use my finger and some lube before moving to the smallest toy.

I take my time, although as I glance at the clock again, I guess it doesn't actually take long, working up to the biggest one. The whole time, I can't help but sneak glances at my door that's open a couple of inches. I left the hallway light on, liking the idea of having less warning that he was here. I'm on top of the covers, spread out, entirely naked on my bed, and even though I know I'm waiting for him, I close my eyes and try to sink into the fantasy.

I'm alone, playing with the toys I got with the hopes of one day hooking up with Adrian. I shift as I finally move a hand to my leaking cock, slowly spreading the precum around as I focus on the sensation on the plug filling me up, stretching me out. I let out a deep moan and wonder what Adrian would think if he were home, if he could hear me.

I want more, so I shift a hand to the base of the plug and slowly pull it back just a little before fucking it into me, shifting it around to try to really enjoy it. Another moan escapes my throat, not that I'm bothering to be quiet.

"What are you doing?" Adrian's voice cuts through my focus on how great that feels.

My eyes fly open to meet his where he's standing in the doorway. He sounded so confused that for a moment, I panic. Did I misunderstand his text? But then he smirks and winks at me, and I relax.

"I heard you moaning, and I thought that maybe you were hurt," he explains, tone just a little too dramatic to sound genuine. "Your door was open. I'm sorry. I didn't mean to intrude, but…" His voice trails off, and I wait, completely frozen as I stare at him for a moment.

But this whole fantasy-come-to-life thing is far too sexy for me to stay still for long. I give another slow stroke up my cock, and Adrian's gaze locks in on the motion, no longer looking surprised as his eyes fill with heat as though that one movement gave him permission to be here, to be a part of things. His focus shifts lower and one of his dimples pops as he smirks.

"Hudson Roy. Is that a plug in your ass?"

I nod, heat pooling low in my gut at the stern way he full-named me. I stay quiet, though, wanting to follow his lead.

"I had no idea that was something you enjoyed, but between the noises you were making and the way your huge cock is leaking right now, I'm going to guess you really like it. Is that correct?"

"Yes," I answer, sounding breathless already.

"Do you want me to leave?" he says slowly, taking a few steps closer as I shake my head. "Good. Because seeing you like this, splayed out on my guest room bed, with a plug up your ass while you play with your thick cock, has to be one of the most erotic things I've ever seen. I don't want to go. Do you want me to just watch? Or do you want me to show you what the real thing feels like?"

I nod eagerly at his suggestion. As hot as him watching me would be, my fantasy was always that he'd offer to join in. "I want you."

"Fuck, Hudson. You have no idea how much I've wanted to hear you say that." He pauses, moving to the edge of the bed. "But I don't know if we should jump right to fucking," he teases. "You were pretty reckless tonight, leaving the door open like that. What if I had brought friends home with me? Anyone could have found you like this."

"Fuck, I'm sorry. I shouldn't have done that. But I would only want you to find me like this. I only want you to show me what it would feel like to have a real cock in my ass."

His smug smile grows, and I might be begging now, but I'm loving every second of this. I know I'll only enjoy it more if he makes me work for it, if he bosses me around a bit first.

"Hmmm. I don't know," he says dismissively, gaze locked back on the plug inside me. "But your ass does look so tempting. I would just hate to reward such bad behavior."

"So don't—don't reward me. Use me. Teach me a lesson," I suggest hopefully. "Fuck me so hard that I won't ever forget to close my door again."

He chuckles. "Wow, Hudson. I had no idea you were so desperate for my cock."

"You have no idea."

He finally moves to undress before joining me on the bed, kneeling between my legs as he slowly gives me a once-over. "Do you promise to behave from now on?"

"Yes. I promise."

"If you ever need to be fucked, I want you to come to me directly. Got it? Don't risk anyone else finding you like I did tonight," he says sternly. It's so fucking hot. He can boss me around and put any claim on me that he'd like. I'm already his. I have been for a long time.

"Only you," I agree easily.

He finally drags his gaze from my ass to meet mine before saying, "Good boy." Fuuuuuck, why was that so hot? He better pick up the pace before I finish from his dirty talk alone. I swear Adrian knows exactly what to say to have me absolutely wild for him.

"Flip over. I want you on your hands and knees."

I eagerly follow his instructions, getting into position with my ass in the air for him. Eventually, he grabs the base of the plug and slowly pulls it back before teasing me with a few shallow advances back in. I bite my lip to prevent myself from complaining. I know that would only encourage him to draw this out even more.

After what feels like forever, Adrian fully removes the plug from inside me, and my ass clenches around nothing, seeking that feeling of fullness again. I manage to not even complain as I watch over my shoulder while he slowly puts a condom on.

Finally, *finally* Adrian positions himself between my legs, up on his knees as he lines up the tip of his dick with my hole. He pushes inside me in one agonizingly slow thrust, his perfect cock teasing my prostate in the best way. When he's fully inside me, he pauses, hands gripping my hips to hold me exactly where he wants me. "Are you ready to be taught your lesson? To find out what happens when you take unnecessary risks like you did tonight."

"Yes. I'm so ready."

He lets out a short laugh, muttering something under his breath that sounds like "perfect" as he pulls almost all the way out of me before slamming back in. He uses his grip on my hips to guide them back to meet each of his punishing thrusts, and I fucking love it.

Usually when we have sex, we're eager for each other, sure, and I really enjoy it when Adrian tells me what to do. But this is a whole new level. This is playing into my fantasy while also fulfilling ones I didn't even know I had. The way that he's fucking me, so much harder and rougher than I'm used to, is amazing.

Everything feels more passionate somehow, more desperate, as Adrian takes everything that he possibly can from me. And I want to give it to him. I want to give him everything. Each hard thrust has his cock teasing my prostate, sending me closer to my climax. The way he's using me right now, not only feels amazing physically, but also makes me feel so incredibly sexy, so desired.

I moan again, and Adrian echoes the sound. "Fuck, look at you," he pants. "You look like every fantasy I've ever had. Isn't this better than that silicone toy?"

I'm nodding before he even finishes. "So much better."

"Are you going to be a good boy and tell me when you need to be fucked again so you can forget all about those toys?"

"Yes. Of course. I promise." My voice sounds so wrecked and even that makes me feel sexier as I think about why it's that way, that Adrian has made me sound so thoroughly fucked.

"Good. Now prove to me how good you really are. Come for me," he demands as he continues to fuck me with his unrelenting pace. Apparently, that was all I needed, and my orgasm crashes into me without anything even touching my dick.

Holy fucking shit. I swear my eyes roll into the back of my head as I completely lose myself to the pleasure of my release. Adrian lets out a long moan as his movements falter, and he finishes inside the condom. I wish it wasn't there. I want to feel all of him. To have him truly claim me and mark me as his.

But I try not to focus on that when I know we aren't there yet. Hopefully soon.

He carefully pulls out and helps me reposition so I'm lying on the bed while avoiding the mess I just made of the sheets. When I'm settled, he disappears for a moment and returns with supplies to clean me up like he always does. I love how he always takes the time to take care of me after sex. Even though he calls it "hookups," the emotional bond between us feels stronger than ever.

He places a soft kiss on my temple as he wraps an arm around me. "You okay?"

"I'm amazing," I answer honestly. "That was even better than my fantasies."

"Me too," he admits. "Should we move to my bed so we don't accidentally roll onto your cum stains in the middle of the night?"

I chuckle. "Probably."

And after we settle in for the night, we fall asleep wrapped around each other like we do every night. I think I like that part even more than the sex.

ADRIAN

I don't want to brag—who am I kidding, yes I do—but this baby shower could be featured in magazines. Hudson has never cared about learning the gender of the baby, though I'm sure Emily knows since she's seen the ultrasounds and is basically a doctor, so everything has been very gender neutral. Obviously, everyone can be a hockey fan, so I've put together the most elaborate Werewolves themed baby shower I could.

There are signs that say "Welcoming The Newest Cub to the Pack" with the Werewolves logo and balloons everywhere in red, black, and white. With it being the playoffs and there being so many players in attendance, there's a huge array of healthy food options alongside the more fun ones for us nonprofessional athletes. My personal favorite is, of course, the giant chocolate fountain with fruit and other desserts to dip in it.

Everyone is dressed to the theme, easy enough when most of the people here basically live in Werewolves merch, and even though Hudson could afford to buy everything himself and asked people to donate to the adoption agency instead, people couldn't help themselves, and almost everyone brought something for

Emily, as well as an outfit or other small gift on top of their donations.

The party is in full swing, and as I look away from the conversation I'm having with some of the WAGs, it's like my gaze is a magnet drawn right to Hudson. He looks so happy, smiling as wide as I've ever seen as he talks to Clark, one of our D men, and his wife and son. That's the whole point of this, right? That Hudson is happy. I think today was so important for him. I know he's close with his team, but as their captain, I think he feels separate from them sometimes, and he forgets how much they all adore him. He might be retiring, but these men and their families aren't going anywhere.

He mentioned how hard it is for him to keep up with his hockey friends because of their busy schedules, but a lot of his ex-teammates are also retired, and a lot of them even came today. Everyone loves Hudson, and I'm so glad he can have this reminder of all the support that exists in his life before he starts this next chapter of parenthood.

He's going to be the best dad, I know that as a fact, but no one should have to face life alone. If he does decide that a relationship isn't what he actually wants from me when our current arrangement is done, I want him to remember that I'm not the only person who wants to be there for him.

I've been trying to repeat everything Beck said to me about Hudson's loyalty and about not letting my past get in my way. But anxieties aren't always logical, and as much as I try to pretend like my childhood wasn't a big deal, that I got over the way my parents so easily kicked me out of their life after ignoring me for so long, apparently, I'm not as unaffected as I'd hoped.

I just don't think I'll ever be able to believe that Hudson really wants to be with me while I'm the easiest option.

I've been calling it a crush for a long time, but I know I've been downplaying my feelings, even to myself. I'm in love with him. I have been for a long time, and our time being together physically has only made those feelings harder to ignore. He really is my dream man, a fantasy come to life. I used to think of Shelby as a black hole, sucking away the best parts of him and dimming his light. I'd like to think I could be the one to reflect it back at him, that our time as roommates has made us both happier people even though we haven't actually been together.

I know I've never been happier.

And I want to believe him when he says he wants to date me. I want that desperately. I haven't been able to stop myself from fantasizing about what life would look like if he really does still want to be with me and if I admitted how much I want that too.

But wanting it doesn't eliminate my concerns, so I need to continue on with our plan. I've tried so hard to not think of today as a possible celebration for a child that could someday be mine, but I couldn't help imagining myself at Hudson's side while opening presents instead of being the person who recorded who got him what gift. I pictured everyone also congratulating me, gushing over what a great dad I'll be, too.

Even if things do work out perfectly, and we do end up together after Hudson's had that time alone to figure things out, I know that wouldn't be any time soon. So, I'll continue in my role as supportive friend and keep the focus of today on Hudson.

It isn't hard when he's always my focus.

I just hope no one else catches on to the hearts that I can feel in my eyes every time I look at him.

That no one realizes just how in love with Hudson I am.

39

HUDSON

May

"And where does this go?" I ask, holding up a frilly looking… sheet? Maybe.

"That's the crib skirt," Adrian explains. "It goes under the mattress so it hangs around the edge, then you can't see under the crib."

"Right. God forbid we see that," I deadpan, earning a laugh from Adrian who's folding up all the clothes I got yesterday at the baby shower he threw with some of the WAGs. I had never been to a baby shower before, but Adrian made it very clear that it was a gender neutral, everyone-included event.

Still, I was surprised that every single player and their families showed up on our off day. I'm going to miss having that kind of support, but a lot of the moms assured me that they weren't going anywhere when I retire. I had to swear that I'd be joining their playgroup before they let me leave, and I didn't hesitate to agree.

Adrian had my parents video call in. He had offered to have them come in person, but my dad had a fever last week, and my mom was too anxious about the trip. I completely understood, and I thought it was really sweet that Adrian had put that much effort in. Apparently, he even helped them pick out a gift, a video baby monitor that he helped my mom set up on her phone so she can check on the baby when she wants to so she can feel like a part of things.

I got a little choked up when he was explaining that to me. Looking at the camera now, where it's already in place above the crib, has me emotional for a different reason. I can't believe today is finally here.

The day I have been both excitedly counting down to and absolutely dreading.

I'm moving into my house.

Honestly, it probably could have happened sooner. Project-wise, things wrapped up a couple of weeks ago, but Adrian was still tweaking things, and the first round of the play-offs ended up being way longer than we'd all hoped, needing all seven games for us to advance. Moving in the middle of that would have been a mess.

Moving in the middle of the play-offs during a winning season is insane from a superstition standpoint in the first place. And believe me, I've contemplated using that excuse to stay with Adrian for even longer, but as much as I have absolutely loved every moment of us physically being together, I'm also desperate for him to admit that what we have is so much more than a hookup arrangement between roommates.

I refuse to use the L word, even to myself, until I'm ready to say it to him, and until I think he might be ready to hear it, but I'm convinced that Adrian is it for me. He's the person I was always meant to end up with, and as strange as it may be, I think the only reason I ever married Shelby was so I could end up here, about to adopt a baby, hopefully with Adrian at my side.

And we were able to win this round in only five games, so I'm using my few days off to move into my new house.

Well, I didn't do any of the moving. I can't risk getting injured because I lift a box the wrong way, but Adrian has organized for the few things I'd ended up with in the divorce to be moved in here, and has furnished the rest of the house perfectly.

The only room with anything left to be done is the nursery, and that's only because Adrian insisted I should be the one "nesting" to prepare for the baby to come.

So that's what we're doing tonight: *nesting*.

I'm just glad Adrian agreed to help. I want him to want to do all these parenting things with me because I really believe he is going to be this baby's other dad. He's thinking about ways to include my parents from another state, and he's picked out everything in this farm themed, gender-neutral nursery.

I really think he wants to be a part of this family he's helping build, he just isn't ready to admit it because he's afraid it could be taken away from him, or maybe that he doesn't belong in it. Whatever the reason, I think it has to do with his shitty parents, and if it wouldn't risk my adoption on the off chance they started a fight they wouldn't win, I probably would have flown to Arkansas by now to give them a piece of my mind about just how horrible they are.

But today is the first step in convincing him that he not only deserves whatever happiness he can find in this world but that he absolutely has a place front and center in my family if he's willing to take it.

That, even if he doesn't, or even if he needs years before he's ready, that spot will always be there.

Adrian has shown me exactly what I've been missing with my other partners in the past. Being with him has made me the happiest I've ever been, and completely ruined me for anyone else. So, if he does walk away when this arrangement ends, I have no plans to replace him.

"Okay, that's the last of it," he exclaims. "You got so many cute outfits! I separated everything by size, so the top drawers have the bibs, hats, and socks. Below that is newborn onesies in this drawer, with shorts in the same size next to that. Zero to three months in the bottom drawers. The outfits are hung up in the closet, also by size, with the size labeled hanger separating them."

"You're amazing," I reply, unable to keep my adoration out of my tone.

He laughs, waving it off. "It was fun. The crib looks like it's ready too. I think the nursery is done! What do you think?"

I look around, taking in the mural of a barn on one wall with little farm animals surrounding it, the baby monitor, the piggy bank that has "Roy" painted on the side, and the humidifier that's shaped like a chicken. All the little touches Adrian added make this feel like the ideal room to bring a baby home to.

"I think it's perfect," I say honestly. "Thank you. This whole house is amazing, but this room… It's really special. It makes it feel so real, ya know? The baby will be here so soon. I couldn't have done any of it without you, thank you."

His dimples are on full display as he smiles. "I'm glad you like it." We both spend a minute admiring the room before Adrian sighs. "I guess this is it, huh? You're moving out, we're no longer roommates, and our arrangement is over."

I've been trying to focus on the positive, the next steps, but in this moment, I'm not ready. "I mean, I think we're still room-mates today, since I woke up in your house," I suggest, sounding desperate even to myself, but I don't care.

He lets out a short laugh. "So, what does that mean? We can hook up one last time?"

I shrug, trying to sound casual even as I plead with my eyes. "If you want to."

He bites his lip. Glancing around before he lets out a short laugh. "Not in the nursery. Do you even have condoms and lube here yet?"

"I was optimistic," I explain with a nod.

He smirks. "Get them. Do whatever you want to clean up and meet me in the kitchen. My first meal here is going to be your ass." He spins, casually leaving the room like that wasn't the hottest thing anyone has ever said to me.

40

ADRIAN

$\mathcal{I}$ take a deep breath, splashing some water on my face at the kitchen sink trying to get my act together.

This could be the last time I have sex with Hudson.

I hope it isn't.

As I was washing all the clothing in infant detergent and folding it to put away by size, I was daydreaming about it being my turn to wake up in the middle of the night to feed and change the baby. Clearly, my fantasies have evolved beyond sexual ones since I've gotten to turn those into reality.

But there's the very real chance that tonight could be my last opportunity to have sex with him. So many things could change between us after he moves out. I need to appreciate tonight for what it is, to take advantage of the opportunity he offered by suggesting it.

Still, I couldn't fuck him in his new bed. That felt too... sacred. Like the beginning of something, rather than its potential end.

Apparently, I thought that the kitchen was a good alternative.

I guess we'll find out.

"So should I bend over the side of the table… or?" Hudson asks, pulling my attention back to the present. I guess that he's still able to sneak up on me in his house, too.

I turn to face where he's casually leaning against one of the chairs, wearing only a towel tucked around his waist. There's a bottle of lube and a few condoms on the table next to him. He's easily the most attractive man I've ever seen, and even after all this time, I can't believe that I've had sex with him and that he's asking me to fuck him again.

"You could," I agree. "But the table has a 600 pound weight capacity. I was picturing you laying on your back with your legs bent up while I sit in one of the chairs at the seat below you where I can lean in and eat you out."

He's already climbing onto the table before I finish, laying the towel down below him.

"One second, let me grab you a pillow." I quickly walk into the living room and borrow a throw pillow, bringing it back to place on the table under his head as he lies down fully.

He smiles. "You always take such good care of me."

I have no idea what to say to that, so I lean in for a kiss, letting it linger as I try not to worry about how many kisses we have left.

When I finally pull away, it's only because I'm already painfully hard, and I can't wait to advance things any longer. I take a seat at the chair positioned between his legs, just like I suggested, and he lifts his head to look down his muscular body at me. He winks and something in my chest squeezes.

I can't look at his perfect face right now; I'm far too close to admitting how I really feel, to saying I'm madly in love with him and we can forget all about my plan. But I promised myself I wouldn't do that, that I would give him the space to move out and decide what he really wanted on his own.

If there's any chance I'll ever believe that we belong together, I need to set him free first.

So I lean in and pour all the things I'm not ready to say into my actions, into hopefully making him feel as good as I possibly can. I don't hold back as I lick and suck around his hole, making the shapes and letters and patterns with my tongue that I've learned over our time together get the biggest reaction from him.

He's quickly moaning and panting and begging for more. I love it. I love knowing that I'm the one earning each of those cries, that I'm the one in control of his pleasure.

When he's relaxed enough, I fuck into him with my tongue, and the moan he lets out sounds like it's straight out of a cheesy porn film.

I slowly add a finger with my tongue, continuing to open him up as he moans for more. I switch to lube, adding more fingers, and far too quickly, he's begging for my dick.

This is it.

"I need to take off my clothes. Get off the table now and bend over it so I can fuck you, but don't forget the pillow," I instruct. The table is low enough that with him bent over, it should be the perfect angle. And yes, I might have considered that when I chose it. Who wouldn't?

He hurries to get off the table, bending over in front of me as I slowly remove my shirt, and then my pants and underwear. The whole time he's bent over, he's squirming, his ass shifting back and forth, seeking me to fill him up. It's such a fucking power trip to know how desperate he is for me.

When I'm naked, I trail my hand up and down his spine, stopping before I get to his hole. The whimper he makes is the sweetest sound. "Adriaaaan, please."

"Please, what?" I tease.

"Fuck me!" he demands.

And as much as I want to, I can't help but tease him a little more, making a tsking sound as I round the table instead. "But you didn't listen to me."

He whips his head in my direction. "What?"

"You didn't listen," I repeat. "I told you to bring the pillow, and you left it all the way over here." I hold it up, now on the opposite end of the table. "Maybe you don't really want me to fuck you."

His jaw drops open, and he stares at me in disbelief. "I absolutely want you to fuck me."

I smirk. "Ask me again. Beg me to fuck you. Maybe if you do it nicely enough, I'll forgive you."

We both know that I'm going to fuck him regardless of what he says, as long as it isn't "no." He's told me countless times by now how hot it is when I boss him around, when I make him beg for it.

And tonight, more than any other night, maybe a part of me needs to hear it. Needs to hear him begging for my cock, begging for me.

Maybe I'm just desperate for anything that might help me believe that it could be true.

"Please, Adrian. I need you. I'm so sorry I didn't listen, will you please fuck me? Pretty please, Charming, I need you to stretch me out and fill me up. I want to picture your dick so far up my ass that I see stars every time I try to eat at this table."

I smile at that thought, round the table again, and grab the condoms and bottle of lube on my way until I'm standing behind him. I open a condom, put it on and slick up my dick with lube before I give his ass any attention. When I finally do tease him with my tip, he rocks back, trying to force me inside of him.

I tsk again. "Hudson, you're such a bad listener tonight," I tease.

"Please, Adrian, baby, I need you."

I freeze, my heart squeezing at the new endearment. He's never called me that before. It's always "Charming" or "Prince" or my name. Which he said with "baby," so he definitely meant it for me.

"I'm sorry. I'll be good, now. Please fuck me."

I don't know what to think after he called me that, but I'm done teasing him. I finally line my dick up with his lubed-up hole and slowly push in.

Despite his promises, he isn't "good," and in almost no time at all, he's rocking back to meet every thrust as I hold onto his hips like my life depends on it. He feels incredible squeezed around my cock. It doesn't matter how many times we've done this, somehow each time, it seems to blow my mind even more with just how amazing it is to be inside of him, how perfectly we manage to fit together.

The sounds he makes are intoxicating. "Right there," "so good," and "oh my god." Each moan or cry sends me closer and closer to the edge. His knuckles are white where he's gripping the edge of the table, using his hold to push himself back onto me with even more force. It's too much, feels too good.

I don't want it to be over. I want to live in this moment, live inside him, forever. But I'm only human, and his ass is squeezing me like it's begging for my release. Hopefully those noises mean he's as close as I am.

When I can't possibly hold back any longer, I reach around to grasp his leaking cock. "Come for me," I command, and on the first stroke, his release is covering my hand and the towel still on the table.

His ass clenches impossibly tighter around my dick as he comes, dragging out my orgasm at last as I continue to thrust into him.

I never want it to end, but far too quickly it's over, I'm pulling out, and tying off the condom. I get us both cleaned up in a daze. It's really happening. Hudson isn't going to come home with me.

We no longer live together.

As I'm pulling my clothes back on, Hudson, still standing there completely naked, is the first to talk. "I was thinking we could test out the TV in my room too, see if it's at an okay angle to watch from the bed."

I shake my head, trying to focus. As great as it would be to keep pretending, to continue with the excuses, that would just be more of the same, more of making myself the convenient option for him.

I let myself have tonight, honestly because I was too weak to say no, but if there's any chance we can do this again, I need to stop doing what's easy.

"I need to go," I finally tell him with a sad smile.

His face falls, but he nods. "Okay, yeah. That was the deal. Can I walk you out at least?"

"You're naked," I remind him with a soft laugh as I shake my head.

"So?"

"So, I'll see you around. Have a good game Sunday." I try to turn to leave, but Hudson rushes forward to grab my hand.

"Hey, don't do that," he says. "Don't pretend like this is the end."

I shrug, desperately trying not to get my hopes up.

"Nothing has changed, Adrian. I still want to be with you. Unless something has changed for you? Do… Do you want this to be the end?"

I offer him my truth, or at least some of it, letting out a soft "No" as I shake my head. I'm not ready to admit just how much I want to be with him aloud, but I can say that much.

He smiles triumphantly. "Good. Then this is just a new chapter for us. The one where I woo you."

I can't help it, a surprised laugh escapes from my throat. "Woo me?"

"Yup!" he answers confidently. "I know I messed up the order of things by doing all the physical stuff first, not that I regret any of that, obviously. But now I get to convince you that I'll still want you without any of that. I'm excited."

And despite myself, and all the reservations and anxiety I have over what's going to happen next for us, I let his excitement rub off on me, just a bit, smiling for real before I squeeze the hand that he's still holding and go up on my toes to kiss his cheek.

"I hope so," I whisper before I turn and leave to spend the first night without Hudson as my roommate in almost ten months.

APPARENTLY, wooing involves a lot of chocolates. And coffee. At least once a day, some sort of gift shows up at my desk or door. And Hudson hasn't pulled back from talking to me at all, it's just more over the phone than it used to be. When he's been at his away games during his downtime, he's suggested watching the same show together while we're on the phone, or even just asks to stay on the phone with me while I'm working so that we can "hang out." He's still the first person I talk to every day and the last one before I fall asleep at night.

When he's in town, he still invites me over to watch our favorite design shows, and it's like we're back in the early days of our friendship, on opposite sides of the couch. Except now, when our eyes meet, Hudson looks at me like I'm special, like he feels lucky to have me sitting on the other end of his sectional.

And every time he does, it feels like a brick is removed from the walls I've been hiding behind, so desperate to protect myself.

Do I really need protecting from him? I know I'll never recover if he changes his mind, but that voice of fear is getting quieter and quieter with every passing day. With every meal his chef still prepares for me and still delivers to my house. With every order of food from our favorite restaurant he gets us at any given opportunity. With every time I hear his voice on the other end of my phone or see his name light up the screen.

Some days it's hard to hear that voice of doubt at all.

I know I'd wanted to give him space, but he's putting in so much effort to eliminate any that it's hard to resist.

"I can't wear this!" I say to my friends as we make our way over to the boxes from the offices where they met me. His latest present arrived today via a very nervous equipment assistant. I swear Hudson has no concern for rumors. Inside the plain bag was a new-to-me, game-worn jersey from Hudson with instructions to wear it to tonight's game.

"You have to: a player gave it to you and told you to wear it," Beck insists seriously. "Not wearing it would be like asking for us to lose tonight. Do you want to be the reason the Werewolves don't get the cup this year?"

My other friends are all smirking at how intense he is, or maybe at the thought of me wearing this giant jersey that's basically Hudson staking his claim on me, but they all nod and murmur agreements. I've told them all by now that we were hooking up when we lived together, but that we're reevaluating everything now that things have changed. Beck so kindly translated that to them all, explaining Hudson wants to date me, and I'm apparently "too hard on myself to believe him." They've all been trying to convince me that his constant texting and various gifts have meant I should give in.

And obviously, I want to. But I need to know this is more than just a challenge for him to win, too. I know how competitive he can be.

Excuses? Who me?

"This is huge on me, and someone is going to say something," I insist.

"No one said anything when you lived with the man and went to public adoption classes with him for months. Everyone in this arena is going to be in Werewolves merch tonight. You're special to all of us, A. But you aren't that special," Lincoln teases.

I stick my tongue out at him playfully. Who let him be in our group anyway?

"Fine. I'll wear it. But if they lose, or I'm in some gossip magazine tomorrow, I'm blaming all of you."

We get to the Caldwell owner's box without incident, and despite how crowded it is, no one in there even bats an eye at what I'm wearing.

"See, A. You're fine," Oakley reassures me before heading to get food.

"I hate when Lincoln is right," I mutter, crossing my arms.

Jordan laughs. "Yeah, but unfortunately he usually is."

The warning buzzer sounds, and we all squeeze out onto the balcony. I'm small enough that people easily let me past to claim our normal seats at the front of the box, and eventually my friends follow.

"He won't even know that I wore it," I grumble as they announce the starting lineup.

"I think it's sweet," Cody insists with his signature smile.

And apparently the jersey wasn't the only gesture tonight.

To my absolute shock and horror, Hudson blows a fucking kiss at our box after he scores.

I'm pretty sure most people missed it, and no one would have any way of knowing that he was directing it at me, but I know. My friends see it, and they know. And it's all any of them talk about for the rest of the night.

Luckily, I manage to stay out of the gossip columns, although there is a picture of Hudson blowing that kiss with speculation as to what "mystery fan" it was intended for. As far as I know, no one caught on that I was actually wearing his jersey, but Hudson definitely knew, and he insisted I keep it when I asked if he wanted it back.

I've been wearing it around the house nonstop. But he doesn't know that part.

HUDSON

Somehow, we manage to win all four of the first games against Nashville in the conference finals. I'm exhausted, but as I pull out my phone in the away locker room, the ten missed calls from Adrian, Emily, Holly, and an unknown number immediately have me on high alert.

I hesitate for a moment, but call Emily first, she picks up on the third ring. "Baby is fine, I'm fine," she says in greeting, but that isn't exactly the most reassuring greeting.

"What happened? I didn't even check my voicemail, I just saw all the missed calls."

"Sorry about that."

"Oh my god, is that him? Does he need me to pick him up at the airport? Hudson, get your ass over here!" Adrian shouts in the background.

"Why are you with Adrian? Where are you?"

"I'm at the hospital," she says casually. "And no rush, but you can come if you'd like. I'm technically in labor, but it could be a while with the induction. I've been trying to explain that to Adrian, but I think he would feel better if you were here."

"You're in labor? But it's too soon, you're not due until next month after the play-offs," I insist, aware that I sound stupid; if she says she's in labor, she is, but I'm so shocked I don't know what else to say.

"My blood pressure was high at my appointment today, so they had me come here for extra testing. My kidney function is still okay, so they aren't calling it preeclampsia, but my blood pressure is still high so they still admitted me to monitor both the baby and I, and they've recommended I be induced."

"I'm still in Nashville, but we're going straight to the airport from here. I'll be there as soon as I can—"

"Everybody hurry up and get your asses on the bus!" Ollie shouts from his spot next to me where he's obviously heard my side of the conversation. "Hudson's baby is coming!"

I smile, nodding at my teammates in thanks as the locker room erupts in applause. "It'll be a few hours, but I'll see you soon."

Traveling home seems to take an eternity, but once we've landed, the team lets me off first to another round of applause, and I get to the hospital in record time. With how late it is, the streets are pretty clear, but I also might ignore a few speed limits.

I check in at the desk, explaining that my baby is on the way, and the security guard escorts me to the elevator and scans their badge to get me to the correct floor. I have to check in again specifically with the labor and delivery people, this time showing my ID and getting a bracelet that I need to keep on at all times. If I don't and try to leave with the baby, it will apparently set off all sorts of alarms.

By the time a nurse shows me to Emily's room, I've been stressed out, adrenaline way too high for hours, and I feel like it's a huge accomplishment that I even made it here. I'm expecting to walk into chaos, but Emily and Adrian are laughing as I enter the room. I look around, no one else is in here, and they're just... watching a movie?

Adrian jumps up when he sees me. "Oh thank god, you made it!"

I look around again. Emily appears to be hooked up to a lot of monitors, but other than that, everything seems pretty chill.

"I thought there would be more happening," I admit, and Emily laughs.

"Sorry to disappoint. I've been trying to explain to Adrian that even though they started the medication for the induction, it can be a long process. Especially with this being a first pregnancy. As long as my blood pressure stays where it's at, and the baby's heart rate remains strong, we could be here for a couple of days before they're born."

"Oh." I let out a sigh of relief and feel my entire body relax. Adrian takes my arm and guides me to sit down on the couch next to him. "Thanks for being here. I wasn't sure if you would want to."

He squeezes my arm. "Of course. That's part of the reason I didn't travel with the team this week. I thought someone should be in town if Emily needed anything, and obviously you can't be." His admission makes my heart feel too big for my chest. Adrian can claim we need space all he'd like, that I was the one acting like we were in a relationship when we weren't, but him staying here when I can't feels very much like something a partner would do. "She called me when you didn't answer, and I knew you were in the middle of your game, so I offered to come keep her company."

I can't hold back, I pull him in for a tight hug, relaxing even more when he wraps his arms around me to squeeze me back. "Thank you."

When we pull apart, way too soon for my liking, he shrugs. "Of course."

"Come on, Charming, don't do that. Don't dismiss how

amazing you are." He blushes, and it's so adorable. I want to kiss his cheeks, to pull him back into my arms and never let go.

Emily clears her throat, reminding me that we aren't alone. "Well, you two are as cute as ever, but now that you're here, Hudson, we should probably try to sleep. It could be a long couple of days."

"Is it okay if we stay? I mean, you don't have to, Adrian, I just…"

"One of you can take the recliner and the other the couch if you'd like. The couch folds down into more of a bed."

Adrian nods. "I'm not going anywhere if you don't want me to. I also put your go-bag in the closet there if you'd like to change."

I smile at him, prepared as always, and when I open the closet, I see that there's a bag for him as well.

He wants this, I have to believe he does, even if he's afraid to say it.

"I'M SORRY, Emily, I know you were hoping to avoid surgery, but the baby's heart is decelerating and you're still only a couple of centimeters dilated," Kathy, Emily's midwife, confirms. "I warned Dr. Owen before I came in here, and I'm sure she's watching the monitor. Let me see if she's secured the OR."

"What does that mean?" I ask, panicked even though they both seem so calm. Emily got an epidural about two hours ago, thank god. Before that, the pain seemed like an absolute nightmare, and she's been calm since, but words like *surgery* and *deceleration* seem like reasons to be more concerned, right?

Adrian is standing quietly at my side, but he reaches out to take my hand, grounding me with his steady support.

Kathy is on her phone, probably talking to this Dr. Owen person, so Emily answers. "See the baby's heart rate on the monitor there." She points to the wave I've been watching all day. "They're okay right now, but the contractions are putting too much stress on them. We're going to have to switch to a C-section. It'll be okay, though, you should even be able to come into the OR if you'd like."

I nod, but my throat feels tight. This is really happening. Today is the day. I'm going to meet my baby *today*.

That shouldn't be so surprising when we're in a hospital literally waiting for them to be born, but the due date wasn't for three weeks, and Emily said that the induction could take a couple of days. I thought I had more time.

"Okay! Dr. Owen is on her way to the OR. Dad, you are welcome to join us, but it's showtime!"

The nurses all jump into action, unplugging things and grabbing equipment, reattaching Emily to what seems like portable monitors.

"What about Adrian?" I ask desperately.

He squeezes my hand. "I won't leave. I'll go as far as they'll let me."

"You can come with us to the pre-op area and help him get into scrubs if you'd like," one of the nurses says as she starts to move Emily's bed. "But only one support person is allowed in the OR, sorry."

"Thank you." Adrian nods, squeezing my hand again. "See, I'll be right in pre-op. You got this."

Getting to the OR is a blur, and before I know it, someone is handing me a set of scrubs. "It'll be a few minutes while we get everything prepared and confirm the epidural placement before you can join us. Put the scrubs on over what you're wearing if you can, otherwise there's a curtain here if you need privacy. I'll come and get you when we're ready. Don't touch anything in the operating room, and if you feel dizzy or faint at all, go toward the exit door and sit on the ground. I won't have you passing out into my sterile field, got it?"

I nod. I got this. I think.

Adrian hands me the scrubs as I pull them on, helping me fit a scrubcap hairnet thing on my head and booties over my shoes. And then, we wait. I try to focus on deep breathing, but I can't stand still, fidgeting as I think about everything that's happening, what today means, that I'll be bringing a baby home with me when I leave, how I wish Adrian was planning to come home with me, too.

He grabs my hand again, rubbing his thumb soothingly as he looks up at me. "Hey, everything is fine. You'll be the very best dad."

I nod, but I can't help voice some of my concern. "How do you know?"

He lets out a soft laugh. "You've done everything you can to prepare, and you're the best person I know. This kid is so lucky to have you." He smiles, and his dimples soothe some of my anxiety. I feel like I can take a full breath for the first time since Kathy mentioned surgery.

But my heart rate picks up again when Adrian adds, "Anyone would be lucky to have you." He's staring up at me with so much adoration and longing, and I'm sick of acting like we don't want to be together, as if Adrian isn't the very best thing that's ever happened to me.

I know that the nurse could come back at any moment, but I have to ask. "What about you?"

Adrian's brows scrunch together as he asks, "What about me?"

I'm done holding back. "You said 'anyone would be lucky to

have me.' Well, what about you?" I ask, voice cracking a little, but I force myself to go on, to tell him everything I'm feeling so he can't brush me off again.

"Adrian, I only want you. I want you to be there for everything, every day. I love that you beat me to the hospital. I love that you were there at every adoption meeting and class, that you got to hear the heartbeat with me, even if it was over the phone. Not because you were helping me out, but because we got to share those things. I love that my memories of this adoption process all include you."

His jaw has fallen open, but he doesn't stop me. "You know how much I want to be a dad, how excited I am that it's actually happening, but it doesn't feel right to think about taking the baby home without you being there to share that moment with. I appreciate every ounce of support you've offered me, but I don't want you there just to help me. You're easily the most helpful person I've ever met, but that isn't why I want you there."

"Then why…?" he asks quietly, blinking up at me still looking confused.

I shake my head. "Adrian, I want you there so that when the baby smiles for the first time, we can both experience that, together. I don't want to call you or text you about the milestones, about how our days were. I want you right there with me cheering them on as things happen. I want to already know every detail of your day as we fall asleep in the same bed together because I was there for it all."

I take his other hand, squeezing them. "I want us to be a family. You said this kid is lucky to have me? Well, I think they would be even luckier to have you. You're the very best thing that's happened to me, and I wouldn't be here today, about to become a dad, if it wasn't for you. I thought I would have more time before the baby was here for more grand gestures, but this is it. And I don't think those were working anyway, because proving to you that you're my first choice isn't about those things."

"It isn't?" he asks in that same confused tone, but his mouth is tilting up the faintest amount in the corners.

"No, because being with someone isn't about big grand gestures. I think it's about all the boring little moments that aren't actually boring because you're with the other person, and being with them makes everything better. You make everything better, Adrian."

He's smiling now, a hint of those dimples peeking through, giving me hope. "I do?"

I nod, my own smile taking over my face. I think this might actually be working, but I'm not done. "Do you remember when I asked you early on why you thought you didn't deserve for people to be nice to you, to take care of you? That it seemed like you're always helping everyone else with no one to look out for you."

He nods, still smiling.

I move a hand to cup his cheek. "Well, now I'm asking if you think you don't deserve to be loved? Because I'm here, begging you to let me be that person, and I'm telling you that you deserve it. That I would like to spend the rest of my life proving to you that you'll always be my number one choice. You are so much more than a convenient option. You're the only option for me. Other than this baby, you're it for me, Adrian. Whether you believe me today or five years from now, my answer won't change, because I'm completely in love with you."

ADRIAN

"**Y**ou love me?" I repeat.

I'm trying to let the words sink in. To really take in everything Hudson just said to me.

I think he's right. The big gestures have only made me more nervous, given me more reasons to believe he only wants to be with me because I'm making him chase me, that when I finally admit how much I want to be with him, he'll feel like he's won and no longer care.

But the little moments? The way his face lit up when he saw me in Emily's hospital room, every time he sends me a picture excited about some tiny detail he's discovered I added to his house that I knew he would love. The fact that his entire body visibly relaxed when they said I could come down here with him, and the way he's been clutching my hand like I'm the only thing giving him comfort as he waits to meet his baby.

Those things add up. They mean something.

They aren't for show. They can't be faked.

And he isn't asking to just date me. He's talking about forever. He said he loves me.

"Of course I love you, Adrian. I've been calling you Prince

Charming for years, and I'm sorry it took me so long to realize I wanted you to be my happily ever after."

I can't help it; I burst out laughing. "Oh my god, that was so cheesy."

He beams back at me. "But you're smiling. Did it work? Have I convinced you that I'm in love with you?" His eyes are lit up, full of so much hope. That isn't for show.

That's for me, because he wants to be with me.

Because he loves me.

I can't believe I've been pushing him away. I wasn't protecting myself. I was hurting us both. The final bricks of my walls disappear, and my heart is his for the taking.

I bite my lip, but give up trying to fight off my own equally cheesy grin. "I can't believe I'm saying this, but I think it did."

He joins in laughing with me. "Really?"

I nod. "I love you too, Hudson. I'm sorry I ever doubted you. I've just been so afraid to hope for that future if it could be taken away."

He moves his other hand so he can hold both sides of my face. "It's yours if you want it. I'm not going anywhere."

I nod, still kind of shocked that this is happening, but I believe him. I trust Hudson, and if he says he loves me, then I think it's okay to admit how much I love him too. If he says that I deserve to be happy, then maybe I do.

Maybe I can have everything I've ever dreamed about.

"Can I kiss you?"

I nod again, and his lips on mine feel like home. Kissing Hudson makes everything he's promising feel real. Like I can really have my very own happily ever after.

"We're ready for you. You'll need to scrub in," the nurse interrupts, and we jump away from each other.

We're both smiling as our gazes meet though.

"I'll see you soon, then?" Hudson says nervously.

I nod. "Go meet our baby."

THE C-SECTION WENT PERFECTLY ACCORDING to the nurse who came out to update me. And despite her being three weeks early, our perfect little girl was born without any complications and doesn't even need to spend any time in the NICU.

Hudson and Emily had spoken ahead of time and agreed on skin-to-skin time with Emily immediately after the delivery, so she's cuddled on her chest when the nurses push her bed back into the post-op area. I immediately burst into tears, and Hudson comes over, wrapping his arms around me from behind to kiss the top of my head before I approach her and wrap her little fingers around my thumb.

"Congratulations, you two," Emily says. "I kind of feel like I get to say, 'I told you so,' but is that rude?"

I laugh. "Thank you. Did Hudson say something, or?"

"Oh, he announced it to the whole OR. It's probably a good thing you had that mask on so none of them could recognize you, Mr. Professional Athlete," she jokes.

"Oh shit, I didn't even think about that," Hudson admits, also laughing. "I don't care who knows though."

I spin to look at him. "Um, I care. If you guys lose the cup, I'm not having the fans blaming me; you know how superstitious people are!"

He shrugs. "I have everything I need now. I don't care if we win."

I playfully slap him. "Well, I do! You might be retiring, but I'm about to get promoted. I want to be president for a cup-winning team, not boring old conference champions."

"I'll do my best," he promises with a wink.

And he does. A couple of days later, we get to bring baby Emily home. Hudson asked Emily if he could give our daughter her mother's name so she knows how grateful he is that she brought her into the world, which she tearfully agreed to, and then the next day, he was suiting up for the finals.

He didn't actually want to leave us at home, and if I hadn't agreed to move in with him before we ever left the hospital, I don't think he would have. But I insisted he finish out the season, and that I could stay with our daughter for a few hours, and he finally agreed.

Six games later, they did it. And Oliver scored the winning goal. The Werewolves officially won the cup, and Oliver celebrated by kissing his boyfriend in front of all the cameras. Apparently, the guy is a fan who Oliver hit it off with after he won a contest earlier in the season.

And baby Em got to sit in the Stanley Cup. Hudson insisted I be the one holding her so he could get a picture of "all of his favorite things."

It's proudly displayed in multiple rooms in our house.

And every time I see it, it's another one of those little reminders that he loves me. That I'm one of his favorite things, and all of this—the perfect man, the dream house, the sweetest baby in the world, are mine. That I'm a part of this family.

That I deserve to be happy.

Hudson
Seven Months Later

"I can't believe you convinced them to move into your condo," I say to Adrian for probably the hundredth time this week.

"Everything is very wheelchair accessible. And you know how much your dad lights up whenever Em is on the screen during our calls."

"Yeah, but I've been trying to convince them to come to Chicago for years. Even before Em was born, they still wouldn't even consider it. Now that I'm with you, they suddenly need to live on the same street as me?"

"What can I say, Em and I are very persuasive."

"Thank you. Just when I think I have everything I could ever want, you somehow manage to make my life even better."

He's organized everything to be moved from their house, installed all the assistive equipment that my dad needs, and he's already set up my old room as a craft room for my mom. I know they'll love it here. With my dad's restrictions, they rarely left the house in Minnesota if they weren't going to a doctor's appointment, and now Adrian has my mom talking about taking Em to the park and enjoying all the shops and things she can walk to while my dad naps or is with his new nurses.

Adrian even organized to have my dad's nurses in Minnesota travel here for two weeks to help train his new ones. They'll make a ton of overtime during the trip to hopefully cover any time between placements, and Adrian helped us write glowing letters recommending them.

The medical van pulls up first. Even though my mom's van is adapted to fit his chair, we all felt better having him make the trip with medical staff, and my mom pulls up a few minutes later.

"Oh my god! My babies!" she shrieks as she gets out of the car. She quickly checks in with my dad before turning to us. "I can't believe we're really here!" She runs up to hug Adrian first, kissing his cheek before she takes Em from my arms. "Well, aren't you just the sweetest? Who's the luckiest grandma in the entire world? I am!" she coos between kisses.

"Hi, Mom," I cut in for my own hug.

"Hello, sweetie. Obviously I'm excited to see you, too!" she assures me.

"Uh-huh." I tease. "I know I'm not the favorite anymore; it's okay. I was at the top for over thirty years. I can handle third place now."

"Third?" Adrian laughs.

"Did you not see her hug you before Em, even? I'm definitely third."

"Oh, stop it, I love you all equally," she insists with a laugh. But I don't miss the wink she aims at Adrian.

I love it.

And as my mom helps my dad hold my daughter for our first family picture all in Chicago, I make sure Adrian is front and center, right next to them.

None of this would exist without him.

He really is the best thing that's ever happened to me, and looking at the pure joy on his face as my mom refers to us as "her sons" to the person who drove my dad here, I think he might finally believe us when we tell him how special he is.

EPILOGUE TWO

Adrian
A Few Months After That

"I can't believe it actually worked," I say, squeezing Hudson's arm as he holds up the thick envelope from the Illinois records offices.

"I'm so happy we got to do it all together."

A couple of days after we brought Em home from the hospital, after the first home visit from the adoption agency, Hudson asked if I would be interested in petitioning to be officially added to Em's adoption. He'd already spoken to Emily and an adoption attorney, and I eagerly agreed, even if I wasn't sure that it would be possible.

Emily had terminated all parental rights with the intention of Hudson adopting her baby, and that didn't change, but the adoption isn't official until months of home visits and further paperwork after the baby is already living with the adoptive parent.

So, after Hudson made an official announcement to the press at the championship parade that he couldn't wait to celebrate with his boyfriend and daughter, we petitioned to have me added to the adoption. And apparently, all those adoption classes I attended, home visits and interviews I was a part of before she was ever born, made adding me a lot easier, because the judge approved our adoption.

After everything with Ollie's dramatic coming out announcement during the season, and the fact that Hudson was already retired, the news of him dating a man went over pretty well. The fact that two queer players won the cup and proudly celebrated with their same-sex partners was celebrated by hockey fans and LGBTQIA+ members and allies everywhere. Hudson hasn't publicly claimed a label, and privately, we've talked about how he doesn't feel like he needs one. He loves me and that's all he seems to really care about.

Hudson's parents are with us today too. We made sure to add a ramp for his dad as soon as they agreed to move here, so he can get around the main level at least, and his mom is holding Emily. I'm glad that they're here for this: our little family doesn't feel complete without them.

Hudson carefully opens the envelope and pulls out the document, tears shining in his eyes as he reads Emily's new birth certificate. "We're officially her parents."

My vision blurs as I see my name right there with Hudson's.

It's real. I'm Emily's dad. Not just Hudson's partner, as much as I love claiming that title, I also love having this tie to her. It feels so official.

"Thank you," I tell him, fighting the tightness in my throat. "For everything, and for letting me be a part of all this."

He puts the document down to wrap his arms around me. "You aren't just a part of it, baby. You're the whole reason we get to have any of this. Thank you."

I let the tears fall. They're happy tears anyway, so why should I fight them?

It's real, this family of mine, and it's so much better than I could have ever dreamed.

THE END

LOOKING for more from Lexi Amber?

CHICAGO Awakenings
Accidentally Joining His Cult *contemporary MM romance*
Accidentally Falling For My Best Friend *contemporary MM romance*
Accidentally Falling For Her- The Girls *contemporary FF romance companion novella*

CO-AUTHORED **With Bec Benson**
Love Without Labels
The Reality of Wanting Him *contemporary MM romance*
The Reality of Wanting My Bully *contemporary MM romance*
The Reality of Ever After *LWL novella expected March 2026*
The bachelor party in Vegas
Wanting My Husband *LWL spin-off expected mid 2026* not on the reality show

ACKNOWLEDGMENTS

Thank you so much to everyone who helped make this book possible!

Both covers were created by the very talented Rebecca at Story Styling Cover Designs and the amazing cover image was done by Wander Agular. Copy edits were done by Raven at Raven Quill Editing. Proofreading was done by Lindsey Middlemiss.

Character images drawn by angki.s_ on socials. Chapter header images and Chibis by Kieran, Kierofoxen on socials— thank you both so much for all of the art you've already done, can't wait to get more!

Sensitivity feedback was done by Jonathan Samuels and Toddles— I can't thank you both enough for the feedback and entertainment in all of your comments!

The biggest shout out and thank you to my beta readers! Bryoni, Charlotte, Brittany, Anna, Debbie, Ashley, and Tori— Thank you all for reading this early and for all of the continued support!

Bec, wow I can't believe this fever dream of a book is real. Hopefully you know how grateful I am to have you as one of my very best friends. I'm so glad that I get to do this author thing with you. Your feedback and emotional support means the world to me.

I'd also like to thank my very supportive husband who always checks to see if I change this sooo I did. You're still awesome.

Thanks to my parents who've been very supportive, even if I hope they never actually read any of my books.

And to my kids thanks for letting mommy work, even after I quit my nursing job to stay home with you guys. I'll love you forever and always no matter what.

ABOUT THE AUTHOR

Lexi is an American author who is obsessed with queer happily ever afters. Most of her time is spent with her two kids, but if they're asleep then she is either reading, writing, or watching hockey.

Professionally trained as a nurse, Lexi decided to start writing when she became a stay at home mom and the characters in her head haven't stopped talking since.

Lexi also loves Diet Coke, traveling, and Halloween. Her house is probably obnoxiously decorated for whatever holiday is next because she thinks that little things that make people smile are important.

For early chapters of upcoming releases check out Patreon patreon.com/LexiAmber

Signed copies of solo work and lots of fun merch at Lexiamber.com

ALSO BY

Lexi Amber

Chicago Awakenings

Accidentally Joining His Cult *contemporary MM romance*

Accidentally Falling For My Best Friend *contemporary MM romance*

Accidentally Falling For Her- The Girls *contemporary FF romance companion novella*

Accidentally Living With The Captain *contemporary MM romance February 2026*

Co-authored With Bec Benson

Love Without Labels

The Reality of Wanting Him *contemporary MM romance*

The Reality of Wanting My Bully *contemporary MM romance*

The Reality of Ever After *LWL novella expected March 2026* The bachelor party in Vegas

Wanting My Husband *LWL spin-off expected mid 2026* not on the reality show

www.ingramcontent.com/pod-product-compliance
Lightning Source LLC
Chambersburg PA
CBHW030142310726
48970CB00005B/1544